DAMNED FOR ETERNITY

Jennan bowed toward the central control pillar where Helva *was*. Helva's personal preference crystallized at that precise moment and for that particular reason: Jennan, alone of all the men, had addressed his remarks directly at her physical presence—even though she could pick up his image anywhere in the ship—regardless of the fact that her body was behind massive metal walls.

Helva didn't understand that she fell in love with Jennan that evening . . . she didn't realize that together they would have to face one of the most grisly holocausts.

But, most important, Helva didn't know that for a spaceship to fall in love was to be eternally damned . . .

". . . A WINNING TREATMENT!"
—*Library Journal*

The Ship Who Sang

Anne McCaffrey

A Del Rey Book

BALLANTINE BOOKS • NEW YORK

A Del Rey Book
Published by Ballantine Books

ACKNOWLEDGMENTS
Revised for this edition are the following sections which
first appeared as listed:
The Ship Who Sang © 1961 by Mercury Press, Inc.
The Ship Who Mourned © 1966 by The Condé Nast
    Publications, Inc.
The Ship Who Killed © 1966 by Galaxy Publishing
    Corporation
The Ship Who Dissembled © 1969 by Galaxy Publishing
    Corporation
Dramatic Mission © 1969 by The Condé Nast
    Publications, Inc.

Library of Congress Catalog Card Number: 69-86390

ISBN 0-345-28505-0

Manufactured in the United States of America

First Edition: March 1970
Seventh Printing: December 1979

First Canadian Printing: April 1970

Cover art by The Brothers Hildebrandt

Contents

The Ship
Who Sang

SHE WAS BORN a thing and as such would be con-
demned if she failed to pass the encephalograph test
required of all newborn babies. There was always the
possibility that though the limbs were twisted, the mind
was not, that though the ears would hear only dimly,
the eyes see vaguely, the mind behind them was recep-
tive and alert.

The electro-encephalogram was entirely favorable,
unexpectedly so, and the news was brought to the waiting, grieving parents. There was the final, harsh decision: to give their child euthanasia or permit it to
become an encapsulated "brain," a guiding mechanism
in any one of a number of curious professions. As such,
their offspring would suffer no pain, live a comfortable
existence in a metal shell for several centuries, perform-
ing unusual service to Central Worlds.

She lived and was given a name, Helva. For her
first 3 vegetable months she waved her crabbed claws,
kicked weakly with her clubbed feet and enjoyed the
usual routine of the infant. She was not alone, for
there were three other such children in the big city's
special nursery. Soon they all were removed to Central
Laboratory School, where their delicate transformation
began.

One of the babies died in the initial transferral, but of Helva's 'class,' 17 thrived in the metal shells. Instead of kicking feet, Helva's neural responses started her wheels; instead of grabbing with hands, she manipulated mechanical extensions. As she matured, more and more neural synapses would be adjusted to operate other mechanisms that went into the maintenance and running of a space ship. For Helva was destined to be the "brain" half of a scout ship, partnered with a man or a woman, whichever she chose, as the mobile half. She would be among the elite of her kind. Her initial intelligence tests registered above normal and her adaptation index was unusually high. As long as her development within her shell lived up to expectations, and there were no side-effects from the pituitary tinkering, Helva would live a rewarding, rich and unusual life, a far cry from what she would have faced as an ordinary, "normal" being.

However, no diagram of her brain patterns, no early I.Q. tests recorded certain essential facts about Helva that Central must eventually learn. They would have to bide their official time and see, trusting that the massive doses of shell-psychology would suffice her, too, as the necessary bulwark against her unusual confinement and the pressures of her profession. A ship run by a human brain could not run rogue or insane with the power and resources Central had to build into their scout ships. Brain ships were, of course, long past the experimental stages. Most babies survived the perfected techniques of pituitary manipulation that kept their bodies small, eliminating the necessity of transfers from smaller to larger shells. And very, very few were lost when the final connection was made to the control panels of ship or industrial combine. Shell-people resembled mature dwarfs in size whatever their natal deformities were, but the well-oriented brain would not have changed places with the most perfect body in the Universe.

So, for happy years, Helva scooted around in her shell with her classmates, playing such games as Stall, Power-Seek, studying her lessons in trajectory, propulsion techniques, computation, logistics, mental hygiene, basic alien psychology, philology, space history, law, traffic, codes: all the et ceteras that eventually became compounded into a reasoning, logical, informed citizen. Not so obvious to her, but of more importance to her teachers, Helva ingested the precepts of her conditioning as easily as she absorbed her nutrient fluid. She would one day be grateful to the patient drone of the subconscious-level instruction.

Helva's civilization was not without busy, do-good associations, exploring possible inhumanities to terrestrial as well as extraterrestrial citizens. One such group —Society for the Preservation of the Rights of Intelligent Minorities——got all incensed over shelled "children" when Helva was just turning 14. When they were forced to, Central Worlds shrugged its shoulders, arranged a tour of the Laboratory Schools and set the tour off to a big start by showing the members case histories, complete with photographs. Very few committees ever looked past the first few photos. Most of their original objections about "shells" were overriden by the relief that these hideous (to them) bodies *were* mercifully concealed.

Helva's class was doing fine arts, a selective subject in her crowded program. She had activated one of her microscopic tools which she would later use for minute repairs to various parts of her control panel. Her subject was large—a copy of the Last Supper—and her canvas, small—the head of a tiny screw. She had tuned her sight to the proper degree. As she worked she absentmindedly crooned, producing a curious sound. Shell-people used their own vocal chords and diaphragms, but sound issued through microphones rather than mouths. Helva's hum, then, had a curious vibrancy, a warm, dulcet quality even in its aimless chromatic wanderings.

"Why, what a lovely voice you have," said one of the female visitors.

Helva "looked" up and caught a fascinating panorama of regular, dirty craters on a flaky pink surface. Her hum became a gurgle of surprise. She instinctively regulated her "sight" until the skin lost its cratered look and the pores assumed normal proportions.

"Yes, we have quite a few years of voice training, madam," remarked Helva calmly. "Vocal peculiarities often become excessively irritating during prolonged intrastellar distances and must be eliminated. I enjoyed my lessons."

Although this was the first time that Helva had seen unshelled people, she took this experience calmly. Any other reaction would have been reported instantly.

"I meant that you have a nice singing voice . . . dear," the lady said.

"Thank you. Would you like to see my work?" Helva asked, politely. She instinctively sheered away from personal discussions, but she filed the comment away for further meditation.

"Work?" asked the lady.

"I am currently reproducing the Last Supper on the head of a screw."

"O, I say," the lady twittered.

Helva turned her vision back to magnification and surveyed her copy critically.

"Of course, some of my color values do not match the old Master's and the perspective is faulty, but I believe it to be a fair copy."

The lady's eyes, unmagnified, bugged out.

"Oh, I forget," and Helva's voice was really contrite. If she could have blushed, she would have. "You people don't have adjustable vision."

The monitor of this discourse grinned with pride

and amusement as Helva's tone indicated pity for the unfortunate.

"Here, this will help," said Helva, substituting a magnifying device in one extension and holding it over the picture.

In a kind of shock, the ladies and gentlemen of the committee bent to observe the incredibly copied and brilliantly executed Last Supper on the head of a screw.

"Well," remarked one gentleman who had been forced to accompany his wife, "the good Lord can eat where angels fear to tread."

"Are you referring, sir," asked Helva politely, "to the Dark Age discussions of the number of angels who could stand on the head of a pin?"

"I had that in mind."

"If you substitute 'atom' for 'angel,' the problem is not insoluble, given the metallic content of the pin in question."

"Which you are programmed to compute?"

"Of course."

"Did they remember to program a sense of humor, as well, young lady?"

"We are directed to develop a sense of proportion, sir, which contributes the same effect."

The good man chortled appreciatively and decided the trip was worth his time.

If the investigation committee spent months digesting the thoughtful food served them at the Laboratory School, they left Helva with a morsel as well.

"Singing" as applicable to herself required research. She had, of course, been exposed to and enjoyed a music appreciation course that had included the better known classical works such as "Tristan und Isolde," "Candide," "Oklahoma," and "Le Nozze di Figaro," along with the atomic age singers, Birgit Nilsson, Bob Dylan, and Geraldine Todd, as well as the curious rhythmic progressions of the Venusians, Capellan visual chromatics, the sonic concerti of the Altairians and Reticulan croons. But "singing" for any shell-person posed considerable technical difficulties. Shell-people were schooled to examine every aspect of a problem or situation before making a prognosis. Balanced properly between optimism and practicality, the nondefeatist attitude of the shell-people led them to extricate themselves, their ships, and personnel from bizarre situations. Therefore, to Helva, the problem that she couldn't open her mouth to sing, among other restrictions, did not bother her. She would work out a method, bypassing her limitations, whereby she could sing.

She approached the problem by investigating the methods of sound reproduction through the centuries, human and instrumental. Her own sound production equipment was essentially more instrumental than vocal. Breath control and the proper enunciation of vowel sounds within the oral cavity appeared to require the most development and practice. Shell-people did not, strictly speaking, breathe. For their purposes, oxygen and other gases were not drawn from the surrounding atmosphere through the medium of lungs but sustained artificially by solution in their shells. After experimentation, Helva discovered that she could manipulate her diaphragmic unit to sustain tone. By relaxing the throat muscles and expanding the oral cavity well into the frontal sinuses, she could direct the vowel sounds into the most felicitous position for proper reproduction through her throat microphone. She compared the results with tape recordings of modern singers and was not unpleased, although her own tapes had a peculiar quality about them, not at all unharmonious, merely unique. Acquiring a repertoire from the Laboratory library was no problem to one trained to perfect recall. She found herself able to sing any role and any song which struck her fancy. It would not have occurred to her that it was curious for a female to sing bass, baritone, tenor, mezzo, soprano, and coloratura as she pleased. It was, to Helva, only a matter of the correct reproduction and diaphragmic control required by the music attempted.

If the authorities remarked on her curious avocation, they did so among themselves. Shell-people were encouraged to develop a hobby so long as they maintained proficiency in their technical work.

On the anniversary of her 16th year, Helva was unconditionally graduated and installed in her ship, the XH-834. Her permanent titanium shell was recessed behind an even more indestructible barrier in the central shaft of the scout ship. The neural, audio, visual, and sensory connections were made and sealed. Her extendibles were diverted, connected or augmented and the final, delicate-beyond-description brain taps were completed while Helva remained anesthetically unaware of the proceedings. When she woke, she *was* the ship. Her brain and intelligence controlled every function from navigation to such loading as a scout ship of her class needed. She could take care of herself, and her ambulatory half, in any situation already recorded in the annals of Central Worlds and any situation its most fertile minds could imagine.

Her first actual flight, for she and her kind had made mock flights on dummy panels since she was 8, showed her to be a complete master of the techniques of her profession. She was ready for her great adventures and the arrival of her mobile partner.

There were nine qualified scouts sitting around collecting base pay the day Helva reported for active duty. There were several missions that demanded instant attention, but Helva had been of interest to several department heads in Central for some time and each bureau chief was determined to have her assigned to *his* section. No one had remembered to introduce Helva to the prospective partners. The ship always chose its own partner. Had there been another brain ship at the base at the moment, Helva would have been guided to make the first move. As it was, while Central wrangled among itself, Robert Tanner sneaked out of the pilots' barracks, out to the field and over to Helva's slim metal hull.

"Hello, anyone at home?" Tanner said.

"Of course," replied Helva, activating her outside scanners. "Are you my partner?" she asked hopefully, as she recognized the Scout Service uniform.

"All you have to do is ask," he retorted in a wistful tone.

"No one has come. I thought perhaps there were no partners available and I've had no directives from Central."

Even to herself Helva sounded a little self-pitying, but the truth was she was lonely, sitting on the darkened field. She had always had the company of other shells and, more recently, technicians by the score. The sudden solitude had lost its momentary charm and become oppressive.

"No directives from Central is scarcely a cause for regret, but there happen to be eight other guys biting their fingernails to the quick just waiting for an invitation to board you, you beautiful thing."

Tanner was inside the central cabin as he said this, running appreciative fingers over her panel, the scout's gravity-chair, poking his head into the cabins, the galley, the head, the pressured-storage compartments.

"Now, if you want to goose Central and do *us* a favor all in one, call up the barracks and let's have a ship-warming partner-picking party. Hmmmm?"

Helva chuckled to herself. He was so completely different from the occasional visitors or the various Laboratory technicians she had encountered. He was so gay, so assured, and she was delighted by his sug-

gestion of a partner-picking party. Certainly it was not
against anything in her understanding of regulations.

"Cencom, this is XH-834. Connect me with Pilot
Barracks."

"Visual?"

"Please."

A picture of lounging men in various attitudes of
boredom came on her screen.

"This is XH-834. Would the unassigned scouts do
me the favor of coming aboard?"

Eight figures galvanized into action, grabbing pieces
of wearing apparel, disengaging tape mechanisms, dis-
entangling themselves from bedsheets and towels.

Helva dissolved the connection while Tanner
chuckled gleefully and settled down to await their arrival.

Helva was engulfed in an unshell-like flurry of
anticipation. No actress on her opening night could
have been more apprehensive, fearful or breathless. Unlike the actress, she could throw no hysterics, china
objets d'art or grease-paint to relieve her tension. She
could, of course, check her stores for edibles and
drinks, which she did, serving Tanner from the virgin
selection of her commissary.

Scouts were colloquially known as "brawns" as op-
posed to their ship "brains." They had to pass as
rigorous a training program as the brains and only
the top 1 percent of each contributory world's highest
scholars were admitted to Central Worlds Scout Training Program. Consequently the eight young men who
came pounding up the gantry into Helva's hospit-
able lock were unusually fine-looking, intelligent, well-
coordinated and adjusted young men, looking forward to
a slightly drunken evening, Helva permitting, and all
quite willing to do each other dirt to get possession of
her.

Such a human invasion left Helva mentally breathless, a luxury she thoroughly enjoyed for the brief time she felt she should permit it.

She sorted out the young men. Tanner's opportunism amused but did not specifically attract her; the blond Nordsen seemed too simple; dark-haired Al-atpay had a kind of obstinacy with which she felt no compassion: Mir-Ahnin's bitterness hinted an inner darkness she did not wish to lighten, although he made the biggest outward play for her attention. Hers was a curious courtship—this would be only the first of several marriages for her, for brawns retired after 75 years of service, or earlier if they were unlucky. Brains, their bodies safe from any deterioration, were indestructible. In theory, once a shell-person had paid off the massive debt of early care, surgical adaptation and maintenance charges, he or she was free to seek employment elsewhere. In practice, shell-people remained in the service until they chose to self-destruct or died in line of duty. Helva had actually spoken to one shell-person 322 years old. She had been so awed by the contact she hadn't presumed to ask the personal questions she had wanted to.

Her choice of a brawn did not stand out from the others until Tanner started to sing a scout ditty, recounting the misadventures of the bold, dense, painfully inept Billy Brawn. An attempt at harmony resulted in cacophony and Tanner wagged his arms wildly for silence.

"What we need is a roaring good lead tenor. Jennan, besides palming aces, what do you sing?"

"Sharp," Jennan replied with easy good humor.

"If a tenor is absolutely necessary, I'll attempt it," Helva volunteered.

"My good *woman*," Tanner protested.

"Sound your 'A'," laughed Jennan.

Into the stunned silence that followed the rich, clear, high 'A,' Jennan remarked quietly, "Such an A Caruso would have given the rest of his notes to sing."

It did not take them long to discover her full range.

"All Tanner asked for was one roaring good lead tenor," Jennan said jokingly, "and our sweet mistress supplied us an entire repertory company. The boy who gets this ship will go far, far, far."

"To the Horsehead Nebula?" asked Nordsen, quoting an old Central saw.

"To the Horsehead Nebula and back, we shall make beautiful music," said Helva, chuckling.

"Together," Jennan said. "Only you'd better make the music and, with my voice, I'd better listen."

"I rather imagined it would be I who listened," suggested Helva.

Jennan executed a stately bow with an intricate flourish of his crush-brimmed hat. He directed his bow toward the central control pillar where Helva *was*. Her own personal preference crystallized at that precise moment and for that particular reason: Jennan, alone of the men, had addressed his remarks directly at her physical presence, regardless of the fact that he knew she could pick up his image wherever he was in the ship and regardless of the fact that her body was behind massive metal walls. Throughout their partnership, Jennan never failed to turn his head in her direction no matter where he was in relation to her. In response to this personalization, Helva at that moment and from then on always spoke to Jennan only through her central mike, even though that was not always the most efficient method.

Helva didn't know that she fell in love with Jennan that evening. As she had never been exposed to love or affection, only the drier cousins, respect and admiration, she could scarcely have recognized her reaction to the warmth of his personality and thoughtfulness. As a shell-person, she considered herself remote from emotions largely connected with physical desires.

"Well, Helva, it's been swell meeting you," said Tanner suddenly as she and Jennan were arguing about the baroque quality of "Come All Ye Sons of Art." "See you in space some time, you lucky dog, Jennan. Thanks for the party, Helva."

"You don't have to go so soon?" asked Helva, realizing belatedly that she and Jennan had been excluding the others from this discussion.

"Best man won," Tanner said, wryly. "Guess I'd better go get a tape on love ditties. Might need 'em for the next ship, if there're any more at home like you."

Helva and Jennan watched them leave, both a little confused.

"Perhaps Tanner's jumping to conclusions?" Jennan asked.

Helva regarded him as he slouched against the console, facing her shell directly. His arms were crossed on his chest and the glass he held had been empty for some time. He was handsome, they all were; but his watchful eyes were unwary, his mouth assumed a smile easily, his voice (to which Helva was particularly drawn) was resonant, deep, and without unpleasant overtones or accent.

"Sleep on it, at any rate, Helva. Call me in the morning if it's your opt."

She called him at breakfast, after she had checked her choice through Central. Jennan moved his things aboard, received their joint commission, had his personality and experience file locked into her reviewer, gave her the coordinates of their first mission. The XH-834 officially became the JH-834.

Their first mission was a dull but necessary crash priority (Medical got Helva), rushing a vaccine to a distant system plagued with a virulent spore disease. They had only to get to Spica as fast as possible.

After the initial, thrilling forward surge at her maximum speed, Helva realized her muscles were to be given less of a workout than her brawn on this tedious mission. But they did have plenty of time for exploring each other's personalities. Jennan, of course, knew what Helva was capable of as a ship and partner, just as she knew what she could expect from him. But these were only facts and Helva looked forward eagerly to learning that human side of her partner which could not be reduced to a series of symbols. Nor could the give and take of two personalities be learned from a book. It had to be experienced.

"My father was a scout, too, or is that programmed?" began Jennan their third day out.

"Naturally."

"Unfair, you know. You've got all my family history and I don't know one blamed thing about yours."

"I've never known either," Helva said. "Until I read yours, it hadn't occurred to me I must have one, too, someplace in Central's files."

Jennan snorted. "Shell psychology!"

Helva laughed. "Yes, and I'm even programmed against curiosity about it. You'd better be, too."

Jennan ordered a drink, slouched into the gravity couch opposite her, put his feet on the bumpers, turning himself idly from side to side on the gimbals.

"Helva—a made-up name . . ."

"With a Scandinavian sound."

"You aren't blonde," Jennan said positively.

"Well, then, there're dark Swedes."

"And blonde Turks and this one's harem is limited to one."

"Your woman in purdah, yes, but you can comb the pleasure houses—" Helva found herself aghast at the edge to her carefully trained voice.

"You know," Jennan interrupted her, deep in some thought of his own, "my father gave me the impression he was a lot more married to his ship, the Silvia, than to my mother. I know I used to think Silvia was my grandmother. She was a low number so she must have been a great-great-grandmother at least. I used to talk to her for hours."

"Her registry?" asked Helva, unwittingly jealous of everyone and anyone who had shared his hours.

"422. I think she's TS now. I ran into Tom Burgess once."

Jennan's father had died of a planetary disease, the vaccine for which his ship had used up in curing the local citizens.

"Tom said she'd got mighty tough and salty. You lose your sweetness and I'll come back and haunt you, girl," Jennan threatened.

Helva laughed. He startled her by stamping up to the column panel, touching it with light, tender fingers.

"I *wonder* what you look like," he said softly, wistfully.

Helva had been briefed about this natural curiosity of scouts. She didn't know anything about herself and neither of them ever would or could.

"Pick any form, shape, and shade and I'll be yours obliging," she countered, as training suggested.

"Iron Maiden, I fancy blondes with long tresses," and Jennan pantomined Lady Godiva-like tresses. "Since you're immolated in titanium, I'll call you Brunehilde, my dear," and he made his bow.

With a chortle, Helva launched into the appropriate aria just as Spica made contact.

"What'n'ell's that yelling about? Who are you? And unless you're Central Worlds Medical go away. We've got a plague. No visiting privileges."

"My ship is singing, we're the JH-834 of Worlds and we've got your vaccine. What are our landing coordinates?"

"Your *ship* is singing?"

"The greatest S.A.T.B. in organized space. Any request?"

The JH-834 delivered the vaccine but no more arias and received immediate orders to proceed to Leviticus IV. By the time they got there, Jennan found a reputation awaiting him and was forced to defend the 834's virgin honor.

"I'll stop singing," murmured Helva contritely as she ordered up poultices for this third black eye in a week.

"You will not," Jennan said through gritted teeth. "If I have to black eyes from here to the Horsehead to keep the snicker out of the title, we'll be the ship who sings."

After the "ship who sings" tangled with a minor but vicious narcotic ring in the Lesser Magellanics, the title became definitely respectful. Central was aware of each episode and punched out a "special interest" key on JH-834's file. A first-rate team was shaking down well.

Jennan and Helva considered themselves a first-rate team, too, after their tidy arrest.

"Of all the vices in the universe, I *hate* drug addiction," Jennan remarked as they headed back to Central Base. "People can go to hell quick enough without that kind of help."

"Is that why you volunteered for Scout Service? To redirect traffic?"

"I'll bet my official answer's on your review."

"In far too flowery wording. 'Carrying on the traditions of my family, which has been proud of four generations in Service', if I may quote you your own words."

Jennan groaned. "I was *very* young when I wrote that. I certainly hadn't been through Final Training. And once I was in Final Training, my pride wouldn't let me fail. . . .

"As I mentioned, I used to visit Dad on board the Silvia and I've a very good idea she might have had her eye on me as a replacement for my father because

I had had massive doses of scout-oriented propaganda. It took. From the time I was 7, I was going to be a scout or else." He shrugged as if deprecating a youthful determination that had taken a great deal of mature application to bring to fruition.

"Ah, so? Scout Sahir Silan on the JS-44 penetrating into the Horsehead Nebulae?"

Jennan chose to ignore her sarcasm.

"With *you*, I may even get that far. But even with Silvia's nudging *I* never day-dreamed myself *that* kind of glory in my wildest flights of fancy. I'll leave the whoppers to your agile brain henceforth. I have in mind a smaller contribution to space history."

"So modest?"

"No. Practical. We also serve, et cetera." He placed a dramatic hand on his heart.

"Glory hound!" scoffed Helva.

"Look who's talking, my Nebula-bound friend. At least I'm not greedy. There'll only be one hero like my dad at Parsaea, but I *would* like to be remembered for some kudo. Everyone does. Why else do or die?"

"Your father died on his way back from Parsaea, if I may point out a few cogent facts. So he could never have known he was a hero for damming the flood with his ship. Which kept Parsaean colony from being abandoned. Which gave them a chance to discover the antiparalytic qualities of Parsaea. Which *he* never knew."

"I know," said Jennan softly.

Helva was immediately sorry for the tone of her rebuttal. She knew very well how deep Jennan's attachment to his father had been. On his review a note was made that he had rationalized his father's loss with the unexpected and welcome outcome of the Affair at Parsaea.

"Facts are not human, Helva. My father was and so am I. And *basically*, so are you. Check over your dial,

834. Amid all the wires attached to you is a heart, an underdeveloped human heart. Obviously!"

"I apologize, Jennan," she said.

Jennan hesitated a moment, threw out his hands in acceptance and then tapped her shell affectionately.

"If they ever take us off the milkruns, we'll make a stab at the Nebula, huh?"

As so frequently happened in the Scout Service, within the next hour they had orders to change course, not to the Nebula, but to a recently colonized system with two habitable planets, one tropical, one glacial. The sun, named Ravel, had become unstable; the spectrum was that of a rapidly expanding shell, with absorption lines rapidly displacing toward violet. The augmented heat of the primary had already forced evacuation of the nearer world, Daphnis. The pattern of spectral emissions gave indication that the sun would sear Chloe as well. All ships in the immediate spatial vicinity were to report to Disaster Headquarters on Chloe to effect removal of the remaining colonists.

The JH-834 obediently presented itself and was sent to outlying areas on Chloe to pick up scattered settlers who did not appear to appreciate the urgency of the situation. Chloe, indeed, was enjoying the first temperatures above freezing since it had been flung out of its parent. Since many of the colonists were religious fanatics who had settled on rigorous Chloe to fit themselves for a life of pious reflection, Chloe's abrupt thaw was attributed to sources other than a rampaging sun.

Jennan had to spend so much time countering specious arguments that he and Helva were behind schedule on their way to the fourth and last settlement.

Helva jumped over the high range of jagged peaks that surrounded and sheltered the valley from the former raging snows as well as the present heat. The violent sun with its flaring corona was just beginning to brighten the deep valley as Helva dropped down to a landing.

"They'd better grab their toothbrushes and hop aboard," Helva said. "HQ says speed it up."

"All women," remarked Jennan in surprise as he walked down to meet them. "Unless the men on Chloe wear furred skirts."

"Charm 'em but pare the routine to the bare essentials. And turn on your two-way private."

Jennan advanced smiling, but his explanation of his mission was met with absolute incredulity and considerable doubt as to his authenticity. He groaned inwardly as the matriarch paraphrased previous explanations of the warming sun.

"Revered mother, there's been an overload on that prayer circuit and the sun is blowing itself up in one obliging burst. I'm here to take you to the spaceport at Rosary—"

"That Sodom?" The worthy woman glowered and shuddered disdainfully at his suggestion. "We thank you for your warning but we have no wish to leave our cloister for the rude world. We must go about our morning meditation which has been interrupted—"

"It'll be permanently interrupted when that sun starts broiling you. You must come now," Jennan said firmly.

"Madame," said Helva, realizing that perhaps a female voice might carry more weight in this instance than Jennan's very masculine charm.

"Who spoke?" cried the nun, startled by the bodiless voice.

"I, Helva, the ship. Under my protection you and your sisters-in-faith may enter safely and be unprofaned by association with a male. I will guard you and take you safely to a place prepared for you."

The matriarch peered cautiously into the ship's open port.

"Since only Central Worlds is permitted the use of such ships, I acknowledge that you are not trifling with us, young man. However, we are in no danger here."

"The temperature at Rosary is now 99°," said Helva. "As soon as the sun's rays penetrate directly into this valley, it will also be 99°, and it is due to climb to approximately 180° today. I notice your buildings are made of wood with moss chinking. Dry moss. It should fire around noontime."

The sunlight was beginning to slant into the valley through the peaks and the fierce rays warmed the restless group behind the matriarch. Several opened the throats of their furry parkas.

"Jennan," said Helva privately to him, "our time is very short."

"I can't leave them, Helva. Some of those girls are barely out of their teens."

"Pretty, too. No wonder the matriarch doesn't want to get in."

"Helva."

"It will be the Lord's will," said the matriarch stoutly and turned her back squarely on rescue.

"To burn to death?" shouted Jennan as she threaded her way through her murmuring disciples.

"They want to be martyrs? Their opt, Jennan," said Helva dispassionately, "We must leave and that is no longer a matter of option."

"How can I leave, Helva?"

"Parsaea?" Helva asked tauntingly as he stepped forward to grab one of the women. "You can't drag them *all* aboard and we don't have time to fight it out. Get on board, Jennan, or I'll have you on report."

"They'll die," muttered Jennan dejectedly as he reluctantly turned to climb on board.

"You can risk only so much," Helva said sympathetically. "As it is we'll just have time to make a rendezvous. Lab reports a critical speedup in spectral evolution."

Jennan was already in the airlock when one of the younger women, screaming, rushed to squeeze in the closing port. Her action set off the others. They stampeded through the narrow-opening. Even crammed back to breast, there was not enough room inside for all the women. Jennan broke out spacesuits to the three who would have to remain with him in the airlock. He wasted valuable time explaining to the matriarch that she must put on the suit because the airlock had no independent oxygen or cooling units.

"We'll be caught," said Helva in a grim tone to Jennan on their private connection. "We've lost 18 minutes in this last-minute rush. I am now overloaded for maximum speed and I must attain maximum speed to outrun the heat wave."

"Can you lift? We're suited."

"Lift? Yes," she said, doing so. "Run? I stagger."

Jennan, bracing himself and the women, could feel her sluggishness as she blasted upward. Heartlessly, Helva applied thrust as long as she could, despite the fact that the gravitational force mashed her cabin passengers brutally and crushed two fatally. It was a question of saving as many as possible. The only one for whom she had any concern was Jennan and she was in desperate terror about his safety. Airless and uncooled, protected by only one layer of metal, not three, the airlock was not going to be safe for the four trapped there, despite their spacesuits. These were only the standard models, not built to withstand the excessive heat to which the ship would be subjected.

Helva ran as fast as she could but the incredible wave of heat from the explosive sun caught them halfway to cold safety.

She paid no heed to the cries, moans, pleas, and prayers in her cabin. She listened only to Jennan's tortured breathing, to the missing throb in his suit's purifying system and the sucking of the overloaded cooling unit. Helpless, she heard the hysterical screams of his three companions as they writhed in the awful heat. Vainly, Jennan tried to calm them, tried to explain they would soon be safe and cool if they could be still and endure the heat. Undisciplined by their terror and torment, they tried to strike out at him despite the close quarters. One flailing arm became entangled in the leads to his power pack and the damage was quickly done. A connection, weakened by heat and the dead weight of the arm, broke.

For all the power at her disposal, Helva was helpless. She watched as Jennan fought for his breath, as he turned his head beseechingly toward *her*, and died.

Only the iron conditioning of her training prevented Helva from swinging around and plunging back into the cleansing heart of the exploding sun. Numbly she made rendezvous with the refugee convoy. She obediently transferred her burned, heat-prostrated passengers to the assigned transport.

"I will retain the body of my scout and proceed to the nearest base for burial," she informed Central dully.

"You will be provided escort," was the reply.

"I have no need of escort."

"Escort is provided, XH-834," she was told curtly. The shock of hearing Jennan's initial severed from her call number cut off her half-formed protest. Stunned, she waited by the transport until her screens showed the arrival of two other slim brain ships. The cortege proceeded homeward at unfunereal speeds.

"834? The ship who sings?"

"I have no more songs."

"Your scout was Jennan."

"I do not wish to communicate."

"I'm 422."

"Silvia?"

"Silvia died a long time ago. I'm 422. Currently MS," the ship rejoined curtly. "AH-640 is our other friend, but Henry's not listening in. Just as well—he wouldn't understand it if you wanted to turn rogue. But I'd stop *him* if he tried to deter you."

"Rogue?" The term snapped Helva out of her apathy.

"Sure. You're young. You've got power for years. Skip. Others have done it. 732 went rogue 20 years ago after she lost her scout on a mission to that white dwarf. Hasn't been seen since."

"I never heard about rogues."

"As it's exactly the thing we're conditioned against, you sure wouldn't hear about it in school, my dear," 422 said.

"Break conditioning?" cried Helva, anguished, thinking longingly of the white, white furious hot heart of the sun she had just left.

"For you I don't think it would be hard at the moment," 422 said quietly, her voice devoid of her earlier cynicism. "The stars are out there, winking."

"Alone?" cried Helva from her heart.

"Alone!" 422 confirmed bleakly.

Alone with all of space and time. Even the Horsehead Nebula would not be far enough away to daunt her. Alone with a hundred years to live with her memories and nothing . . . nothing more.

"Was Parsaea worth it?" she asked 422 softly.

"Parsaea?" 422 repeated, surprised. "With his father? Yes. We were there, at Parsaea when we were needed. Just as you . . . and his son . . . were at Chloe. When you were needed. The crime is not knowing where need is and not being there."

"But *I* need *him*. Who will supply my need?" said Helva bitterly. . . .

"834," said 422 after a day's silent speeding, "Central wishes your report. A replacement awaits your opt at Regulus Base. Change course accordingly."

"A replacement?" That was certainly not what she needed . . . a reminder inadequately filling the void Jennan left. Why, her hull was barely cool of Chloe's heat. Atavistically, Helva wanted time to mourn Jennan.

"Oh, none of them are impossible if *you're* a good ship," 422 remarked philosophically. "And it is just what you need. The sooner the better."

"You told them I wouldn't go rogue, didn't you?" Helva said.

"The moment passed you even as it passed me after Parsaea, and before that, after Glen Arhur, and Betelgeuse."

"We're conditioned to go on, aren't we? We *can't* go rogue. You were testing."

"Had to. Orders. Not even Psych knows why a rogue occurs. Central's very worried, and so, daughter, are your sister ships. I asked to be your escort. I . . . don't want to lose you both."

In her emotional nadir, Helva could feel a flood of gratitude for Silvia's rough sympathy.

"We've all known this grief, Helva. It's no consolation, but if we couldn't feel with our scouts, we'd only be machines wired for sound."

Helva looked at Jennan's still form stretched before her in its shroud and heard the echo of his rich voice in the quiet cabin.

"Silvia! I *couldn't* help him," she cried from her soul.

"Yes, dear, I know," 422 murmured gently and then was quiet.

The three ships sped on, wordless, to the great Central Worlds base at Regulus. Helva broke silence to acknowledge landing instructions and the officially tendered regrets.

The three ships set down simultaneously at the wooded edge where Regulus' gigantic blue trees stood sentinel over the sleeping dead in the small Service cemetery. The entire Base complement approached with measured step and formed an aisle from Helva to the burial ground. The honor detail, out of step, walked slowly into her cabin. Reverently they placed the body of her dead love on the wheeled bier, covered it honorably with the deep blue, star-splashed flag of the Service. She watched as it was driven slowly down the living aisle which closed in behind the bier in last escort.

Then, as the simple words of interment were spoken, as the atmosphere planes dipped in tribute over the open grave, Helva found voice for her lonely farewell.

Softly, barely audible at first, the strains of the ancient song of evening and requiem swelled to the final poignant measure until black space itself echoed back the sound of the song the ship sang.

The Ship
Who Mourned

WITH EYES THAT did not register what they saw,
Helva watched stolidly as the Regulus Base personnel
broke ranks at the conclusion of Jennan's funeral. Never
again, she vowed, would she be known as the ship who
sang. That part of her had died with Jennan.

From somewhere very far away from her emotional
centers, she impassively watched the little figures separate, pair off, walking rapidly to continue interrupted
tasks or moving slowly back to the barracks. Some, passing, looked up, but she did not interpret their glances. She
had nowhere to move to and no desire to move anywhere
away from the graveside of her dead partner.

"It cannot end like this," she thought, anguish over-
powering the stupor in her heart. "I cannot be like this.
But what do I go on to now?"

"XH-834, Theoda of Medea requests permission to
enter," said a voice at the base of her lift.

"Permission granted," Helva said automatically.

So absorbed in her grief was Helva that by the time
the lift had deposited the slender female figure at the
lock, Helva had forgotten she had permitted entry. The
woman advanced toward the central shaft behind which

Helva was embedded in her shell. In her hand she held
out a command reel.

"Well, insert it," snapped Helva when the woman
made no other move.

"Where? I'm not regular service. The tape explains the
mission but . . ."

"In the northwest quadrant of the central panel, you
will observe a blue slot; insert the tape with the wind tab
in position nearest the center red knob of the panel. Press
the blue button marked 'relay' and if you are unaware of
the text and are cleared for it, press the second yellow
button marked 'audio.' Please be seated."

Dispassionately and with no more than a fleeting
awareness that she ought to have put Theoda at her ease
or made some attempt at graciousness, Helva watched
the woman fumble before she was able to insert the tape.
Theoda sank uncertainly into the pilot's chair as the tape
began.

"XH-834, you will proceed in the company of Physiotherapist Theoda of Medea to the NDE, System Lyrae
II, Annigoni IV, and present all aid possible in rehabilitation program of Van Gogh space plague survivors. All
haste. All haste. All haste!"

Helva slammed the stop signal on the tape and called
Central Control.

"Does Physiotherapist Theoda constitute my replacement?"

"No, XH-834, Theoda is not in Service. Your replacement is delayed in transit. Proceed in all haste, repeat, in
all haste, to Annigoni."

"Request permission for immediate lift."

Established routine procedures took Helva through
takeoff before she consciously realized what she was doing. Leaving Regulus was the last thing she wanted to do,
but she had her order-tape and she had heard the imperative "all haste" repeated.

"All areas clear for lifting. Proceed. And XH-834. . .?"

"Yes?"

"Good luck."

"Acknowledged," said Helva, ignoring the softened, unofficial farewell. To Theoda, she explained briefly how to strap herself into the pilot chair, following the woman's nervous fingers as they stumbled over the fastenings. Finally assured Theoda would be secure during acceleration, Helva lifted, her rear screen picking up the base cemetery as long as vision permitted.

It no longer made any difference to Helva what speed she attained, but when she found herself increasing acceleration in an unconscious desire to finish her mission quickly and return to Regulus Base—and Jennan—she sternly measured her rate against Theoda's tolerance. Journey speed achieved, she told Theoda she could leave the chair.

Theoda unsnapped the harness and stood uncertainly.

"I was sent here so quickly and I've traveled 24 hours already," she said, looking down at her rumpled, dirty uniform.

"Quarters are aft the central column," and Helva gasped inwardly as she realized Theoda would inhabit the place so recently vacated by Jennan. Instinctively she glanced in the cabin. Someone had already removed Jennan's personal effects. Not one memento remained of his tenancy, no souvenir of their brief happiness. Her feeling of desolation deepened. How could they? When had they? It was unfair. And now she must endure this fumbling female.

Theoda had already entered the cabin, throwing her kit bag on the bunk and entering the head. Helva politely withdrew her vision. She tried to make believe the homey noises of showering were Jennan's, but her new passenger's ways were completely different.

The difference, oh, the difference to me, cried Helva, mourning.

Lost in an elegy, she became only gradually aware of the quiet in the ship and, scanning discreetly, saw Theoda stretched out on her back in the limp, deep slumber of the exhausted. In repose, the woman was older than Helva had initially assumed. Now, too, Helva justly attributed the ineptitude and fumbling to the true cause, exhaustion. The face was deeply lined with sorrow as well as fatigue; there were dark smudges under the closed eyes. The mouth was dragged down at the corners from familiarity with pain. The long, blunt-ended fingers twitched slightly in reflex to a disturbing dream and Helva could see the inherent strength and sensitivity, the marks of use in odd scars on palm and fingers, unusual in an age where manual work was mainly confined to punching buttons.

Jennan had used his hands, too, came the unbidden comparison. Mourning reclaimed Helva.

"How long did I sleep?" Theoda's voice broke into Helva's reminiscences as the woman wove sleepily into the forward cabin. "How much longer is the trip?"

"You slept 18 hours. The tape estimates an elapse of 49 hours galactic to Annigoni orbit."

"Oh, is there a galley?"

"First compartment on the right."

"Umm, is there anything you require?" Theoda asked, halfway to the galley.

"My needs are supplied for the next hundred years," Helva said coldly, realizing as the words were formed that her critical need could not be met.

"I'm sorry. I know very little of you ships," Theoda apologized. "I've never had preferential treatment like this before," and she smiled shyly.

"Your home planet *is* Medea?" inquired Helva with

reluctant courtesy. It was not uncommon for a professional person to claim the planet of his current employer.

"Yes, Medea," Theoda replied. She made immediate
noise with the rations she held, banging them onto the
table with unnecessary violence. Her reaction suggested
some inner conflict or grief, but Helva could recall
nothing of great moment connected with Medea, so
she must assume Theoda's problem was personal.

"I've seen your type of ship before, of course. We of
Medea have reason to be grateful to you but I've never
actually been in one," Theoda was talking nervously, her
eyes restlessly searching over the supplies in the galley
cupboards, rearranging containers to see the back of the
shelves. "Do you enjoy your work? It must be a tremendous satisfaction."

Such innocent words to drop like hot cinders on
Helva's unhealed grief. Rapidly Helva began to talk, anything to keep herself from being subjected to another
such unpredictably rasping civility.

"I haven't been commissioned long," she said. "As
a physiotherapist you must certainly be aware of our
origin."

"Oh, yes, of course. Birth defect," and Theoda looked
embarrassed as if she had touched on a vulgar subject.
"I still think it's horrible. *You* had no choice," she blurted
out, angrily.

Helva felt suddenly superior. "Initially, perhaps not.
But now, it would be very difficult to give up hurtling
through space and be content with *walking*."

Theoda flushed at the almost scornful emphasis of the
final word.

"I leave that to whoever is my brawn," and Helva inwardly cringed as she reminded herself of Jennan.

"I've recently heard about one of your ships who
sings," said Theoda.

"Yes, I have, too," said Helva unencouragingly. Must
everything remind her of Jennan's loss!

"How long do you live?"

"As long as we wish."

"That is . . . I mean, who's the oldest ship?"

"One of the 200s is still in active service."

"You're not very old then, are you, being an 800."

"No."

"I am," said Theoda, staring at the empty ration unit she held in one hand. "I am near my end now, I think." And there was no regret in her voice, not even resignation.

It occurred to Helva that here, too, was someone with deep sorrow, marking time.

"How many more hours until planetfall?"

"47."

"I must study," and abruptly Theoda rummaged in her kit for filmfile and viewer.

"What is the problem?" Helva asked.

"Van Gogh in Lyrae II was hit by a space plague similar in manifestation to that which attacked Medea 125 years ago," Theoda explained.

Suddenly Helva knew why Theoda had seen Service ships. She microscoped her vision on Theoda's face and saw the myriad tiny lines that indicated advanced age. Theoda had undoubtedly been alive on Medea at the time of their plague. Helva recalled that the plague had struck a heavily populated area and swept with terrific violence throughout the entire planet in a matter of days—its onslaught so fierce and its toll so great that medical personnel often collapsed over the sick they tended. Others inexplicably survived untouched. The airborne disease spores struck animal as well as human, and then, as suddenly as it had come, almost as if the disease were aware that the resources of a galaxy were on the way to subdue its ravages, it disappeared. Medea had been decimated in the course of a week and the survivors, both the ones hardy enough to endure the intense fever and pain, and those who were curiously immune, spent their years trying to discover source or cause, cure or vaccine.

From her capacious trained associative recall, Helva found seven other different but similarly inexplicable plague waves, some treated with better success than Medea's. The worst one to be recorded had hit the planet Clematis, eliminating 93 percent of all human life before help arrived. Clematis had been placed under eternal quarantine. Helva thought that was rather locking the barn and never bothering to track down the missing horses.

"You had, I gather, sufficient experience with Medea's plague so that your presence may be of help to Van Gogh's people?"

"That is the thought," said Theoda, wincing. She picked up her filmviewer purposefully and Helva realized that more discussion was out of order. She knew, too, that Theoda had painful word associations even at the end of a long life. Helva could not imagine a time centuries hence when mention of Jennan would not hurt.

Annigoni swam into view precisely as the trip chronometer edged onto 67 hours, and Helva found herself immediately answering a quarantine warning from an orbital monitor.

"You have Physiotherapist Theoda on board, do you not?" Helva was asked after she identified herself.

"I do."

"Your landing should set you down as close to the hospital city of Erfar as possible. There is, however, no space field in that vicinity and a meadow has been set aside for your use. Are you able to control your dangerous exhausts?"

Helva wryly assured them of her ability to land circumspectly. They gave her the latitude and longitude and she had no difficulty in bringing herself to a stand in the patch-sized meadow so indicated. A powdery white road led to a long white complex of multiwindowed buildings, half a kilometer away. From the complex came a land vehicle.

"Theoda," said Helva as they awaited the arrival of the

landcar, "in the effects compartment under the control panel, you will find a small gray button. With it attached to your uniform, you can maintain communication with me. If you would be good enough to rotate the upper section of the button clockwise, I can have two-way contact. It would afford me some satisfaction to be in on the problems you encounter."

"Yes, certainly, of course."

"If you rotate the bottom half of the button, I have limited scope vision as well."

"How clever," murmured Theoda, examining the button before attaching it to her tunic.

As the car drew to a halt, Theoda waved at the occupants from the high lock and stepped onto the lift.

"Oh, Helva, thank you for the journey. And my apologies. I'm not good company."

"Nor have I been. Good luck."

As Theoda descended, Helva knew that for a lie. They had been perfect company, each locked in separate miseries. Somehow it had escaped her that grief was a frequent visitor in the universe, that her inability to aid Jennan was scarcely unique. Her sister ships had all had such experiences and were still at their jobs.

"None of them ever loved their brawns as I did Jennan," she soliloquized sullenly, perfectly conscious of how ill her sentiment befitted her steel, yet unable to extricate her thoughts from their unconscious return to misery.

"Request permission to board," came a rough voice at the lift bottom.

"Identification?"

"Senior Medical Officer Onro, Detached Regulus Base. I need to use your tight beam."

"Permission granted," replied Helva after a rapid check of the name in the MedOff roster on file.

MedOff Onro plunged into her lock and, with the briefest of salutes at her central shaft, lunged into the pilot's chair and slapped home the call button on the beam.

"Have you any honest-to-god coffee?" he grated out, swiveling the chair to launch himself from it toward the galley.

"Be my guest," murmured Helva, unprepared for such vigor after several days of Theoda.

Onro's shoulder took a bruising as he careened off the threshold of the galley, wrenched open the cupboards, knocking containers about.

"Coffee may still be in its accustomed place on the third shelf of the righthand locker," Helva remarked drily. "Excuse me; a container just rolled onto the floor."

Onro retrieved it but cracked his head smartly on the corner of the cupboard door he had left open. The stream of invective Helva half expected did not come. The man carefully closed the cupboard with the controlled patience of the much-put-upon and, breaking the heat seal, immediately stalked back to the central cabin and resumed his seat, watching the dial on the tight beam as it warmed slowly to peak, never blinking as he gulped the now steaming hot coffee. Even as he swallowed, the springs in his taut frame began to unwind.

"Creatures of habit, aren't we, XH? I've been dreaming of coffee for 18 mortal days and nights. The stuff they use in its place on this lousy lump of ill-assorted metals makes ME sleepy. Coffee is not as potent as benzedrine nor half as rough on the system. Ah, there they are. I swear these beams take longer every time I have to fool with the damned things."

"Central Base Regulus."

"XH-834 reporting," announced Onro.

"Who?" gasped an unofficial voice.

"Onro talking."

"Yes, sir, didn't recognize your voice."

"Did you think Helva had a cold?"

"No, sir, that wasn't what I thought."

"Well, never mind the chitchat. Put this on the computers and let it do a little brainstorming. I'm too tired. You better check the computerese, too. I haven't been asleep much lately." He turned to Helva, "How d'ya like the luck? First home leave in three galactic years and I have to time my arrival with the plague's. I wonder if I can get a rebate on vacation time." He turned back to the beam. "Here's the garbage," and he rapidly dictated the material. "Now here's a verbal to check it."

"Disease unidentifiable on the Orson scale as a known virus or variation thereof. Patients thoroughly tested and apparently perfectly healthy can develop clinical symptoms in 10 hours; complete deterioration of muscle control, presence of high fever, excessive spinal pain follow in 3 days. Death caused by 1) brain hemorrhage, 2) heart failure, 3) lung collapse, 4) strangulation or in case where medical help has been late in arriving 5) starvation. All survivors unable to make muscular coordinations of any kind. Extent of brain damage negative. But they might as well be dead."

"Impairment to intellect?" asked Central Control.

"Impossible to ascertain except to hope that the injury to the brain has, as usual, left the intellect alone."

"Julie O'Grady and the Colonel's Lady are sisters under the skin," muttered Helva for she could see through the MedOff's words that the victims of the plague were not as robbed of their bodies by disease as she had been by birth defects.

"Our skintight friend is closer to the truth than she knows," Onro snorted. "Except for infants, there isn't one of them that wouldn't be better off in a shell right now. They aren't going to go anywhere the way they are."

"Do you wish to stand by for report?" asked Central Control.

"Take long?"

"You could get a little sleep," suggested Helva blandly. "These reports don't usually take too long," she added, tapping out a private distress signal to Central as she spoke.

"Not long, MedOfficer Onro," said Central on cue.

"You'll get a crick in your neck, Onro," remarked Helva as she saw him stretch out his long legs and scrunch down in the pilot chair for a catnap. "Use the pilot's bed. I'll give you a jolt as soon as the message returns."

"You'd better or I'll unscrew your safety panel," Onro snapped, lurching drunkenly toward the bunk.

"Yes, of course." Helva watched as he took the two deep breaths that were all that were needed before he was oblivious.

Her contact with Theoda began, sight and sound. Theoda was bending over a bed, her strong fingers soothing the motionless frame of the woman there. Flaccid muscles, lack of reflexes, pasty skin, unfocusing eyes, loose mouth; the chords of the neck strained briefly as the patient made some incoherent sound deep in the throat.

"There is no sensation in the extremities that we can discover," the voice of an out-of-sight person said. "There is some reaction to pain in the torso and in the face but we can't be sure. The patient, if she understands us, can give us no sign."

Helva noticed, and she hoped that Theoda did, that the half-closed eyelids made an almost imperceptible downward motion, then upward. Helva also observed the flaring of the nostrils.

"Theoda," she said quietly so as not to startle her. Even so, Theoda straightened quickly in surprise.

"Helva?"

"Yes. In the scope of my limited range of vision, I could see a twitch of the eyelids and a motion of the nostrils. If the paralysis is as acute as I have learned from MedOff Onro, these bare flickers may be the only muscle controls the patient has. Please ask one of the observers to concentrate on the right eye, another on the left and you observe only the nostrils. Establish a pattern of reply and explain it to the patient and see if she understands you."

"Is that the ship?" an off-sight person demanded irritably.

"Yes, the XH-834 that brought me here."

"Oh," was the disparaging reply, "that's the one that sings. I thought it was the JH or GH."

"Helva is not an 'it'," said Theoda firmly. "Let us try her suggestion, since her vision is considerably more acute than ours and her concentration far superior."

To the patient, Theoda said quietly and distinctly, "If you can hear me, please try to lower your right eyelid."

For an age-long second, there was no movement; then as though the effort were tremendous, the right lid slowly descended the barest fraction.

"In order to be sure this was not an involuntary motion, will you try to dilate your nostrils twice."

Very slowly, very slowly Helva caught the motion of the nostrils. She also saw, which was more important, the tiny beads of perspiration on the upper lip and brow, and quickly called attention to them.

"What a tremendous effort this must be for that imprisoned mind," said Theoda with infinite compassion. Her blunt-fingered hand rested softly on the moist forehead. "Rest now, dear. We will not press you further, but now we have hope for you."

Only Helva was aware of the disconsolate sag and then straightening of Theoda's shoulders as she walked to the next bed.

Helva accompanied Theoda through the entire tour of the plague hospital, from the men's and women's wards to the children's and even into the nursery. The plague had been no respecter of age, and babies of a few weeks had been affected.

"One would have hopes that in the younger and more

resilient body those tissues that were damaged, if any have been, would stand the best chance of regeneration," remarked one of Theoda's guides. Helva caught part of a gesture that took in the 50 cribs of motionless infants in the ward.

Theoda leaned down and picked up a small pink, blonde infant of 3 months. The flesh was firm, the color good. She tweaked the pectoral fold with unnecessary force. The baby's eyes widened and the mouth fell open. A slight croak issued from the throat.

Quickly Theoda snatched the child to her breast, rocking it in apology for the pain. Sight and sound were muffled by the blanket but not before Helva, too, had seen and realized exactly what Theoda had.

Theoda was rocking the child, so that Helva caught only elusive fragments of a violent discussion. Then her scope of sight and sound returned as Theoda laid the child in the crib on its stomach and carefully started to move the child's arms and legs in an approximation of the crabbed action that is the beginning of independent loco- motion.

"We will do this with every child, with every person, for one hour every morning and every afternoon. If necessary, we will commandeer every adult and responsible adolescent on Annigoni for our therapists. If we are to reach the brain, to restore contact between intellect and nerve, we must repattern the brain centers from the very beginning of brain function. We must work quickly. Those poor imprisoned people have waited long enough to be released from their hells."

"But . . . but . . . on what do you base your premise, Physiotherapist Theoda? You admitted that the Medean plague has fewer points of similarity than originally thought."

"I can't give you a premise right now. Why must I? My whole experience leads me to *know* that I am right."

"Experience? *I* think you mean 'intuition'," continued

the official stuffily, "and we cannot, on the basis of one
woman's intuition, conscript the workforce needed from
busy citizens . . ."

"Didn't you see the beads of sweat on that woman's
face? The effort required to do so simple a thing as lower
an eyelid?" demanded Theoda tartly. "Can any effort
required of *us* be too much?"

"There is no need to be emotional," Theoda was told
testily. "Annigoni has opened herself to these survivors
with no thought of the danger of exposure to the same
virus . . ."

"Nonsense," Theoda said. "Before your ships approached Van Gogh you made certain that the plague
had passed. But that is neither here nor there. I will return to the ship and contact Central Control. I'll have
your premise and authorization all neatly printed out."
She whirled around, facing back into the ward so that
Helva could see the respectfully waiting wardnurses. "But
any of you who love children and trust another woman's
instinct, do as I just did whether it is authorized or not.
There is nothing to be lost and the living to be released."

Theoda stormed out of the hospital, brushing aside the
complaints and temporizing of the officials. She stumbled
into the landcar, ordering it back to the ship. Her tight,
terrible voice made the driver hold his tongue. Helva
could see her strong fingers washing themselves, straining
in a tense clasp of frustration, never idle, groping, grasping, clenching. Then Theoda reached up to the button
and cut the contact abruptly.

Unconcerned, Helva switched to the wide vision of her
exterior scanners and picked up the landcar as it sped
toward her. The car discharged its passenger and left. But
Theoda did not step onto the lift. Somewhat at a dis-
advantage because of the angle, Helva could only watch
as Theoda paced back and forth.

In the bunk, Onro slept on and Helva waited.

"Permission to enter," said Theoda finally, in a low voice.

"Granted."

Stumbling again, one hand in front of her as if feeling her way, Theoda entered the ship. Wearily she sagged into the pilot's chair and, leaning forward on the console, buried her head in her arms.

"You saw, Helva," muttered the therapist, "you saw. Those people have been like that for upward of 6 weeks. To move an eyelid with a commensurate effort of budging a ton. How many will come out of this sane?"

"They have an additional hope, Theoda. Don't forget, once you can establish that the integral intellect remains, the body may be bypassed. There are advantages to that, you know," she reminded the therapist.

Theoda's head came up and she turned in her chair, looking in amazement at the panel concealing Helva's shell-encased body.

"Of course. You're a prime example, aren't you?"

Then she shook her head in disagreement.

"No, Helva, it's one thing to be bred up to it, and another to be forced into it as the only expedient."

"The young would experience no shock at shell life. And there are, I repeat, advantages, even distinct gains, to be made. Witness my ability to follow your tour."

"But to have walked, and touched, and smelled, and laughed, and cried . . ."

"To have cried . . ." gasped Helva, "to be able to weep. Oh, yes," and an unendurable tightness filled her mind as her brief respite from grief dissolved.

"Helva . . . I . . . in the hospital . . . I mean, I'd heard that you had . . . I'm sorry but I was so lost in my own problem that I just didn't realize that you were the ship who sang, and that you'd . . ." Her voice trailed off.

"Nor did I remember that at Medea the virus didn't just isolate the intellect in the body; it destroyed it, leaving only a mindless husk."

Theoda turned her head away.

"That baby, that poor baby."

"Central Control to the XH-834, are you receiving?"

Theoda, startled by the voice at her elbow, jerked back from the lighted tight-beam face.

"XH-834 receiving."

"Prepare to tape computer report on MedOfficer Onro's request."

Helva activated the apparatus and gave the a-ok.

"Verbal?" asked Theoda in a stage whisper.

"Verbal requested," Helva relayed.

"No correlation between age, physical stature, health, ethnic group, blood type, tissue structure, diet, location, medical history is indicated. Disease random, epidemic force. No correlation muscle, bone, tissue, blood, sputum, urine, marrow in postplague postmortem. Negative medication. Negative operation. Possible therapy."

"There!" cried Theoda in triumph, jumping to her feet. "Therapy the only positive."

"Only 'possible'."

"But the only *positive* factor, nonetheless. And I'm positive it's repatterning."

"Repatterning?"

"Yes. It's a bizarre therapy and it doesn't always work, but the failure may have been because the intellect had retreated in desperation," Theoda argued with vehement confidence. "To be trapped, unable to make even the simplest communication—can you imagine how ghastly that must be? Oh, what am I saying?" she said, turning in horror toward Helva's presence.

"You're quite right," Helva assured her blandly with inner amusement. "It would be intolerable if I could no longer control the synapses as I do now electronically. I think I should go mad having known what it is to drive between the stars, to talk across light-years, to eavesdrop in tight places, maintaining my own discreet impregnability."

Theoda resumed her restless pacing.

"But you don't really think," Helva said, "that you are going to get those skeptics to do the necessary recruiting on the basis of the computer report?"

"The therapy was a positive factor," Theoda insisted, her face set in stubborn lines.

"It was a 'possible'. I'm not arguing with your position, only pointing out their reaction," she added as she saw Theoda gathering breath to protest. "I'm convinced. They won't be and it also won't be the first time when good samaritans have decided to rest on their laurels prematurely, convinced that they have in conscience done all they could."

Theoda set her lips.

"I'm positive those people can be saved . . . or at least enough of them to make every effort worthwhile."

"Why? I mean, why do you think repatterning will do the trick?"

"It's a 20th century technique, used before the correction of the majority of prenatal defects and with some severe brain or neural accidents. I took my degree in physiotherapeutic history. So many of the early problems in the field no longer exist, but occasionally, of course, an ancient disease reappears suddenly. Like the epidemic of poliomyelitus on Evarts II. Then the old skills are revived.

"This plague, for instance, is like the Rathje Virus, only the original strain attacked sporadically and recovery was slow but certain. Perhaps because therapy was initiated as soon as the painful phase passed. Also, I believe that the paralysis was not so acute, but the strain has obviously mutated in the centuries and become more virulent.

"However, the similarity cannot be denied. I brought my tapes, Helva," Theoda said eagerly, enthusiasm giving her face a semblance of youth. "The Doman-

Delacato repatterning was used with great effect on the victims of the Rathje Virus.

"You don't suppose," and Theoda stopped dead in her tracks, "we could also prove that the space plague spores had passed by old Terra at that time. Have you any details on galactic spiral patterns?"

"Stick to medical and physiological aspects, Theoda," laughed Helva.

Theoda scrubbed at her face with her hands as though she would wash away fatigue and stimulate her tired brain to inspiration.

"Just one child, one proof is all I need."

"How long would it take? What age child is best? Why a child? Why not that poor woman of the eyelid?"

"The medulla handles reflex action at birth. The pons, maturing at 20 weeks, directs crawling on the stomach. By 25 weeks, the midbrain has begun to function and the child begins to learn to creep on hands and knees. By 60 weeks, the cortex begins to act and controls walking, speech, vision, hearing, tactile and manual competence."

"A year would be too young . . . no understandable speech," Helva mused outloud, remembering her first birthday without effort. But she had already been "walking" and "talking."

"The best age is 5," said another voice. Theoda gasped as she saw Onro standing in the galley, a warming container in one hand. "Because that is the age of my son. I'm Onro, MedOfficer. I sent for you, Physiotherapist Theoda, because I heard you never give up." His face, still creased with blanket folds, turned hard, determined. "I won't give up either until my son walks, talks, and laughs again. He's all I have left. What a way to spend a happy vacation." Onro laughed bitterly, then gulped at the steaming coffee.

"You're Van Goghian?" Theoda demanded.

"By chance, and one of the immunes."

"You heard what I was saying? You agree?"

"I've heard. I neither agree nor disagree. I'll try anything that sounds even remotely feasible. Your idea is reasonable and the computer has only the one positive suggestion—therapy. I'll bring my son."

He turned when he reached the lock, shook his fist back at Helva. "You drugged me, you silver-plated sorceress."

"An inaccurate analysis, but the insult is accepted," Helva said as he disappeared, scowling, down the lift.

Elated, Theoda snatched out her viewer and carefully restudied the films of the technique she would try.

"They used steroids as medications," she mumbled. "Have you any?"

"No medication was indicated on the report," Helva reminded her, "but you can get Onro to steal what you require from the synthesizer in the hospital. He *is* a Senior MedOfficer."

"Yes, yes, that helps," and Theoda lapsed again into fierce concentration. "Why did they use . . . oh, yes, of course. They didn't have any conglomerates, did they?"

Fascinated, Helva watched as Theoda scanned the film, winding and rewinding, rechecking, making notations, muttering to herself, pausing to gaze off into space in abstracted thought.

When Theoda had been through her notes the fourth time, Helva insisted with authority that she eat something. Theoda had just finished the stew when Onro returned with the limp body of a redheaded child in his arms. Onro's rough face was impassive, almost rigid in its lack of expression as the child was tenderly laid down on the bunk. Helva noticed the almost universal trait of the victims, the half-closed eyes, as if the lids were too heavy to keep open.

Kneeling down beside the bunk, Theoda turned the boy's face so that her eyes were directly on a level with his.

"Child, I know you can hear. We are going to work

your body to help you remember what your body could do. Soon we will have you running under the sun again."

Without more ado and disregarding Onro's guttural protest, she placed the boy on his stomach on the deck, seized one arm and one leg and signaled to Onro to do likewise.

"We are taking you back to the time when you were a baby and first tried to creep. We are making your body crawl forward on your belly like a snake."

In a patient monotone, she droned her instructions. Helva timed the performance at 15 minutes. They waited a full hour and repeated the drill. Another hour passed and Theoda, equally patient, droned instructions to pattern the child's body in a walking, upright position, alternating the left hand with right foot, and right hand with left foot. Another hour and she repeated the walking. Then back to the crawling, again and again in double repetition: the two therapists caught naps when they could. Surreptitiously, Helva closed her lock, cut the cabin audio on her relays and ignored the insistent radio demands from the hospital that she put Theoda or Onro on the radio. After 24 hours, Theoda alternated the two patterns, and included basic muscular therapy on the lax body, patiently, patiently manipulating the limbs in the various attitudes and postures, down to the young toes and fingers.

By the 27th hour, Onro, worn by previous exhaustion, frustration and increasing hopelessness, dropped into a sleep from which violent shaking could not rouse him. Theoda, looking more and more gray, continued, making each repetition of every motion as carefully and fully as she had the first time she started the intensive re-patterning.

Helva ignored the crowd outside. She paid no attention to the muted demands, threats, and entreaties.

"Theoda," Helva said softly in the 30th hour, "have

you noticed, as I have, the tendency of the neck muscles to contort?"

"Yes, I have. And this child was once so far gone that a tracheotomy was necessary. Notice the scar here," and she pointed to the thin mark. "I see, too, that the eyelids describe a slightly larger arc than when we began the therapy. The child knows we are helping him. See, his eyes open . . . ever so slightly, but it is enough. I was right! I knew I was right!"

"You won't have much more time," Helva said. "The authorities of Annigoni have called in a Service Craft and it is due to land beside me in half an hour. I will be forced to open or risk damage to the ship, which I am conditioned to avoid."

Theoda looked up, startled.

"What do you mean?"

"Look in my screen," and Helva turned on the picture at the pilot's console so that Theoda could see the crowd of people and vehicles clustered at the base of the ship. "They are getting a bit insistent."

"I had no idea."

"You needed quiet. I could at least supply that," Helva replied. "But to all intents and purposes, their Senior Medical Officer, his son, and their visiting technical adviser are imprisoned inside me and they suspect that my recent . . . that I am turning rogue."

"But didn't you tell them we were conducting therapy . . ."

"Naturally."

"Of all the ridiculous . . ."

"It's time for therapy. Every minute is necessary now."

"First he must be fed."

Theoda carefully inserted the concentrated solution in the thin vein, smoothing down the lump that formed as the nutritive spray entered.

"A sweet child, I imagine, Helva, from his face," she said.

"A young hellion, with all those freckles," snorted Helva.

"They are usually the sweetest inside," Theoda said firmly.

Helva noticed the eyelids droop down on the cheek and then raise again. She decided she was right, not the therapist. Imagine calling red hair and freckles sweet!

Again the patient routine, the assisted patterning. Then a loud thud startled Theoda. It shook the sleeping form of the doctor where he lay on the deck. Helva, with one eye outside, had expected the blow. Onro roused himself garrulously, unaware at first of his surroundings.

"Whassa matter?"

A second dull thud.

"Whatinell's happening? Who's knocking?"

"Half the planet," remarked Helva drily and tuned up the exterior visual and aural. She immediately cut down the nearly deafening noise.

"All right, all right," she said loudly to the audience, her voice amplifying easily over their angry roars.

"DEMAND PERMISSION TO ENTER, XH-834," squalled someone at her base. She meekly activated the lift and opened the lock. Onro stamped to the opening and leaned down, shouting.

"Whatinell's the matter here? Go 'way, all of you. Have you no decency? What's the bloody fuss about? Can't a man get some sleep around here? Only quiet place on the whole lousy planet."

The lift had by then come abreast of him with the brawn from the service ship and the stuffy hospital official of Theoda's tour.

"MedOfficer Onro, we feared for you, particularly when your son was discovered missing from his bed."

"Administrator Carif, did you expect that the lady therapist had kidnapped me and my son and was holding us hostage on a rogue ship? Romanticists all. Hey, what are you doing . . . you young squirt," he demanded as the brawn made a pass at the protected panel of Helva's shaft.

"I am following orders from Central Control."

"You warm up that tight beam and tell Central Control to mind its own damned business. Weren't for Helva here and the peace and quiet she maintained for us, don't know where we'd be at."

He stalked into the cabin, where his son again lay on the floor, with Theoda painstakingly applying her Doman-Delacato therapy.

"Don't know how many we'll save this way, but it does work and you, young man, will tell Central Control, after you've told them to go to hell for me, that they will issue authority to Theoda to recruit any and all . . . if necessary . . . of this planet's population as a therapy force to activate her rehabilitation program."

He got down on his knees by his son.

"All right, boy, crawl."

"Why, that child will catch a cold in this draft . . ." the official exclaimed.

Some woman was trying to get Helva to lower the lift for her but Helva ignored her as the beads of sweat started on the child's face. There was no muscular movement, not so much as a twitch.

"Son, try. Try. Try!" pleaded Onro.

"Your mind remembers what your body once could do, right arm forward, left knee up," said Theoda, with such control that no hint of the tension she must feel showed in her calm, gentle tones.

Helva could see the boy's throat muscles moving convulsively but she knew the watchers were expecting more dramatic motions.

"Come on, momma's sweet little freckled-face boy," she drawled in an irritatingly insulting voice.

Before the annoyed watchers could turn to remonstrate her, the boy's elbow had actually slid an inch on the floor and his left knee, slightly flexed by Theoda's hands, skidded behind as the throat worked violently and a croaking sound issued from his lips. With a cry of inarticulate joy, Onro clasped his son to him.

"You see, you see. Theoda was right."

"I see that the child made a voluntary movement, yes," Carif was forced to agree. "But one isolated example is . . ." He spread his hands expressively, unconvinced.

"One is enough. We haven't had time for more," Onro said. "I'll put it to the people out there. They'll be the workforce."

Carrying his son to the lock, he yelled down what had happened. There was great cheering and applause. Then the little group at the base of the ship kept pointing urgently to the woman who had begged for the lift.

"I can't hear you," Onro called, for many people were shouting at once, all trying to get across the same idea.

Helva sent the lift down and the woman came up it. As soon as she was halfway to Onro she shouted her message.

"In the nursery, we did as Therapist Theoda suggested. There is already some improvement among the children. Not much, not much and we want to know what we are doing wrong. But four of the babies are already able to cry," she babbled, stepping into the ship and running to Theoda, where the woman leaned wearily against the door jamb. "I never expected to be happy to hear a baby cry again. But some are crying and some are making awful sounds, and one little girl even waved a hand when she was diapered. Oh, we've done just what you said."

Theoda looked her triumph at Carif and he, shrugging acceptance of the accomplishment, nodded.

"Now, Carif," said Onro briskly, stepping into the lift, his son still cradled in his arms, "this is what we'll do. How we'll organize. We don't have to take everyone on your very busy planet. The Youth Corps can be called in from Avalon. Just their bag of tricks."

"Thank you for believing in me," Theoda told the nurse.

"One of the babies was my sister's," the woman said softly, with tears in her eyes. "She's the only one alive from the entire town."

The lift had come back up and the "brawn" and the nurse took it. Theoda had to pack her gear.

"The easy part is over, Helva. Now it's all uphill, encouraging, instructing, upholding patience. Even Onro's son has a long, long way to go with therapy before he approaches his preplague physical condition."

"But at least there is hope."

"There is always hope while there is life."

"Was it *your* son?" asked Helva.

"Yes, and my daughter, my husband, my whole family. I was the only immune," and Theoda's face contorted. "With all my training, with all the skill of years of practice, I couldn't save them."

Theoda's eyes closed against that remembered agony.

Helva blacked out her own vision with a deep indrawn mental breath as Theoda's words echoed the protest she herself had voiced at her ineffectuality. It still burned in her mind: the searing memory of Jennan, looking toward her as he died.

"I don't know why one makes a certain emotional adjustment," Theoda said wearily. "I guess it's the survival factor forcing you to go on, preserving sanity and identity by a refocusing of values. I felt that if I could learn my profession so well that never again would I have to watch someone I loved die because of my ineffectiveness, then the ignorance that killed my family would be forgiven."

"But how could you have turned a space plague?" Helva demanded.

"Oh, I know I couldn't have, but I still don't forgive myself."

Helva turned Theoda's words over in her mind, letting their significance sink into her like an anesthetic salve.

"Thank you, Theoda," she said finally, looking again at the therapist. "What are you crying for?" she asked, astonished to see Theoda, sitting on the edge of the bunk, tears streaming unheeded down her face.

"You. Because you can't, can you? And you lost your Jennan and they never even gave you a chance to rest. They just ordered you up to take me here and . . ."

Helva stared at Theoda, torn with a variety of emotions: incredulous that someone else did understand her grief over Jennan; that Theoda was, at the moment of her own triumph, concerned by Helva's sorrow. She felt the hard knot of grief coming untied and she was suddenly rather astonished that she, Helva, was the object of pity.

"By the Almighty, Helva, wake up," shouted Onro at her base. Helva hurriedly sent down the lift for him.

"What on earth are you crying for? Don't bother to answer," he rattled on, charging into the cabin and snatching Theoda's kitbag from her limp hands. He plowed on, into the galley. "It's undoubtedly in a good cause. But there's a whole planet waiting for your instructions . . ." He was scooping up all the coffee containers he could find and stuffing them into the kitbag, and his pockets. "I promise you can cry all you want once you've given me the therapy routine." He made a cradle of her hands and piled more coffee cans on. "Then I'll lend you my shoulder."

"She's got mine any time she wants," Helva put in, a little unsteadily.

Onro stopped long enough to glance at Helva.

"You're not making sense either," he said in an irascible voice. "You haven't *got* a shoulder."

"She's making perfectly good sense," Theoda said stoutly as Onro started to push her toward the lock.

"Come on, Theoda, come on."

"Thank you, my friend," Theoda murmured, turning

back to Helva. Then she whirled away, allowing Onro to start the lift.

"No, no, Theoda, I'm the one who's grateful," Helva called as Theoda's head disappeared past the edge of the lock. Softly, to herself, she added, "I needed tears."

As the landcar zoomed back toward the hospital complex, Helva could see Theoda's arm waving farewell and knew Theoda understood all that hadn't been said. The dust settled down on the road to the hospital as Helva signaled Regulus Base of the completion of her mission and her estimated return.

Then, like a Phoenix rising again from the bitter ashes of her hundred hours' mourning, Helva lifted on the brilliant tail of exploding fuel toward the stars, and healing.

The Ship
Who Killed

EVERY DIVERTED SYNAPSE in Helva's shell-
encased body vibrated in unconditional revolt against the
autocracy of Central Worlds Service.

"All haste, all haste," she snarled in impotent revolt to
her sister ship, the 822, on the private ship-to-ship band
on which not even Cencom could eavesdrop.

The Seld-Ilsa snorted unsympathetically. "You're doing something, which is more than I can say in Mediation
Service. I've spent weeks and weeks on end waiting for
them to make up their minds which planetary crisis is
most crucial. By the time we get there, critical mass has
been reached and we have a helluva mess to clean up."

"You think MedServ doesn't procrastinate?" Helva retorted sharply. "Why Jennan and I . . ." and she stopped,
startled to have been able to mention his name.

Ilsa took advantage of the brief pause and grumbled
on, oblivious to Helva's stunned silence.

"You'd think they'd've briefed us better in training.
When I think of the situations I've already encountered
that were never even mentioned! Theory, procedure,
technique, that's all we handled. Not a single practical
suggestion. Just garbage, garbage, trivial garbage. They
don't need brain ships, they need computers!" The

822 ranted on. "Stupid, senseless, unemotional computers."

Helva spotted the fallacies in the 822's complaints but remained quiet. She and Ilsa had been classmates and she knew from past experience the voids in the other's personality.

"I *heard*," the 822 said confidentially, "that your mission has to do with that blue block building in the hospital annex."

Helva adjusted her right fin scanner but the oblong structure was devoid of any unusual feature that would indicate its contents.

"Have you *heard* when I'm supposed to hasten away from here again?" she asked Ilsa hopefully.

"Can't talk now; here comes Seld back. See you around."

Helva watched as the 822's brawn-half ascended to the airlock and the SI-822 lifted off Regulus Center Base. Seld had partied with Jennan in Helva one time when both ships were down at Leviticus IV. Seld had a passable bass, as she recalled it. Envy briefly touched her. She flicked back to the ambiguous hospital annex, savagely wondering what kind of emergency this would be. And would she remain an X-designate the rest of her service life?

She had set down at the end of the great Regulus field, the farthest edge from the Service Cemetery. Despite her resignation to Jennan's loss, despite Theoda's healing tears, Helva could not bring herself to grind more salt into her sorrow by proximity to Jennan's grave. Perhaps in a century or so . . . Consequently, waiting around on Regulus was painful. And with the 822 gone, she could no longer divert her pain into anger at the prolonged wait she must endure.

"KH-834, your 'brawn' is on her way with assignment tape," Cencom alerted her.

Helva acknowledged the message, excitement stirring

within her. It was almost a relief to receive a double-
initial call, the pleasure overriding her twinge of regret
that her "brawn" partner was feminine. It was a relief,
too, to experience any emotion after the numbing of
Jennan's death. The Annigoni experience had broken her
apathy.

A ground car zipped out from the direction of the massive Control and Barracks complex, skidding to a stop at
her base. Without waiting, Helva lowered the lift and
watched as a tiny figure hefted three pieces of baggage
onto the platform.

"K" meant to stay a while, Helva decided. The lift
ascended and shortly her new brawn was framed in the
open lock, against the brilliant Regulan sky.

"Kira of Canopus requesting permission to board the
XH-834," said the young woman, saluting smartly toward Helva's position behind the titanium bulkhead.

"Permission granted. Welcome aboard, Kira of Canopus."

The girl kicked the limp lump of a fabric bag uncere-
moniously aboard. But she carefully carried the other two
back to the pilot's cabin. The odd-shaped one Helva
identified, after a moment's reflection, as an ancient
stringed instrument called a guitar.

"Naturally they'd send me someone musically oriented," she thought, not at all sure she was pleased with his
infringement on her most cherished memories of Jennan.
She ruthlessly suppressed this unworthy thought with the
admonition that the majority of service personnel were
musically oriented. The infinite possibilities of the art
passed traveltime admirably.

Kira flipped open the other compact case and Helva,
surreptitiously peeking, noticed it was full of vials and
other medical equipment. Kira inspected the contents
with quick fingers and, closing the case, strapped it with
care against the rigors of acceleration on the shelves behind the bed.

Kira was, in form and nature as well as sex, the antithesis of Jennan. Since she was in a carping mood, Helva wondered how much of that was intentional. But that would mean Cencom had more sensitivity than Helva decided, privately, they were computationally blessed with.

Kira of Canopus couldn't weigh more than 40 kilos fully suited. Her narrow face with slanted cheekbones had a delicacy which appeared ill-suited to bear the designation brawn. Her hair, dark brown, was braided tightly in many loops around her long, oval skull. Her eyes, wide set and almond shaped, were of a clear, cool, deep green, thickly lashed. Her fingers, slim and tapering, were as dainty as her narrow feet, oddly graceful in heavy shipboots. Her movements, swift and sure, were quicksilver, full of restless energy, dartingly inquisitive.

Kira reentered the main cabin. Helva, used to Theoda's lethargic movements, had to adjust quickly.

Kira inserted the order tape, locking it into its niche in the pilot's board. As the code ran through, a startled exclamation was wrung from Helva.

"Three hundred thousand babies?"

Kira's laugh was a staccato arpeggio of mirth.

"Assignment Stork, by the holies!"

"You're only temporary?" questioned Helva, trying to keep the irritation out of her voice. There was a magnetism about Kira that appealed to Helva.

Kira smiled wryly. "This assignment will take some time. Only 30,000 are collected already. Even in this day and age, it takes time to make babies."

"I haven't got facilities . . ." Helva began aghast at the thought of becoming a nursery. She broke off as the tape elaborated on the condition of the proposed cargo. "Babies in ribbons?"

Kira, who had had previous briefing on their mission, laughed at Helva's outraged reaction.

The tape continued remorselessly and Helva understood the significance of the miles of plastic tubing and tanks of fluid that had been placed in her not-overgenerous cargo spaces.

In the system of the star Nekkar, an unexpected radiation flare had sterilized the entire population of its newly colonized planet. A freak power failure had resulted in the total loss of the planet's embryo banks. The KH-834's mission was to rush embryos to Nekkar from planets that had answered the emergency call.

In the very early days of space travel, when man had still not walked on Mars, or Jupiter's satellites, a tremendous advance had been made in genetics. A human fetus in its early stages was transferred from one womb to another, the host mother bringing the child to term and giving it birth without having an actual relationship to it. A second enormous stride forward in propagating the race of man occurred when a male sperm was scientifically united with female ova. Fertilization was successful and the resultant fetus was brought to term, the child growing to normal, well-balanced maturity.

It became a requirement of those in hazardous professions, or those with highly desirable dominant characteristics of intelligence or physical perfection, to donate sperm and ova to what became known as the Race Conservation Agency.

As civilization expanded onto newer, rawly dangerous worlds, the custom was for young men and women to leave their seed with the RCA on reaching their majority. It was good sense to have such a viable concentration of genetically catalogued seed available. Thus, given a lack, say, in a generation of a particularly desirable ethnic group, sufficient additional embryos could be released to restore the ecological balance.

On an individual basis, the young wife, untimely widowed, might bear her husband's children from his seed on file at the RCA. Or a man, wishing a son of certain pronounced genetic characteristics to perpetuate a family name or business, would apply to the bank.

There were, of course, ridiculous uses made of the RCA facilities: women in the thrall of a hysteria over a noted spaceranger or artist would apply to the RCA for his seed if the male in question was agreeable. But naturally conceived children were the rule rather than the exception. Helva herself had been the naturally inseminated child of her parents.

Generally, the RCA served Central Worlds as a repository in case of just such an emergency as had arisen at Nekkar: the inability of individuals to propagate the race. An appeal had reached the Main RCA on Earth to locate and deliver 300,000 fertilized ova of genetic type similar to the Nekkarese. RCA had 30,000 on hand and had forwarded the call to all major RCA banks throughout the Central Worlds asking for contributions, which the KH-834 would pick up and deliver to Nekkar.

The tape ended with a silent hold cue to Helva. It took her a moment to realize that, though she had the mission information, she had received nothing on her new partner. No matter how temporary this assignment, it would take time. Some basic biography would be essential for Helva to function effectively in partnership with Kira. Obediently she cut the tape, activating a record-store of the balance for later playback. It would appear there were many unusual factors in this assignment. Central Worlds moves in mysterious ways, itself to sustain.

"Well," Helva exclaimed, to end the brief silence after the mission portion of the tape was silent. "I hadn't expected motherhood at my tender age. I see I have underestimated the demands Central Worlds makes of its minions."

Her attempt at levity touched off a violent response in Kira and Helva wondered what under a first magnitude star had she got for a partner.

"Read this tape on me before we proceed with the mission," Kira said in a dead voice, all her previous vivacity wiped out.

She slammed the store button, shunting the mission tape to the ship files, and inserted a second reel. With an almost savage twist she turned on the audio, sitting stiffly erect and motionless as the tape played back, either deaf or impervious to the biograph.

Kira Falernova Mirsky of Canopus had finished all but a year of brawn training. She came of a Service-oriented family that had brought up 10 generations to illustrious ——and once, exalted——careers in Central Worlds' service branches. She had left the Training School on marital leave that had lasted two years, ending at her husband's death. A long term of hospitalization and therapy followed, during which time, the tape noted, Kira had asked for and taken medical training but did not reapply for brawn education. She had responded to a high level request to take this temporary assignment, since her training had matched perfectly the needs of this particular emergency.

Then followed a rattle of personal indices, emotional, psychological and educational, which Helva translated, as she was expected to, to mean that Kira Mirsky of Canopus would make an unusually fine brawn if she gave herself half a chance. The tape ended abruptly, as if there should be more. The omission, probably on the last tag of the mission reel, seemed to sing out its absence far louder than the tritest concluding evaluation or recommendations. Central Worlds had many devious facets and perhaps such an obvious omission was one. Surely Kira sensed it. That damned biograph left too much unsaid, particularly apparent to a brawn trainee. Helva's mind danced with the possibilities and gnawed mental teeth against the silent hold-cue. In the meantime, Helva was faced with a very awkward situation, her new partner stiff with anticipation and predisposed by Central Worlds to make a bad first adjustment to Helva.

Helva made a rude, sibilant noise and was relieved to see Kira react in surprise to it.

"Brains they got?" Helva demanded contemptuously. "I don't call that a proper tape. They forgot half the garbage anyway. Ssscheh!" and she repeated her exasperation noise. "Oh, well, I expect we'll do fine together if only because they left out the usual nonsense. Besides, the mission *is* temporary."

Kira said nothing, but the woodenness left her slender body as if an anticipated ordeal had been canceled. She swallowed hard, licking her lips nervously, still unsure of her position, having steeled her nerves for something unpleasant.

"Let's get the cargo aboard and turn me into a rocking ship."

Kira rose, her body awkward, but she managed to smile at Helva's column. "With pleasure. Have your holds been outfitted?"

" 'With yards and yards of lacing/and a bicycle built for two on it,' " Helva replied, quipping from an ancient patter song. She was determined to establish a comfortable empathy.

Kira's smile was less tentative and her body motion became more fluid.

"Yes, it would look like that, I guess."

"Of course I've never seen a bicycle built for two . . ."

"Or a purple cow?" and Kira giggled girlishly.

"Hmmm. Purple cow, my dear brawn, is an all too apt analogy for our present occupation," Helva replied, ignoring the edge to Kira's laughter. "And don't tell me I'll have room for 300,000 mechanical teats in the cargo space Central Worlds saw fit to give me."

"Oh, no," Kira said. "We don't have but the first 100,-000 accounted for as of the time the tape was cut. We'll swing out from Regulus toward Nekkar, picking up donations as we go, deliver them within the 4-week time limit when the fetuses must be either implanted or decanted, and swing around the Wheel until we do meet the quota."

Helva knew this from the tape. "Three hundred thousand isn't a very big number for a planetary population of a million that needs to expand."

"My dear KH-834," and Kira savored the name, "the word 'temporary' particularly when used by our beloved Service, has elastic qualities of infinite expansion. Also, another team, with drone transports, is recruiting orphans from unsocialized worlds to insure the proper age variations. But born children aren't *our* concern."

"The heavens be praised!" Helva muttered under her breath. She did not have room to transport many active live bodies nor the inclination, not so soon after Ravel.

Kira smiled back at Helva over her shoulder as she contacted the Hospital Unit to request transfer.

"Will you activate the pumping equipment?" she asked Helva, who was in the process of doing just that.

The miles of plastic tubing, once filled with the tiny sacs of fertilized ova, would contain the nutritive and amniotic fluids necessary for the growth of the embryos.

The continuous ribbon of tiny compartments, each with its minute living organism, was prepared for the voyage with the caution and care of a major surgical operation on a head of planet. Each segment must contact an intake point for the nutritive fluid and an outgo valve for the dispersal of wastes. Each meter of ribbon was inspected to insure that the proper contact was made. The ribbon and its fluids as well as the encasing tube buffered the embryos with more invulnerability against the rigors of space travel than had they been carried in a natural womb. As long as the KH-834 made the journey to Nekkar within the 4 weeks, all 30,000 fetuses would live to be born.

It became apparent to Helva that Kira was dedicated, in a detached if professional way, to the assignment. Central Worlds might be relying on a maternal instinct as additional insurance for the mission. Helva, to her inner amusement, found herself, the pituitarily inhibited shell-person, rising nobly to the challenge. Kira, obviously young enough to some day enjoy motherhood, was completely uninvolved. Yet the affinity Helva felt toward these minute voyagers was basically a shell reaction. They were, after all, encapsulated as she was, the difference being that they would one day burst from their scientific husks, as she never could nor even desired to. Still, she felt a growing protectiveness, above and beyond the ordinary, toward her passengers. The situation didn't appear to touch Kira's psyche, and that puzzled Helva.

She struggled to identify the coldness of Kira's reaction and could not. Then the technicians who had effected the installation of the precious cargo withdrew, and Helva was busy with the mechanics of takeoff.

It was a pleasure to have a passenger who knew how to take care of herself. Not that Theoda had been a burden in the psychological sense of the word, but Kira knew the procedures and Helva did not need to spare a thought toward her. Takeoff was under minimum thrust, not that the triply buffered embryos could suffer damage had she blasted off with all power, but Helva preferred to take no unnecessary chances and there was plenty of time to reach Nekkar in Böotes' sector.

First planet of call would be Talitha, where 40,000 future citizens of Nekkar had been prepared. After lift, Kira made a careful check on all circuits in the nursery, confirmed her findings with Helva's remote monitors and informed Cencom that they were clear of Regulus and driving toward Talitha.

The formalities ended, Kira swung slowly around in the gimbaled pilot's chair. Her slenderness lost in the padded armchair, she seemed both too fragile and young for her responsibilities.

"The larder is well stocked," Helva suggested.

Kira stretched leisurely, moving her shoulders around to ease the taut muscles across her back. She shook her head sharply, sending a shower of hair fasteners slithering across the cabin as her braids came tumbling out of the

coronet. Helva watched, fascinated. Shoulder-length hair
was the common fashion among spacewomen. The tips
of Kira's braids brushed the floor. Whatever maturity she
possessed departed with the severe coiffeur. Like the
prototype of an ancient fantasy creature, Kira rose from
the pilot's chair and moved across the deck to the galley.

"You wouldn't by any remote computational factor
stock a beverage known as coffee?" Kira asked wistfully.

Helva chuckled, remembering Onro. It seemed to
be an occupational necessity.

"I have three times as much as normal Service inventory suggests," Helva assured her.

"Oh," and Kira's eyes rolled upward in mock rapture,
"you *know!* The ship that brought me here was a pro-
vincial transport from Draconis and hadn't a drop on
board. I nearly perished."

Kira flipped open the proper cabinet and broke the
heatseal, sniffing deeply as the fragrant aroma rose from
the heating liquid. She gulped down a sip, grimacing
against the heat. With an expression of intense relief,
she leaned against the counter. "You and I are going to
do nobly together, Helva. I'm sure of it."

Helva caught the rasp of fatigue in the lilting voice.
Would she always receive passengers in the advance
stages of exhaustion? Or was something the matter with
Helva that all her visitors tended to fall asleep once
aboard her? As a nursery ship this could be an asset,
Helva thought acidly.

"It's been a long day for you, Kira. Why don't you get
some rest? I'm staying up anyway."

Kira chuckled, knowing that the brain ships never
slept. She glanced toward the cargo holds.

"I'll listen with all ears perked," Helva reassured her.

"I'll just finish my coffee and take a short snooze,"
Kira agreed. At the cabin door she turned back toward
Helva's column, cocking her head slightly, her green eyes
sparkling.

"Helva, do you peek?" Her expression was prim to the pursing of her lips.

"I assure you," Helva replied with great dignity, "I am a very properly mannered ship, Scout."

"I shall expect you to conduct yourself decorously at all times as behooves a person in your position in life," Kira replied so haughtily that Helva imagined her pedigree sprinkled with royal ancestors.

Head high, Kira stepped into her cabin only to trip on one of her swinging braids and tumble into the room. Helva was sorely tempted to get a glimpse of Kira's face.

"Don't you dare look in!" Kira exclaimed, her voice breaking with laughter.

Helva had promised nothing about tuning off sound and heard Kira giggling softly. In a short while only the sound of a sleeper's shallow, slow breathing broke the stillness of the ship.

Helva took out of file the portion of the tape which followed the hold-cue. The excerpt was brief and enigmatic.

"Scout Mirsky is a practicing Dylanist, accepting this assignment in Central World Service without suspension of her craft. Accordingly she is not to be permitted shore leave on the following planets, as her activities constitute an infringement of planetary laws restricting proselytization of government groups and/or an embarrassment to Central World Service: Ras Algothi, Ras Alhague, and Sabek. Subject Scout and Ship designate are not, repeat, are not, to approach planets of stars Baham and Homan in the Pegasus Sector or planets of stars Beid and Keid in the Eridanus Sector."

Nothing could be clearer than that, but the reasoning behind such restrictions was unfathomable. And Kira was a practicing Dylanist, whatever that was. The name had a familiar ring and the guitar that Kira cherished suggested a musical group of some sort. Well, mused Helva, she'd let it come up in conversation naturally.

The 6 days to Talitha were livened by Kira's rapid switches of mood and manner, from gamine to queen, welcome to Helva after Theoda's stolidness and as counterpoint to her painful memories of Jennan. Helva literally did not know what Kira would do next. However, when it came time to check their passengers, Kira was deftly professional and painstakingly thorough.

Dubhe, the second planet on their tour, called in to confirm a contribution of 40,000 fertilized ova, to be ready at touchdown. Kira checked computations on ETA at Dubhe, arriving at the same figure simultaneously with Helva. Child she might look, child she might play, but Kira's working mind was sharp and accurate.

The transfer at Talitha went without undue incident because Kira's acute attention to detail averted the one possible accident. An attendant, too eager to finish his assignment, tripped over the leads to a fluid tank in the now-crowded cargo hold.

Kira lit into him with a furious catalogue of his ancestors, his present worth, his future career potential, and his probable imminent demise if he repeated his awkwardness. She did so in three languages other than Basic that Helva knew and several that had the advantage of sounding ever more vicious. Yet the minute she had exhausted her choler, she turned, coolly collected, to the head of the detail with apologies.

Once lifted from Talitha, Kira shook loose the pins that held her braids and settled in the pilot's chair with a sigh of relief.

"I caught three of your descriptions of him, but the others were beyond me."

"I find that old Terran Russian, mixed with liberal neumagyarosag, is extremely vitriolic in sound," Kira said. "Actually I was only repeating a recipe for a protein dish called paprikash. It sounds much, much worse, doesn't it?" She grinned broadly at Helva, her green eyes wide.

"Effective, too. The oaf positively blanched."

"Thorn . . . ." and Kira cut off her words, pressing her lips firmly together, her face, for one tiny moment, showing inner pain. "I think," she murmured, closing her eyes, "I'm hungry." Her voice was breathless, like a child's. "And," her eyes flashed open, her face composed again, "I think I shall make paprikash! Since, you realize, I have just furiously remembered the accurate receipe." She danced across the floor. "Taught me by an old gypsy." She waggled her finger at Helva. "Promise not to peek. It's a family secret."

She pivoted on her toes, round and round into the galley, laughing breathlessly as she caught the counter for support.

"Doesn't it smell heavenly?" Kira demanded of Helva, later pausing with the dish raised to Helva's column. "Be better with noodles and thick crusty bread. Hmmm!" she mumbled happily over a full mouth. "Oh, perfect. I have not lost my touch." She put her fingers to her lips, releasing a kiss to the air in the extravagance of gustatory enjoyment. "Marvelous." She curled her legs under her on the wide pilot's chair and ate quickly, licking her fingers occasionally when the stew splashed.

"You make me wish I wasn't nourished by a bunch of flagons," Helva remarked. "I've never seen anyone enjoy the simple business of eating as much as you do. And you don't seem to suffer from excess calories."

Kira shrugged negligently. "Excellent metabolism. Absolutely unalterable. That's me!" That fleeting edge of bitterness crept into the gay voice.

Helva began to suspect that these sudden switches of mood were less the product of a naturally volatile spirit than the elaborate defenses of a badly hurt woman, struggling to suppress her pain by overriding all references to it.

Helva remembered how carefully the guitar case had been stowed in the closet. Not so much as a hint had

Kira made that it was there, silently waiting. Was this
out of deference to Helva's recent tragedy?—for surely
Kira knew of Jennan's death and the legends that had
already begun to cling to the 834. Or was Kira avoiding
the guitar for a reason of her own?

Kira had finished her meal. The dish lay on her lap.
Her face was brooding, eyes fixed on a spot at the base of
the control console.

Her whole attitude was apathetical and unhealthy.
Helva knew she must break this mood. Kira had somehow been touched on too vital a point—despite the
overtly innocuous conversation—to help herself.

Softly, without conscious choice from her wealth of
musical references, Helva began to sing an old air:

> "Music for a while
>   Shall all your cares beguile;
>   Wond'ring how your Pains were eas'd."

"How my pains are eased?" hissed Kira, her eyes great
green globes glittering with hatred at the titanium column. "Do you know how my pain will be eased?" She
was on her feet in such a violent upward heave that there
seemed to be no intermediate motion of rising. Tall in
fury, Kira frightened Helva with the sudden strength in
the slight body. "In death! In DEATH!" and she held her
arms straight up, wrists turned toward Helva so that she
saw the thin white scars of arterial cuts.

"You," and Kira's arms dropped rigid to her side.
"You had the chance to die. No one could have stopped
you. Why didn't you? What kept you living after *he*
died?" the girl demanded with trenchant scorn.

Helva drew in her breath sharply, against the tanta-
lizing memory of an anguished desire to dive into the
clean white heart of Ravel's exploding sun.

"Do you realize that even if a person wants to die, it
is not allowed! *Not allowed!*" Kira began to pace wildly,

graceful even in this savage mood. "No. You promptly are subjected to such deep conditioning you cannot. Anything else is permitted in our great society except the one thing you really want—if it happens to be death. Do you realize that I have not been left alone in three years? And now . . ." Kira's face was contorted in ugly anger and contempt, " . . . now you're my nursemaid. And don't think for one moment I'm not aware you have had a confidential report on my emotional instability."

"Sit down," Helva ordered coldly and activated the final section of the mission tape with its restriction. As the import of the message reached Kira, she did sit, slumped lifeless in the pilot chair, her face drained of all emotion.

"I'm sorry, Helva. I'm really sorry." She raised trembling hands in apology. "I just didn't believe they would leave me alone at last."

"They are very good at conditioning," Helva remarked softly. "They must be and they have to be. They can't have ships or people going rogue from grief. But I think they have let you alone. They've merely made sure you can't get to those few worlds where ritual suicide is permitted, like Baham, Homan, Beid and Keid. And they can't allow you to suicide because the ethos of Central Worlds is dedicated to extending life and propagating it wherever and whenever possible. I'm a living example of the extremes to which they are willing to go to sustain a human life. The RCA is another aspect of the same ethos. For you to seek suicide means a breakdown in this ethos which cannot be permitted. Even the Pegasus and Eridani planets limit the conditions under which suicide is condoned and proscribe certain grotesque ceremonies to insure that only the most desperate attempt it.

"You'd think," Helva sighed with exasperation, "they'd figure out some way to alleviate loss, since death is the one thing the great and glorious Central Worlds hasn't been able to cure."

Kira's tumbled hair hid her face from Helva's view.
Even the slim fingers were motionless. The girl had
abandoned herself to grief and suddenly Helva was immeasurably irritated with this immolation in self-pity.
True enough, she had been tempted to suicide, but her
conditioning had held. She had keened her loss to black
space, but she had lifted with Theoda to Annigoni and
gone on with the business of living. Just as Theoda had
after her own tragedy. As many people had, all over the
universe and throughout time. When her medical advisers
had realized that Kira was wallowing in sorrow, they
should have applied a block . . . oh, no, not when Kira
had nearly finished brawn training, Helva remembered
that factor. She had been made block-resistant so the only
therapy was intensive conditioning. They couldn't erase,
only inhibit.

Helva looked dispassionately at her brawn, furious at
her situation, realizing that Central Worlds had known
exactly what they were asking of Helva when they assigned Kira to her. That, too, was part of the ethos. Use
what you have that will get the job done.

"Kira, what is a Dylanist?"

The lowered head jerked up, the curtaining hair falling
away from the face. The scout blinked and turned to
stare at Helva's bulkhead.

"Well, that is the last question I would have expected,"
she said in a quiet voice. She gave a little snort of laughter
and then tossed her head, shaking her hair out of her
way. She looked at Helva thoughtfully, speculatively.
"All right. I'll absolve you of the guilty crime of psychotherapy. Although," and Kira pointed an accusatory
finger at the column, "I was coerced to make this mission
and I thought it awfully suspicious *you* were my ship."

"Yes, that would follow logically, wouldn't it?" Helva
agreed calmly.

Kira laid a slim hand on the bulkhead, on the square
plate that was the only access to Helva's titanium shell

within the column. It was a gesture of apology and entreaty, simple and swift. Had Helva been aware of sensory values it would have been the lightest of pressures.

"A Dylanist is a social commentator, a protester, using music as a weapon, a stimulus. A skilled Dylanist, and *I* wasn't one," and from the emphasis on the pronoun, Helva assumed that Kira considered her husband, Thorn, had been one such, ". . . can make so compelling an argument with melody and words that what he wants to say becomes insinuated into the subconscious."

"Subliminal song?"

"Well, haven't *you* been haunted by a melody?" Kira paused at the door of her cabin.

"Hmmm, yes, I have," Helva agreed, not sure that the theme from Rovolodorus' Second Celestial Suite was exactly what Kira had in mind. Still the point was well taken.

"A really talented Dylan stylist," Kira continued, returning with the guitar case, "can create a melody with a message that everyone sings or hums, whistles, or drums *in spite* of himself. Why, you can even wake up in the morning with a good Dylan-styled song singing in your head. You can imagine how effective that is when you're proselytizing for a cause."

Helva roared with laughter. "No wonder you'd be considered an embarrassment to Central Worlds on the Ophiuchus circuit."

Kira's grin was impish. "I got the chapter, verse, and section on *that*, plus what a waste of time, talent, and ability that could be put to worthwhile use in service to C.W."

She made a face as she struck chords, sour from the instrument's long disuse. She tightened the keys, tuning up from the bass string, her expression unexpectedly tender as she worked. She struck a tentative chord, tightened the E string a fraction more, to nod satisfaction at the resulting mellow sound.

With flashing strong fingers she wove a pattern of chords and notes, drawing more volume from the instrument than its fragile structure suggested. To Helva's amazement she recognized an ancient Bach fugue just as Kira struck an angry discord, clamping both hands on the strings to keep them from resonating.

"Achh," she exclaimed, sharply flapping her hands and then clenching them into tight fists. "I haven't played since . . ." She struck a major chord, then modulated to a diminished minor. "I remember we spent one entire night . . . till noon the next day, actually . . . trying to analyze an early Dylan song. The trouble was, you weren't supposed to analyze Dylan. You had to feel him and if you tried to parse what he was saying into Basic or into psychological terms, it . . . it was meaningless. It was the total imagery of the music and the words that made the gut react. That was the whole purpose of his style. When the gut reacts the mind gets the whiplash and another chip is knocked off the solid block within."

"I'd say his work might be good therapy," Helva remarked dryly.

Kira flashed her an angry look that dissolved into a grin. She made her guitar laugh. "The trouble with therapy is you tend to find too many confusing alternative meanings to the simplest motions and words, and then you're so confused, you suspect everyone and everything." And Kira's guitar echoed the pitch of her words derisively.

A red warning light flashed on the panel simultaneously with an impulse to Helva's internal monitors. The guitar was the sole occupant of the pilot's chair and Kira was halfway down the passageway to the No. 3 hold before Helva could activate her own visual check.

Kira paused at the hold door long enough to assess the damage before she spun to the farther hold, where their additional supplies were stored.

The clumsiness of the technician had, to all scrutiny,

been remedied at the time of the accident by securing the tubing in the demijohn of nutritive fluid. What had not been apparent at that time was that the closure at the other end of the line had been loosened. Sufficient of the fluid had dripped away from the weakened joint to register on the telltale. Helva anxiously checked with her magnified vision along the section of embryos serviced by that tank. There was loss at the joint, but the ribbon was still full.

Kira was back with new tubing and joints. Deftly she removed the faulty equipment, careful in her transfer to prevent air bubbles seeping in along the ribbon. Then she checked the entire length of ribbon and each minute sac under magnification to make certain there were no visible bubbles or disruption to the contact between sac top and the nutritive nipple fastening.

Then she checked the joints in the other ribbons, each line, each flask, every connection. It was a job of several hours' duration but she made no attempt to hasten the process.

Reassured, she and Helva did another check of the internal monitors before she closed the hatch.

"I should have cut him up and made him into the paprikash. That would have served him right!" Kira muttered as she disappeared into the privacy of her cabin.

Helva eavesdropped until she heard the slow, even breathing. All the while the mute guitar stared back at her from the pilot's seat, threads of that haunting melody plaguing Helva as she maintained her vigil.

At Dubhe, Kira insisted on an elaborate spectrum inspection on the disturbed ribbon to make sure none of the several thousand fetuses within the strand had suffered impairment. Whatever emotional problems tormented Kira, she held them apart from her professional life. Her objectivity was the more appreciated by Helva because she had had a glimpse of Kira's personal turmoil.

The KH-834 sped onward from Dubhe to Merak, where another 20,000 waited. On the short voyage between Dubhe and Merak, neither Kira nor Helva mentioned what Helva styled "the paprikash" incident. Kira did not put the guitar away but spent some time every "evening" giving Helva additional samples of Dylanist wit and social penetration, from the ancient dream songs of the Protest Decade in early Atomic history to contemporary examples.

When the call from Alioth came, it interrupted Kira's masterful rendition of a very early Dylan, "Blowin' in the Wind."

Kira carefully laid aside her guitar and answered the call, her face registering polite surprise at the origin.

"Fifteen thousand?" she repeated for confirmation, and received what Helva felt was an unnecessarily curt rejoinder and cutoff.

While Kira had been dealing with the call, Helva had activated the ship's memory files for facts on the planet.

"That's odd," she remarked.

"How so?" asked Kira, jotting down eta computations.

"There's no record of their having a bank. Grim planet. In a highly unstable volcanic period. Use a lot of molten mining techniques. Highest mortality rate in the Central Worlds."

"I think," commented Kira dryly, "you'd better see what Cencom has to say about *our* landing there."

"It's not on the restricted list, Kira," Helva replied, but she activated the tight beam.

"Alioth?" Cencom exclaimed, surprised out of its formal voice. "The mayday didn't go out to them. We've no record of a bank there. Ethnically speaking, it's possible. Hold."

Kira cocked an eyebrow at Helva. "They're checking with I know who. Two gets you one they abort the call."

"Two gets me one of what?" jibed Helva.

"KH," Cencom returned. "Proceed to Alioth. No bank

listed but traders report improvements in mining techniques indicate technological advances at proper level for race propagation. Religious hierarchy powerful, so do not antagonize. Repeat, do not antagonize. And report soonest."

"You just lost two whatever it was you bet," Helva taunted.

"Okay," Kira said with a shrug. "Filmbank have any clips?"

Helva flashed them on the viewer. The first were aspects of the small spaceport. The main city was dominated by an enormous temple built against the side of an extinct volcano; the broad multiple steps leading to it reminding Helva of a ziggurat. She didn't much care for worlds with a religious hierarchy, but she was aware that her opinion was at the moment jaundiced. Too many religions were gloom and doom. Alioth, fourth planet of its solar system, was far enough out from its primary to get little of its brightness and its volcanic era predisposed it to Dantean excesses. One last scene showed a procession of torch-bearing cowled figures crossing a huge central plaza in front of the temple.

"A truly cheerless place," Kira said, making a face. "Well, with only 15,000, we can't have to stay long." She strummed a gay tune to counteract the morbid pictures.

"They *are* in the ethnic group required by Nekkar," Helva remarked dubiously.

"Can't see a thing with all those hoods," Kira said. "You don't suppose the embryos come complete with cowl, do you? That'd be a facer for the Nekkarese," and she giggled, adding a guitar laugh.

"You should say, born with a caul."

Kira threatened Helva with the guitar, then made her inspection of the three holds.

"This extra 15,000 will crowd us a little, with the 20,000 at Merak," Kira said as she worked.

"Alioth is spatially aligned with Nekkar. We can make it there with time to spare. Then, hoiyotoho off on another stork run."

Kira straightened, wrinkling her nose in Helva's direction.

"Hoiyotoho is utterly inappropriate to a stork run."

"For you, maybe, but not for me. I am, after all, an armored maid."

"Ha!" Kira fell silent as she peered through a magnifying lens at a joint.

When the two had finished the inspection, Kira paused at the galley, reaching absently for coffee. She wandered, moody for the first time in nearly a week, into the main cabin and plunked herself down on the pilot's chair, curling her feet under her and sitting quietly, only the vapor of the heating coffee moving.

"Stock run!" she said finally. "D'you realize, Helva, I'm the same ethnic group, too? Those pieces of life are the children of people like me. Only unlike me. Because they have left seed and I have none."

"Don't be ridiculous," Helva snapped, hoping to ward off a Kiran explosion. "You made your RCA duty when you reached your majority, didn't you?"

"No," Kira snapped back. "No. *I* didn't. I had met Thorn by then and *I* was going to have all my children. I didn't need any agency to insure the propagation of those chromosomes that are essentially Kira Falernova Mirsky of Canopus. As a matter of fact," she said sardonically, "I even wrote a Dylan on the RCA, full of wit and drollery, with candid cracks about the uncanned child."

She swung the chair around to face Helva, her eyes narrowed in self-contempt.

"One of the many items my so-censored biograph left out was that my only child died aborning, from his mother's womb untimely ripped, ripping it and rendering her completely barren."

Kira spanned her tiny hips with slender hands. "No life in these loins, ever . . . not implanted nor impregnated. No nothing of Thorn or all we had together. That," and she snapped her fingers, "for our supreme egotistical self-assurance."

It was for such accidents that the RCA recommended seed donations from every young adult. It was pointless to remind Kira of this. She was all too patently aware of her folly.

"That's why I returned to medicine after Thorn's death rather than the Service. But all my studies proved that there was no rebirth in me nor birth for me. Science can do many wonders, make many adjustments, but not that."

She sighed heavily but her bitterness was not as frantic as that first explosion. Helva wondered if Kira had resigned herself to barrenness as she had not, from appearances, resigned herself to living.

"Which is why, dear Helva, it is ironic for me, of all people, to be assisting this particular cargo around the Great Wheel."

Helva refrained from any remarks. Kira finished her coffee and retired to rest. Within a few hours there would be Merak to deal with, then on to Alioth.

They cleared Merak in record time, the technicians being both quick and careful. Alioth was only a few days onward before the last spatial hop to Nekkar. Scout and ship had now achieved a pleasant routine in which Helva filled gaps in her classical and ancient musical repertoire with Kira's comprehensive acquaintance with folk music from old Terra and the early colonial periods of the now major worlds.

Helva woke Kira just before touchdown on Alioth. The scout dressed quickly in a somber tunic, braiding her hair so closely to her scalp Helva wondered her head didn't ache.

Touchdown was not auspicious. To begin with, the

spaceport was overshadowed by the jagged, glowing peaks of Alioth's active continental spine. They were told to touch down some distance from the small rectangular building that housed what spaceport control and administration the inhospitable planet required. Kira protested they were too far from the building to effect a quick transfer and was brusquely informed she was to await the arrival of a ground vehicle. It took its time in arriving, a huge transport truck loaded with cowled figures who took positions around Helva's base, elbow to elbow. Their belligerent attitude and presence seemed an insult to a ship bearing Helva's markings.

"What is the meaning of mounting a guard on a Scout Ship in Central Worlds Medical Service?" Kira demanded in firm tones to the control tower.

"For the protection of your cargo."

At this moment the charge officer of the guard contingent requested permission to enter the scout ship.

"Well?" Helva asked softly of Kira.

"I don't see we have much choice but I suggest you tape this and tight beam it back to Regulus."

"My thought, too," Helva agreed. "And I think I'll play silent."

"A good idea," Kira said, adjusting a contact button on her cloak.

There were many backward planets where the partnership of the mobile brawn scout and his brain ship were improperly understood. On such worlds it often had been to the advantage of the partners to keep the brain's abilities unknown until needed, if needed. The button would allow Helva to keep in sight and sound contact with Kira.

The officer, an ominous, tall figure in his black cowl, appeared at the airlock, which Helva opened. The man, his face unseen, towered above Kira. A thin hand was extruded from the draperies and made a gesture toward breast and hidden face that could be interpreted as a salute of sorts.

Kira responded in kind, waiting for him to speak first.

"Second Watch officer Noneth," he finally intoned.

"Medical Scout Kira of Canopus," Kira replied with dignity. Helva did not fail to note that the girl clung to her planetary designation, rather than a ship-partner identity as KH-834.

"Your presence is required at High Temple to discuss the donation," Noneth said in hollow, measured tones.

"Time is of the essence in a transfer of this nature," Kira began smoothly.

"Time," intoned the officer, "is at the disposal of Him Who Orders. It is at his command you are to come."

"The seed is ready for shipment?" Kira asked, insistent on some information.

A shudder rippled the fabric surrounding the figure of Noneth.

"Do not blaspheme."

"Unintentional, I assure you," Kira said, calmly refusing to offer further apology.

"Come," ordered the officer in a voice of command that crackled with authority.

"He Who Orders bids you come, woman," a sepulchral, harsh voice echoed shrilly through the tiny cabin.

Kira won another mark of respect from Helva when she gave no indication of surprise at that awesome bellow. The scout's eyes flicked briefly over the smooth oval fastening on Noneth's hood. Helva as well as Kira recognized the device for what it was, a two-way control similar to the one Kira wore: a type issued only to Service personnel.

There'd be a nova of a scandal when Central Worlds discovered who was distributing these restricted designs on backward planets.

"The order must be obeyed. The Temple itself has spoken," Noneth cried in a voice quavering with reverence. "Dally not."

The Temple was feminine, Helva realized, having appraised the timbre of the voice.

"I am under orders," Kira said evasively.

"That is the Eternal Truth," Noneth replied, nodding solemn accord, as Kira apparently responded in a manner consonant with his religion. He raised his hand in a stylized gesture and added, "May Death come to you at the moment of your triumph."

Kira, about to make a graceful obeisance, halted and stared up at the hidden face, her eyes wide with shock.

"May Death come to you at the moment of your triumph?" she murmured. The blood drained from her face.

"Is not Death the greatest of blessings?" asked the priest, mildly surprised at her ignorance.

It was all Helva could do to remain silent but a deep instinct stifled her half-formed groan of protest. It took little extra interpolation to surmise that death on Alioth would be the greatest of blessings: relief from the terrible drudgery, the grim and gloomy aspect of the planet, with its hovering, smoking mountains. The normal perils of molten mining plus the daily anxiety of a volcano emerging and erupting underfoot had emphasized the brevity of existence until the emphasis had swung toward death as a welcome respite from grinding toil and miserable conditions. Was Cencom out of its alleged mind when it did not ban Kira from landing on Alioth, knowing her compulsion? She wouldn't even have to strain against her conditioning.

"Yes, Death is the greatest of blessings. That is Eternal Truth," Kira repeated, trancelike.

"Come with me," Noneth enjoined, gently persuasive, his gaunt hand beckoning to Kira. "Come," echoed the sepulchral voice greedily.

The ground car had no sooner left the base of the KH-834 than the guard began to move.

"She will see Him Who Orders," one sighed enviously. "The bareface harlot will be given an unjust reward. Now! Up the lift and let us secure the cargo. Think of it! Thousands more to die to expiate the sin against Him Who Orders."

That was sufficient for Helva. She locked the lift controls and slid the airlock securely tight. Curse, hammer, buffet though those Aliothites might, Helva was invulnerable against such weapons as Alioth's technology possessed. She activated the tight beam to Cencom. Alioth would rue the day its religious hierarchy decided to hijack the cargo of a Service ship—much less kidnap its brawn.

Dispassionately Helva took account of the matter of Kira's departure. The girl had, in the extremes of grief, sought death. But Helva doubted Kira would betray her service. For one thing, she couldn't, although the Aliothites didn't realize the ship was capable of independent thought and action. Having enticed the brawn away, they assumed the ship was grounded, impotent, and they could take their time forcing Kira to accede to their designs on the embryos.

I could just leave, Helva thought. If death is the reward these zealots seek, then I don't need to have any compunctions about burning the guard detail to its due merits. But I cannot leave Kira. Not yet. I have time. What was the matter with Cencom? They were never around when you needed them! And why in the name of little apples did they permit Kira to land on a death-dedicated planet? You idiot, Helva told herself, because they didn't know that's the way the religion turned.

The ground rumbled beneath her. Far to the north a fireball zoomed heavenward, bursting in a shower of lighted fragments. Other fireworks followed, as well as more ominous movement beneath Helva's tailfins. She held herself ready for an instant liftoff if her balance was shaken beyond the normal recovery in her stabilizers. Somewhere to the northeast, another volcano answered the eruption of the first.

Helva saw the ground car carrying Kira reach the central building and she muttered ineffective mental commands for Kira to snap out of her trance and switch on the contact button.

The guard, impervious to the massed eruptions, went right on trying to force the lift mechanism. Their cowls kept falling from their faces and they kept replacing them as if a bare face were indecent. The red light from the fireballs that continued to light the sky illuminated gaunt, ascetic faces, dirty with ingrained volcanic dusts, dull-eyed from improper nutrition and continual fatigue.

Kira alighted from the transport and, flanked by guards, was escorted to a smaller vehicle that disappeared from Helva's augmented vision into the complex of city buildings. The transport turned back to the field and Helva.

An enterprising guard urged his fellows to bring a gantry rig against the ship. Slowly and with much effort, they wheeled the cumbersome frame from a far side of the field.

Helva watched the performance with grim amusement. Their own fault for insisting we set down so far from the facilities of the port. Perhaps they couldn't see in the gloom of Alioth's perpetual twilight that the lock was closed tight, too.

She tried to rouse Cencom on the tight beam, cursing at that delay because she was so worried about not reaching Kira on the contact.

"Contact button," she muttered to herself, recalling the anomalous appearance of one on Noneth's hood. Now, if it were a Service issue or a true imitation, she ought to be able to use it. That Temple female had utilized one to second Noneth's commands to Kira.

Helva wasted no time in throwing open the wide-wave on the contact band. As hastily, she closed it, dazed with the resultant chaotic kaleidoscope of sight and sound that besieged her. Mentally reeling from the impact on her senses, she wondered painfully how she had managed to get several hundred thousand contacts at once. Quickly she scanned the scurrying guards, still trying to wrestle the gantry frame to her. Each one had a button securing his hood at the neck.

"Great glittering galaxies," moaned Helva. "This religion must be composed of schizoids to deal with that kind of chaos."

Holding tightly to her sanity, Helva opened the band a fraction, wincing at the confusion of sound and sight. She tried to focus in on one contact alone but felt herself drowning in the myriad pictures that returned. It was like trying to focus on a pinpoint through the faceting of a fly's eyeball.

Grimly she refined vision to one small area, forcing herself to accept only one of the conflicting and overlapping images that returned to her. She cut out the sound completely. Fortunately every wearer in the selected segment was converging on one location, crossing a huge plaza, crowded with gyrating, swaying cowled figures, their robes flapping around them as they approached the wide deep steps that led up the side of the dead volcano. This was the ziggurat Helva had noticed in the tape clip.

Suddenly everything and every figure tilted. It took Helva a moment to realize she too was rocking with earthquake as three more volcanoes spewed out their guts skyward. She waited, alert, lest the instability of the spaceport field became too critical for her to remain planetbound.

An ecstatic, moaning roar wafted through the air, now hazy as the earth's minute shifts released gases from narrow fissures in the floor of the plaza. Helva, already confused, did not at first catch the significance of the gas or the fact that the ululation was reaching her ship's outer ears, not issuing from the dumb contact circuits.

Helva increased power in the tight beam, desperately trying to raise Cencom over the volcanic interferences.

Simultaneously she cut in the narrow contact, anxious not to lose Kira. Everyone in the plaza was now waving arms aloft, hoods thrown back from joyful faces raised to the spark-filled, gas-fogged skies. Then the Aliothites wheeled, ducking their heads to breathe deeply of the rising gas fumes. Incredulous, Helva watched, as more and more people pushed and crowded around the fissures; inhaling deeply, staggering away; faces rapt, arms aloft, movements erratic. Then Helva realized that the gases were either hallucinogenic or euphoric, doubly dangerous at a time of mass volcanic eruptions. Yet the exposed open plaza was rapidly filling with bodies either already intoxicated or frantically trying to be.

The significance of gas eruptions in the plaza before the Temple of this demoniac religion was not lost on Helva. Obviously, this effect was known and calculated by the temple hierarchy. Helva was revolted and enraged by such depravity and she redoubled her efforts to locate Kira and her escort. They would have to leave the vehicle and enter the plaza on the south side. One multiexposed group caught her searching eyes. There couldn't be two such slender hoodless figures on this mad planet. Kira was just entering the plaza, her inexorable progress toward the ziggurat steps impeded by the jerking, jolting freak-inebriates.

Fully alarmed, Helva widened the band, trying to skip from contact to contact, forward toward Kira. The effect was maddening, like seeing thousands of film tapes all interlocking fuzzily, playing on the same master screen. For the first time in her life, Helva felt vertigo and nausea. Her sense of impending disaster deepened as she tried to reach Kira before she entered the Temple of Death. Placed as it was on the top of the massive ziggurat, right next to the old volcano, it must be heavy with the hallucinogenic gases. Helva thanked the Service for the small blessing that Kira had been desensitized to such hazards as hallucinogens, but the girl was as immobile in her trance as if she were susceptible.

Helva groaned at her inability to reach Kira, spiritually or physically.

"Ooooh," an answering groan rose from the multitude. "The Temple weeps," the garbled cry went up from a thousand throats. Even the guards at the spaceport, wrestling with the gantry frame, echoed the chant.

"Oh," Helva gasped. Her surmise that she was broadcasting to all the Aliothites, was confirmed as this new exclamation was repeated by the crowd. She had been mistaken for the voice of their Temple female.

Oblivious to the multivision, Helva stared at the cylindrical top of the Temple and recognized what she had not consciously identified before. The cylinder was a ship on its long axis, nose and fins buried in the lava of the old eruption. The Temple entrance was nothing more than an airlock, and by the entrance, Helva could trace the faintly visible designation of a Central Worlds brain ship.

As clear as the day she had heard it, the day Jennan had died, Helva recalled what Silvia had told her about another grief-stricken ship. This had to be the 732. And what better place to mourn than a red-dark violent world, so conducive to the immolation of grief? Or had the 732 aimed at the fiery maw of the erupting volcano and somehow been deflected from the seething cone at the last moment, lodged immovably in the lava-flow at its base? Had the 732 turned her tortured mind on the grim world and urged thousands to die in expiation for the death of her beloved?

The requirements of duty were suddenly lucid to Helva and the plans to discharge it sprang to mind. With the genius of sheer desperation, Helva began to sing, her voice a deep, caressing baritone, coloring her resonances with minor-keyed longing, suspending reason to the dictates of sheer instinct.

"Death is mine, mine forever,"

she intoned, repeating the phrase a third above as the responsive Aliothites chanted the first phrase in obedient mimicry. It was like having an incredibly well-rehearsed world-chorus at your disposal. Helva exploited the phenomenon ruthlessly.

> "Sleep I cannot, rest eludes me."

And down a fifth

> "Dreams to plague me, tortured I."

Up to an augmented seventh as the chorus chimed in on a dissonance, calculated to raise inner hackles and pierce the gut with longing.

> "Let me sleep, let me rest, let me die."

Helva sang, her voice sliding into the edged timbre of a harsh, yearning tenor.

Down again to the original musical phrase, but this time the baritone quality was tinged with scorn.

> "Death is mine, mine forever.
> Let me sleep, let me rest, let me die."

The last word became a vibrant crescendo of derision, diminishing to a mocking whisper long after the supporting chorus had completed its cry on the augmented seventh.

"Cencom calling KH-834, will you acknowledge? ACKNOWLEDGE!" the hard official voice of Regulus Base Cencom broke through Helva's fantastic musical improvisation.

"Mayday, mayday," Helva replied in a jolting soprano on both tight beam and the Aliothite contact band. The chorus obediently shrilled out the resounding emergency challenge. Helva caught her breath as she saw Kira stagger with instinctive reaction to the cry.

"Mayday?" Cencom demanded. "You bet—with a cratty fool Dylanizing on Alioth?"

With a shock, Helva realized that was exactly what she was doing, Dylanizing. Her appeal to Kira, though couched musically, the one medium with which she could hope to reach the entranced scout, had crystallized further into the subliminal form of a Dylanesque protest. Exultant, she knew how to manipulate this to her own ends. With a barely perceptible increase in tempo, she repeated her first phrase, no longer a longing legato, but a mocking staccato. As the chorus responded idiotically true to its model, she hurriedly reported to Cencom.

"Alioth's religious head is the rogue ship 732; the religious motivation is death!"

"The brawn, where is your brawn?" Cencom crackled.

"What is the release word for the 732?" Helva hissed, then chanted the second phrase of her Dylan, again picking up the tempo so that the beat as well as the sound had urgency to it.

"Report!" Cencom demanded.

"I don't have time to report, you nardy fool. The release word!" Helva snarled. She jumped her voice an octave and a half, switching registers to heldentenor, her phrase ringing through the plaza in an arrow of sheer emotion-packed sound to pierce the trance of her scout.

Kira's guards were lurching now, half-dazed by the treacherous fumes that filled the plaza. They had Kira by the arms, and Helva, trapped in the background of the mighty chorus, couldn't tell whether they were restraining Kira or hanging onto her for support. The girl alone was unaffected by the hallucinogen.

"Let me sleep, let me rest, let me die!"

Helva's tenor rang, scornfully, lashing viciously at Kira's deathwish.

"You fool," Cencom said. "She *wants* to die!"

"GIVE ME THE RELEASE WORD!" Helva cried at the tight beam in a strident soprano, then projected her voice, bitterly powerful, angrily compelling, thundering the protest:

> "Let me sleep, let me rest, let me die!"

The phrase echoed tauntingly through the plaza. The chorus, unable to imitate the incredible pitch of Helva's voice, dropped to the lower octave. The challenge rocked back across the plaza, punctuated by the massive thunder of erupting volcanoes.

With a sudden, soundless, soul-shattering wrench, the massed glimpses of chaos dissolved and Helva was suddenly of single sight—Kira!—in a darkly curtained chamber, unevenly lit by red braziers. Increasing her dark vision, Helva penetrated the gloom, her attention focused on the hideous object that dominated the room.

On a raised, black basaltic slab lay the decomposing remains of what had once been a man. The teeth were bared whitely through the decayed flesh in a travesty of a smile. The tendons of the neck were stark ridges and the cartilage of his esophagus ended in the indestructible fabric of a scout coverall. His hands, crossed on the chest cavity crumpled by a massive fatal blow, were linked by the intertwined overgrowth of fingernail. The 732's dead brawn lay in state.

And Helva was seeing him through Kira's contact button . . . at last.

A wailing chant filled the chamber, a meaningless, mournful dribble of sound, emanating from the walls, the ceiling, the floor. The mad brain encased in its indestructible titanium shell, had all circuits open, keening, oblivious to everything.

In as soundless a whisper as she could broadcast, Helva muttered swiftly to Kira. "It's the rogue 732. It's gone mad. It's got to be destroyed." It was easier somehow for Helva, knowing what she must do, to think of the 732 as an impersonal "it," rather than the female the brain had once been.

Kira swayed, making no reply.

For one paralyzing demisecond, Helva wondered if the girl had inadvertently opened the contact, if Kira were still in the thrall of the powerful death wish. Had Helva's Dylan protest pierced Kira's self-destructive trance with its mockery? Had Helva succeeded in jolting her brawn to sanity? The release word would be no mortal use if she did not have her mobile brawn's co-operation to immobilize the rogue.

With slow steps Kira approached the bier and its ghastly occupant. The keening grew louder, the mumbling became articulated.

"He has been taken. He Who Orders has been taken," chanted the 732 and the crowd echoed the chant as readily as they had Helva's. "He is gone. Seber is gone."

Not helpless again? Helva cried, silently, her mind overwhelmed by hopelessness.

Eerily another sound was superimposed over the 732's wail.

"Now that dwarf presents a definite problem, Lia," the wowwing, muffled words could barely be distinguished. "I wouldn't be surprised . . ."

It was a man's voice, Helva realized, played back at a lagging speed which distorted the words into a yawing parody. The ship was broadcasting, had broadcast this tape so many times that the sound of Seber's taped voice was as decayed as his corpse on the bier.

Kira continued to sway in her graceful circumnavigation.

"Speak, O Seber, in singing tones that thy servant, Kira, may hear the music of thy beloved voice," Kira crooned, making an obeisance to the column behind which lay the shell of the mad 732.

Helva barely managed to suppress the cry of intolerable relief at the cues Kira was feeding her.

"CENCOM, THE RELEASE WORD!" Helva pleaded on the tight beam just as the 732's crooning broke off abruptly. Helva could almost feel the ship's held breath.

Delay! Delay! Where was Cencom!

"Lia, the interference on my contact is incredible. Can't you clear up the relays? That dwarf is wreaking havoc . . ."

Even Kira jumped involuntarily as Helva, deepening her voice to a baritone approximation of Seber's, adlibbed frantically.

"Can't seem to read you clearly. Lia? Lia? You got wires crossed?"

"Seber? Seber?" shrieked the rogue ship, her voice wild with incredulous hope. "I'm trapped. I'm trapped. I was thrown off course when the edge of the volcano blew. I tried to die. I tried to die, too."

Kira was fumbling with the draperies at the bulkhead. Her escort, roused from their euphoria as they sensed sacrilege, dove toward Kira. Her swift hand caught one on the voice box in a deadly chop. She ducked under the other man, using her body to throw him against the bier so squarely that his head cracked ominously against the stone and he slumped down.

"KH, the release is na-thom-te-ah-ro, watch the pitch!"

And Helva, knowing she was in effect executing one of her own kind, broadcast the release word to the 732. As the syllables with their pitched nuances activated the release of the access panel, Kira caught the plate, reached in deftly and threw the valve that would flood the inside of the shell with anesthesia.

"I can't see you, Seber. Where are . . ." and the 732's despairing wail was stilled in longed for oblivion.

Kira whirled, the panel clinking behind the concealing draperies as cowled figures lurched into the main cabin from the quarters behind.

"Hold!" Helva commanded in Lia's voice. "He Who Orders has decided. Take the barefaced woman back to the ship. Such blasphemous seed is not for the chosen of Alioth."

Kira, again trancelike, followed the dazed hoods back down the steps.

"Helva, what in the fardles is happening there?" Cencom demanded within the 834.

"He has decided," the fanatical mob in the plaza groaned and swayed in the thrall of the hallucinogenic fumes.

"Helva!" snapped Cencom.

"Oh, shut up all of you," said Helva, near a breaking point.

"He has ordered. That is Eternal Truth."

She watched just long enough to be sure that the reeling, freak-drunk Aliothites would not interfere with Kira's return. How they could, Helva couldn't imagine, for they were dropping by the hundreds, exhausted by fumes and frenzy.

"You better have a good explanation for deliberately abrogating specific restrictions in your journey tape regarding Dylanistic. . . ."

"I'll Dylanize you, you fatuous oaf," Helva cut in angrily. "The end justifies the means, and might I remind you that for some reason, unknown forever to God and man, your list of restricted planets did NOT include Alioth, as by the fingernails of that God they should have!"

Cencom sputtered indignantly.

"Control yourself," Helva suggested acidly. "I found your long-lost rogue and I have killed her. And I did some rough but effective therapy on your precious Kira of Canopus. What more do you want of one brain shell? Huh?"

Cencom maintained silence for 60 stunned seconds.

"Where is Kira?" and Helva could swear Cencom sounded contrite.

"She's all right."

"Put her on."

"She's *all right!*" Helva repeated with weary emphasis. "She's on her way back from the Temple."

The spaceport rocked under a multiple eruption just as the vehicle bearing Kira screeched to a halt at the lift. Helva unlocked the mechanism and Kira leaped on before the guards came to their senses. The ground danced under the ship's stabilizers and, as Kira dove from airlock to pilot's couch, Helva slammed the lock shut and precipitously lifted from grim Alioth.

In the tail scanners they saw the guards retreating to safety as the gantry tumbled leisurely down. Bright jewels dotted the receding planet as it gave them a volcanic sendoff.

"Scout Kira of the KH-834 reporting," the slender girl said crisply to Cencom, shedding her cloak. Helva half-expected a shower of hairpins to follow but Kira remained tautly erect before the tight beam. She gave a terse report, demanding to know why traders had not reported the presence of Service-type contact buttons plainly visible on every Aliothite. And why—a far more criminal omission—the hallucinogenic gas eruptions had not been reported.

"Hallucinogenic gas?" Cencom echoed weakly. Such instances were the nightmare of colonization; entire populations could be subjected to illegal domination by such emissions, as indeed had happened on Alioth.

"I recommend strongly that all traders dealing with Alioth in the last 50 years be questioned as to their motives in suppressing such information from Central Worlds. And discover who was the semi-intelligent CW representative who cleared this freak-off planet for colonization."

Cencom was reduced to incoherent sputters.

"Stop gargling," Kira suggested sweetly, "and order an all-haste planet-therapy team here. You've got an entire society to reorient to the business of living. We'll file a comprehensive report from Nekkar, but now I've got to inspect our children. That was a rough take-off. Over and out." And Kira closed the tight beam down.

With a fluid motion she propelled herself to the kitchen, shaking her braids free and massaging her scalp with rough fingers.

"My head is pounding!" she exclaimed, reaching for coffee. "That gas was unbelievably malodorous." She leaned wearily against the counter, her shoulders sagging in fatigue.

Helva waited, knowing Kira was sorting her thoughts.

"The closer I got to that temple, the deeper the terrible miasma of grief. It was almost visible, Helva," she said, and then added scathingly, "and I wallowed in it. Until that Dylan of yours reached me, Helva."

Her eyes widened respectfully. "The hair on the back of my neck stood up straight. That final chord got me, right here," she groaned, jabbing at her abdomen with a graphic fist. "Thorn would have given his guts to compose such a powerful Dylan." Her shoulders jerked spasmodically in a violent muscle spasm.

"That awful corpse!" She closed her eyes and shuddered, shaking her head sharply to rid herself of the effect. "I think . . ." she murmured, her eyes narrowing with self-appraisal, "I have been thinking—I had done the same thing to Thorn."

"I think perhaps you had," Helva agreed softly.

Kira sipped at her coffee, her face tired but alive, the mask of vivacity replaced by an inner calm. "I have been so stupid," she said with trenchant self-contempt.

"Not even Cencom is infallible," Helva drawled.

Kira threw back her head in a whoop of laughter.

"That's Eternal Truth!" she crowed, dancing back into the main cabin.

Helva watched the victory dance, immeasurably pleased with the outcome of the affair as far as Kira was concerned. She could not regret that she had had to kill one of her own peers. Lia had really died years before with her scout: that tortured remnant had peace at last, and so had Kira. She and Helva would continue together on their stork run, picking up the seeds from . . .

Helva let out a yip of exultation. Kira stared at her, startled.

"What hit you?"

"It's so ridiculously simple I can't imagine someone never suggested it to you. Or maybe they did and you rejected it."

"I'll never know unless you tell me what it is," Kira replied caustically.

"One of the facets of your grief psychosis . . ."

"I'm over it now," Kira interrupted Helva, her eyes flashing angrily.

". . . Ha to that. One of the facets has been the lack of progeny from your seed and Thorn's? Right?"

The scout's face turned starkly white, but Helva plunged on.

"Neither one of your parents was stupid enough to have ignored their RCA duty. Right? So their seed is on file. Take some of your mother's and his father's and . . ."

Kira's eyes widened and her jaw dropped, her face lighting with incredulous radiance. Tears streamed down her cheeks. Delicately she stretched out her hand, touching the access panel softly.

Helva was ridiculously, embarrassingly delighted at

her acceptance of the idea. Then Kira drew her breath in sharply, her face concerned.

"But for you . . . wouldn't you take *your* mother's and . . ."

"No," Helva said sharply, then added more gently, "that won't be necessary." She knew in mind and heart now that the resolution of grief is highly individual: that both she and Kira had reached it by different means, just as Theoda had.

Kira looked unaccountably stricken, as if she had no right to take the solution Helva offered if Helva did not, too.

"After all," the ship chuckled, "there aren't many women," and Helva used the word proudly, knowing that she had passed as surely from girlhood to woman's estate as any of her mobile sisters, "who give birth to 110,000 babies at one time."

Kira dissolved into laughter, crowing with delight over Helva's analogy. She snatched up her guitar, strumming a loud introductory arpeggio. Then the two, ship and scout, surprised the stars with a swinging Schubert serenade as they sped toward Nekkar and deliverance.

Dramatic
Mission

Helva turned the sound down, pleased that all the embryo-tube racks and the great beakers of nutrients were being pulled out, but not at all pleased with the mauling the crewmen were giving her in the process.

They didn't really need to add to the scars already made by the metal frames on her decks, or the strains of spilled nutrients on her bulkheads. But she was silent because even the pilot's cabin showed unmistakable marks of long tenure and Kira Falernova had been a tidy person. However, Helva had no wish to go to Regulus and show this shoddy interior to whichever brawns were waiting to team up with her.

She said as much to the other brain ship sitting near her, to one side of the commercial pads at the Nekkar spaceport.

"That's a silly waste of credit, Helva," Amon, the TA-618, replied, his voice slightly peevish. "How'd'you know your new brawn will like *your* taste? Let him, or her, pay for it out of his quarters' allowance. Really, Helva, use some sense or you'll never buy free. And I don't see why you're so eager to be saddled with a brawn anyway."

"I like people."

Amon made a rude noise. Since he'd landed, he had steadily complained to her about his mobile partner's deficiencies and shortcomings. Helva had reminded herself that Amon and Trace had been together over 15 standard years and that was said to be the most difficult period of any long association.

"When you've had a series of brawns aboard you as long as I have, you won't be so philanthropic. And when you know what your brawn is going to say before he says it, *then* you'll have a little idea of the strain *I'm* currently under."

"Kira Falernova and I were 3 years on this stork-run . . ."

"Doesn't signify. You *knew* it was a short-term assignment. You can put up with anything on that basis. It's the inescapable knowledge that you've got to go on and on, 25 to 30 years' worth . . ."

"If he's all that bad, opt a change," Helva said.

"And add a cancellation penalty to what I'm already trying to pay?"

"Oh, I forgot." Her reply, Helva realized the moment the words were out of her mouth, was not very politic. Among his many grievances with the galaxy at large, the extortionate price of repairs and maintenance made by outworld stations ranked high. Amon had run afoul of a space-debris storm and the damage had required a replating of half his nose. Central Worlds had insisted that the cause was his negligence, so it was therefore not a service-incurred or compensable accident.

"Furthermore, if I opted," Amon went on sourly, "I'd *have* to take whoever is up next for assignment with no refusal right."

"That's too true."

"I'm not fat with double bonuses from grateful Nek-karese."

Helva swallowed a fast retort to such an unfair remark and meekly said she hoped that things would soon look up. Amon wanted a sympathetic listener, not an adviser.

"You take the advice of one who's been around, Helva," Amon went on, mollified by her contrition, "and take every solo assignment you can get. Rack up bonuses while you can. *Then* you'll be in a position to bargain. I'm not. Oh, here he comes!"

"He's in a hurry, too."

"Wonder what lit *his* jets." Amon sounded so disagreeable that Helva began to wonder just how much the brawn was at fault. Brain ships were people, too.

Just then, Helva could her the brawn's excited greeting over the open ship-to-ship band.

"Amon, man, get us cleared and lifted. We got to get back to Regulus Base on the double. I just heard . . ."

The band went dead.

It was so like Amon to be selfish with good news, too, that Helva did not take offense. Good luck to him, she thought as she turned on the outside scanners and watched him lift off. If he did get a good assignment and the delivery bonus, he could pay off his debt. He might even resolve most of his problems with his brawn. The man had seemed nice enough when he'd paid a courtesy call on Kira and herself the day they arrived at Nekkar. But it was petty of him Helva thought . . . If the brawn had heard, the news could not come via tight beam.

"Nekkar Control, XH-834 calling."

"Helva? Had my hand on the switch to call you. Our ground crew treating you right? Anything you want them to do, you just let 'em know," answered the affable com man.

Considering Nekkar's recent disaster, you'd think *they'd* be as sour as Amon.

"I was wondering if you could tell me why the TA-618 left in such a hurry."

"Say, yes, that's something, isn't it? Never know who's around in the next system over, do you? I always said, a galaxy's got room for all kinds. But who'd ever think people . . . I guess you could call 'em people . . . would want any old archaic plays. Can you imagine that?" and infuriatingly the com man chuckled.

Amon had problems knowing ahead of time *what* his man'd say? Helva thought, impatiently waiting for this jovial soul to say anything worth listening to.

"Well, not really, because you haven't told me what you heard yet," Helva cut in as the man seemed likely to continue editorializing.

"Oh, sorry. Thought you ships'd all have your ears . . . oh, pardon the slip . . . to the rumor-block. Well, now, generally my sources are very reliable and this came to me from two sources, as I was telling Pilot Trace. A survey ship out Beta Corvi way registered some regulated-energy emissions. Pinpointed them to the sixth planet which had . . . of all improbabilities . . . a methane-ammonia atmosphere. Never heard of any sentients before developing in that kind of environment, have you?"

"No. Please go on."

"Well, before the crew could get an exploratory probe treated to withstand that kind of air; ha, ha, air, that's good."

"Consider that what we breathe might be poisonous to them," Helva suggested.

"Oh, true, too true. Any rate, before the crew could shake a leg, the Corviki had probed them. What do you think of that?"

"Fascinating. I'm hanging on your words."

"Well, those Survey men are on their toes, I'll tell you. Didn't let an opportunity like this slip from their grasp. Offered to exchange scientific information with the Beta Corviki and invited 'em to join the Central Worlds Federation. Say," and the man paused to think, "how'd the survey know they were high enough on the Civ-scale to qualify right off if they hadn't even got a probe down to the surface of the planet?"

"If the Beta Corviki could contact our survey ship, and if they are fooling around with regulated-energy emissions detectable outside their solar system, we might not qualify on their Civ-scale."

"Oh. Hadn't looked at it from that angle." The man's resilience was incredible, for he paused only briefly before taking up again. "Well, we *have* something they want badly," and he sounded as pleased as if he had himself invented this commodity. "Plays!"

"Plays?"

"That's right. Guess it'd be hard to develop any art forms on a methane-ammonia planet. At any rate, the story is that they will exchange some energy-process of theirs that we need for our old plays."

"New lamps for old?" Helva murmured.

"How's that?"

"That doesn't explain why the TA shot out of here so fast."

"Oh, well, that's easy. Calls are going out all over the sector for you ships to report in. Say, you being the ship who sings and all, this ought to be right up your alley."

"Possibly," Helva temporized. "But I'm due to be assigned a new brawn partner and they woudn't send a green team out on a mission of this importance."

"You mean, you don't want it? Trace said there was a triple bonus attached that any ship in its right mind would fight for."

"I am in my right mind but there is something else more important to me than a triple bonus."

The com man's silence was more eloquent than any cliché he could utter. Fortunately the tight-beam channel warmed up and Helva excused herself to open her end of it.

The transmission began with a mission code, so she flipped on the recorder and monitored the message.

She was directed to proceed immediately to Duhr III, en route to Regulus Base. She was to receive four official passengers at the University Spaceport, Lock No. 24, and proceed with no further delay to base.

"If those were orders, ma'am," the com man said when she returned to his channel, "I can give you instant clearance."

"Not quite yet, pal. I've got to pick up some passengers and I'm not going to go looking like a tramp ship. You did say that if there was anything I wanted . . ."

"Yes, yes, and we mean it," the Nekkarese assured her.

So Helva flashed toward Duhr III, at speeds no human passenger could have endured, with holds and cabins gleaming and fresh, and bunks for full-sized humans placed where cradles for hundreds of embryos had recently swung.

She had borne in mind Amon's sour comments and prevailed upon the willing foreman to make certain judicious chemical additions to the standard paints. The soft greens in the pilot's cabin had been impregnated with pumice from Thuban, so that by changing light-tones, she could alter the shade enough to suit any personality. She'd had the galley done in a good strong orange, a thirsty color but one calculated to make people eat fast and leave. The main cabin was an off-white with blue tones and the others blues and beige. Trouble with Amon was, Helva reflected, he didn't use his wits. Or maybe, she amended tolerantly, he simply hadn't thought of using color-psychology on his brawn. The burden of adjustment, she'd been told, rested with the resident partner.

It hadn't taken long to refurbish her interior once the finishes were mixed, for the foreman and his crew were efficient. The neat, clean interior would have been worth a far longer delay in her estimation, and made her unashamed to be carting passengers to Regulus. In fact, she looked forward to the trip. It was always stimulating to meet new people. And new brawns, she added firmly to herself. However, the carrier fee of these official passengers would pay for the spray job, so erase Amon's advice.

And he wanted Pay-off, huh? Helva mused as she hurtled through space toward the far wink of Duhr. Well, even a brain ship had to have some incentive. Idly she ran a check on her own indebtedness and was agreeably surprised at its rapid reduction.

How extraordinary! If she could keep going at even half her present rate as a brawnless ship, presumably she could buy herself back from Central Worlds within 3 standard years. Her own mistress after 10 years of service? It didn't seem possible. Why, Amon had been in service close to 150 years and he complained bitterly about the size of his debt. Of course, he was the complaining type, so she could discount a lot of his statements as exaggeration. And there were "free" ships. The YG-635, in Amon's class, was free. He did general work for the Scorpii Federation and had been modified to handle their environment.

Then, too, she'd had some lucky breaks. The bonus for that fateful Ravel mission was blood money, even if it was charged on the credit side of her ledger. She'd drawn full salary for the Annigoni plague assignment, plus an efficiency bonus. And, while she and Kira had been partnered on the RCA Nekkarese stork run, she'd drawn double pay because Kira was hired by RCA. The Alioth incident had carried a finders' credit on the 732 and now the staggering Nekkarese gratuity. She'd had no major repairs—not that she ought to, being recently commissioned—so her financial position was very rosy, in spite of the unbelievable expenditures for her early care and maintenance.

Even if Helva did clear the backlog of debt, she would undoubtedly contract herself back to Central Worlds service, for she enjoyed the work. Of course, it would be rather soul-satisfying to be able to tell Central World to go into a tight orbit once in a while. And then, she could hire or fire a brawn as she chose.

Yes, it would be worthwhile to Pay-off for such indulgences.

She still couldn't see why Amon didn't just take the penalty if Trace was such an irritant. It wasn't as if Central Worlds would disown a deeply indebted ship. . . . Well, not her problem. But there'd better be a brawn for her when she touched down at Regulus with her passengers. She had rights, indebted or not.

Despite her speed, having no need to keep day separate from night, the run seemed endless: she never slept and the chronos measured off meaningless hours. She was conditioned for a partner, for someone to take care of, to do for, to live with. She liked emotional involvement with other humans: the interchange of ideas, yes, even the irritation of contemptuous familiarity. These were all experiences she wanted first-hand, not sourly from a disenchanted old brain.

The spaceport of Duhr was partly hidden in an imposing mountain range in the northeastern hemisphere. On the other side and within the mountain itself was the tremendous administration complex of the university planet.

Landing at Lock No. 24, Helva identified herself, and the extendible worm-maw of lock facility unerringly sought her passenger hatch. Two men waited for the connection to be made: one lounging against the trundlecart stacked with baggage, the other occupied solely with twitching at various parts of his tunic or glancing at his wrist unit.

"No time to waste, now. You know which luggage goes where?"

The porthand didn't bother to confirm, but smartly guided the trundler onto the ship, across the main cabin and down the corridor.

"Why, it looks freshly commissioned," the official-type murmured, looking about him in considerable surprise and grudging approval. He paused in his inspection at the galley and peered around, looking into closets and drawers. "Where's the supply key on this class ship?" he asked the porthand, who was stowing the cases in the cabin.

"Ask the ship," the porthand said. "Or hadn't you noticed this is a BB?"

"Oh, good heavens," the official gasped. "I beg your pardon, sir or madam."

Helva noticed tolerantly he still didn't know where she was actually located, for he did a kind of circular bow, designed to catch every corner of the main cabin.

"Are you provisioned to serve four normal humans all the way to Regulus Base?"

"Yes."

"Well, that's a relief. We'd no idea what transport would be coming, this has all happened so fast. And a BB ship! Well, that is flattering. You *can* adjust internal gravity in flight, can't you?" he asked, glancing up from the notations on his wrist unit.

"Yes. What are the requirements? I have had no briefing."

"None?" This concerned him deeply. "Oh, but you should have. You really should have. No, that's wrong. Cancel that. Although the Solar did request . . . well, as you can adjust that's no problem then, is it?"

Not *another* scatterwit, Helva groaned to herself. "If you will indicate the gravity required . . ."

There was an eruption of applause and cheers at the top of the lock tunnel. The official glanced apprehensively towards it. "They're coming now. The Solar will tell you, or Miss Ster, his medical attendant. You must be prepared to take off immediately, you know."

The porthand jauntily crossed back through the main cabin, flipping Helva's column a cheery salute as he exited. "Gear's all stowed for takeoff."

"Very good," his superior mumbled absently as he followed him to the lock. The slight frown was immediately replaced by a fixed smirk just as the noisy party started down the corridor.

The four people in the front rank must be her passengers; they wore shipsuits. Helva enlarged the picture and it was easy to see which one needed controlled gravity. Half-grav, at least, she decided. The man walked with that terrible exertion of someone unused to and uncomfortable in full grav, whose muscles strained to work against the heavy drag. Helva could see that even his face muscles sagged: a pity, for he was a handsome man. Yet he kept his shoulders erect, his head high, too proud to permit physical disability to rob him of dignity.

She was so interested in him that she got only a glance at the other man and the two women before everyone had swept up to the lock.

The port official stepped hastily out of the way as a very distinguished older man with a cluster of academic knots on his tunic held out his hand to the striking woman beside him.

"Here's your personal magic carpet, to carry you to Regulus Base. May I say that it has been a great personal pleasure, Ansra Colmer, to meet you? Officially, the University of Duhr appreciated your willingness to interrupt a personal visit with Solar Prane to give our students the benefit of your art. Your Antigone was inspired: your Phorus II monologue made me appreciate for the first time the vital interplay of color, odor, and rhythm. You're an amazingly versatile exponent of your art and one, I trust, soon to receive the accolade, Solara."

The smile on Ansra Colmer's carefully composed face seemed to stiffen slightly and there was absolutely no echo of humor in her glittering eyes.

"You are too kind, Director, particularly since Duhr has its own Solar," and she made a half turn towards the grav-sufferer. "How can you bear to part with him?" And, not waiting for an answer, she strode past the lock and into the main cabin. With her back to the noisy well-wishers, Helva could see that her expression was now one of suppressed anger and hatred.

The Director cleared his throat as if understanding all too well her innuendo. He bowed gravely toward the Solar.

"You can't be dissuaded, Prane?"

"Central Worlds has made too strong a representation of its needs, Director. It is my duty to my profession to accept, hoping that any honor merited in the undertaking reflects on you for your many kindnesses." Prane's voice was rich, resonant, the voice of the trained professional performer. If Helva noticed the odd hollowness, the occasional wispiness as if the tone were half-supported, her sensors were keener than the ears of the adoring crowd of young students and patient officials.

"Solar Prane will be back in triumph before the term is ended," said the other male passenger, "preserved by the skill of Miss Ster."

"Truly spoken, Davo Fillanaser," the Director agreed heartily, turning now to shake the hand of the young woman beside Solar Prane.

Helva was fascinated by the various undertones in this farewell scene. It ought not be a boring trip, at any rate.

"We must not hold up the pilot any longer," Solar Prane said. With a charmingly apologetic smile, he waved broadly to the crowd, which sighed of its sorrow and murmured regrets, even shed a few tears, as he stepped backward into the lock, his arm hooked through Miss Ster's.

The man addressed as Davo Fillanaser ranged himself beside them, smiling and waving, too.

Solar Prane turned his head toward the young woman and Helva saw him mouth a quick sentence.

"I can't stand much longer, Kurla. Tell the pilot to close the lock."

Immediately Helva activated the lock portal.

"Help me, Davo," Kurla cried, as the crowd was shut from view. She threw her arm around the Solar's waist as the man's large frame seemed to collapse against her.

"Damn fool," Davo muttered, but he used extreme care in assisting . . . as if he were concerned about hurting Prane.

"I'm all right. I'm all right," Prane insisted in a hoarse whisper.

"That farewell party was madness in your condition and in full grav," Kurla said.

"The hero must have a hero's farewell," drawled Ansra Colmer. The smile on her face as she turned toward them was sincere now, sincerely vicious; and her eyes sparkled with intense pleasure at Prane's debility.

"The hero is not yet on his shield, Ansra," the Solar replied, almost as if he relished the notion of defying her. He put Kurla from him, touched Davo's supporting hand, which fell away, and slowly, carefully, crossed the cabin.

"Misfire, Ansra?" Davo asked, following the Solar at a discreet interval.

"Ansra's steel gives me backbone," the Solar chuckled, and Helva could have sworn, again, that these bitter undercurrents were therapeutic. The Solar's medical attendant evidently did not agree.

"That is quite enough," she said with a professional impersonality and, disregarding Prane's independence, threw an arm around his waist and supported him the rest of the way toward the couch. "This ought to be a shock-mattress," she said, flipping back the mesh blanket. "Good." Deftly, she turned the Solar, easing him down to the bed. She then extracted a medical recorder from the pouch at her side. Her expression was detached and her eyes intent as she ran a check on him.

Helva peeked at the dials and gauges and was a little puzzled by some of the readings. The heart strain was not at all excessive, although the pulse was rapid from exertion. The blood pressure was too low for someone under stress, and too high for a man apparently used to low grav conditions. The more perplexing reading was the eeg. Prane was trembling now with reaction to extreme muscular stress: supine, he looked old and tired.

"What are you giving me now, Kurla?" he demanded sharply, rousing as he saw her preparing an i.v. spray.

"A relaxant and . . ."

"No sedations, no blocks. I forbid it."

"I'm the medical attendant, Solar Prane," she said in a firm, impersonal voice.

His hand trembled as he grabbed for her wrist, but Helva could see the fingers pressed deeply into her flesh. Kurla Ster looked him directly in the eye.

"You cannot tolerate liftoff without some sedation, after exerting yourself for that party . . ."

"Give me the relaxant, Kurla, but nothing more. I can cope with the discomfort . . . alone. Once in space, the pilot can adjust the gravity."

It was a contest of wills, with Davo an interested spectator. Curiously enough, Helva noticed that Davo had been on Prane's side, judging by the sigh the man exhaled as the young m.a. replaced the other vials to her pouch and injected but one medication.

"Where is that pilot?" she demanded of Davo as she left the cabin, sliding the door firmly shut behind her.

"Pilot?" Ansra Colmer repeated, idly swinging the pilot's chair on its gimbals. "You were too engrossed in adoring worship of the Solar's classic profile to heed what journey briefing we received."

"Oh, for Christ's sake, Ansra, sheathe your claws. You're becoming a bore," Davo said, propelling Kurla to a seat with a warning smile. "This is a brain ship, Kurla. No other pilot is necessary. We need only settle ourselves down for the trip."

"Miss Colmer, if you don't . . ."

"And be quiet," Davo added firmly to Kurla, his hand on her forearm, cautioning obedience. "The sooner we take off, the better it is for Prane, right?"

She subsided, still rebellious. To aggravate matters, Ansra Colmer smiled triumphantly at her capitulation.

"Let's go," Davo said, nodding over his shoulder toward Helva.

"Thank you, Mr. Fillanaser, and welcome aboard the XH 834," Helva said quietly, achieving an impersonal tone with some difficulty. "Fasten your harness for takeoff." Ansra Colmer interrupted her swinging only long enough to comply. "Miss Ster, may I inquire if Solar Prane's disability will be affected by standard takeoff velocities?"

"Not when he is cushioned by the shock-mattress."

"And by drugs," added Ansra snidely.

"Solar Prane is not under sedation," the m.a. snapped, trying to rise, and restrained by her harness.

"Ansra, leave her alone! Prane is not on drugs and never has been!"

"I am receiving clearance for lift-off," Helva said, mendaciously forestalling another exchange. She even leaked a little engine noise into the main speakers.

As she began to jockey into position, Helva kept an eye on Prane. He was cushioned by the shock-mattress, all right, but if he could barely tolerate full grav, blast-off would rack him with pain. She decided a fast take-off would spare him more than a gradual acceleration. She piled on the power and watched him black out from pain in a brief minute.

The instant she was free of Duhr's attraction and on course for Regulus, she cut all thrust, even the little spin she usually maintained for the comfort of her passengers. He was unconscious, but the pulse in his throat beat regularly.

"I've got to get to him," Kurla was saying in the main cabin.

When Helva looked there, the medical attendant was ludicrously flattened against the far wall of the main cabin.

"Then move slowly," Davo was advising her. "You've been in half-grav long enough to know violent action brings equally violent reaction."

"If you only knew how asinine you looked," Ansra said.

"Solar Prane passed out before maximum thrust, Miss Ster," Helva reported, "but he appears in no distress."

"I must get to him." Kurla was insistent. "His bones are so soft."

An orthopedic problem? And he was permitted in space? Were they out of their minds? Then why such cerebral excitement?

"Shall I return gravity? The shock-web will . . ."

"No, no," Kurla protested.

"If you think I'm going to travel free-fall all the way to Regulus, you've another think coming," Ansra said, the amusement wiped from her face.

"The longer he has without any gravitic stress . . ."

"Too bad," Ansra snapped back. "I know what happens to *me* in constant free-fall and I'm not having . . ."

"Flabby muscles, dear?" Davo grinned at her. "You can always join us in a thrilling workout of isometrics. And you'd better get used to free-fall. You certainly heard it mentioned in our briefing . . . since you're so attentive to briefings . . . that the company will play entirely in free-fall. Get used to it."

"I also heard it mentioned that our minds were what

would be transferred. It's my body that's involved at present."

"And it's Solar Prane's body that must rest now," Kurla flung back, managing to move forward toward the cabin. "He *is* only the director of the entire company."

"In the interests of compromise, ladies," Davo said, "let's use half-grav while we're awake, and free-fall when we're all snugly meshed in at night and don't know any better."

"Can that be arranged?" Kurla looked hopeful. "The unit had to be kept at half full grav on Duhr because of the power required."

"Half-grav suit your gracious supremacy?" Davo asked Ansra, mocking her with a bow.

"He won't last, half-grav or free-fall," she said, grimacing as she heard the cabin door click shut behind Kurla.

Ansra flipped off the harness, twisting in the chair for the most comfortable position from which to regard Davo unobstructedly.

"I don't know why you continue to defend a dying man, Davo. Don't argue; his mind has been affected. I can see it. Don't forget, I knew him rather well." Her smile suggested many intimacies. "And it's his mind that must be transferred." Suddenly her whole attitude changed subtly. "Had you never considered being more than just a supporting actor, Davo?"

Helva took a closer look at the man. She'd thought him a friend or assistant of Prane's, not another actor. He had none of the obvious professional mannerisms the other two displayed.

"You've an excellent reputation in the Guild as a fine classicist," Ansra was saying. "Why do you continue to let Prane dominate and dictate your life?"

Davo regarded her imperturbably for a moment before he smiled carelessly. "I happen to respect Prane Liston professionally and personally. . . ."

Ansra made a rude noise. "You've fronted for him like an understudy on matinee day. Taken his lectures while he 'experimented' in null-grav movement! Ha! Covered for him so the rank and file would not know their hero's frailties!"

"My motives are not as suspect as yours, detouring two months away from your last engagement to 'visit' your old friend, Prane Liston? Ha for you."

Helva detected the flush of anger under the woman's cosmetized skin.

"My visit, Davo Fillanaser, was most opportune," she replied with a saccharine smile. "And according to our briefing, once one is transferred to the . . . how was it phrased, empty envelope? . . . to the envelope awaiting each of us on Beta Corvi, external appearance will not matter. Ability will. I always thought you showed poor judgment to opt the classics, Davo, for you have such a lean and hungry look that you must always be Iago or Cassius. You could be . . . Romeo . . . on Beta Corvi." Her smile was dazzling.

"Not, of course, while Prane Liston remains director *and* Romeo, huh?" Davo leaned toward her, his eyes sparkling, but his lean, dark face inscrutable. "You won't believe the truth, even when you hear it, will you, Ansra? And you just can't believe that Prane Liston is no longer besotted with Ansra Colmer."

"*That* is not at issue," she said, with lofty indifference.

Davo merely smiled. He leaned back in the couch and matched her mood. "You've got your own director lined up, huh? One who'll let Juliet dominate? Then, with a grateful but weak Romeo like me, you'll look twice as good without having to work half as hard as Prane makes you. Oh, come off it, Ansra," he advised, impatient with her machinations. "Prane always could drag the very best performances out of your lazy hide.

"But that's not important, not in this production. There's more at stake than your self-consequence. Or did you really listen to the briefing at all? Those Beta Corviki can regulate the half-life of any unstable isotope they choose. If Central Worlds gets such techniques, it'll revolutionize pile-drives and get us across the galactic seas. . . ." He paused, gave a derisive laugh. "Why, if our petty prancing pleases them, you might play in the Horsehead Nebula next season, Ansra Colmer. Or," and his eyes narrowed speculatively, "should I say, Solara Ansra?"

"Then think carefully, Davo," she urged, her pose alert and tense, "of *all* that is involved. I don't care for altruism: it signs no contracts and pays no salaries. I wouldn't have considered this tour for a moment if it weren't for that Corviki transfer device."

Davo stared at her with such sharp attention that she smiled slightly.

"Really, Davo, what possible significance could things like those Corviki find in Romeo and Juliet, an outmoded love story of an improbable social structure."

"You're more the hypocrite than even I'd thought you."

"Delusions are what we create, not what we believe. And, with a mind-blasted Romeo, the whole thing would be worthless but for those transfer things. Why, if that device can work in a methane-ammonia atmosphere, it can work anywhere. It could open a whole new audience dimension . . ."

"And Solara Ansra as top-ranking performer in the new medium?" Davo asked, his dark eyes intent on hers.

Helva wondered if he had caught the fallacy in her argument.

"Why not? I don't need to be an m.a. to see Prane's dying. He's so weak he'll dissolve under pressure. Why, his headbones are so soft with mindtrap . . ."

"Bones, yes, but not his brain . . .," Davo snapped. "And not mine. *I* remember what I owe the man, dead or dying, and I'm with him all the way. Remember

that, Ansra Colmer. And if you don't cease needling
that nice child, if you don't prove to me that you're
going to integrate into the company, I'll cite a jeopardy
clause on you. There *is* too much at stake in this far-
out dramatic mission to risk a dissident among us. The
computers picked Prane, remember, on the basis of
performance and ability. With all his medical handicap,
he still came out the highest on the probability profile. You shape up, Ansra, or I'll give the computers
a few bits of psychodata on you to update your profile."

He swung himself from the chair far too energetically
for the half-grav and bounded toward the ceiling. He
corrected and slow-stepped toward the galley.

"Auto-pilot, erase the previous conversation between myself and Davo Fillanaser," Ansra commanded in a hard, angry voice. "Is that order clear?"

"Yes," Helva replied, careful to sound dry and mechanical.

"Comply. Which cabin has been assigned to me?"

"Number Two."

As Helva watched the erect figure of the actress
undulate down the corridor, she felt an odd, atavistic
satisfaction in having lingered for refurbishing at Nekkar and in knowing that her interior was, as always, in
order: shipshape.

It was not a pleasant evening, certainly not what
Helva had anticipated when the orders were taped in.
Davo was silent and hyper-alert, watching Kurla and
Ansra, unobtrusively passing Prane's open cabin frequently. Kurla was distressed though she tried to con-
ceal it. Helva, however, had heard Prane reject medical
assistance, and, by her sensors, knew he was feign-
ing sleep to prevent argument. Ansra's sullen cold
looks followed the young medical attendant everywhere.
Helva spoke only when spoken to, accepting the part
of an automated ship, though Davo presumably knew
what she was.

His discussion with Ansra had done nothing to aid Prane, antagonizing her and adding to the tension within the ship. Helva wondered if he had deliberately led the woman on to expose her ambitions, with herself, Helva, the unsuspected witness to the actress' intentions. Yet if he wanted Ansra to compromise herself before witnesses, why give her the second chance? Did Davo really trust the woman enough to think she'd reform?

Well, this wasn't Helva's problem, although she would play back that interlude if necessary. Let another ship worry about the conniving actress, the lovelorn m.a., and the dying actor. Amon could have the whole bit. "Romeo and Juliet," at free-fall in a gas atmosphere! Shakespeare for stabilizers? Helva concurred with Ansra; the whole idea was ridiculous!

A long, shuddering sigh broke into her reveries. A restless sleeper? No, Prane was not asleep though everyone else was secure under the mesh blanket. And Prane needed rest the most.

> " 'Amen, amen! but come what sorrow can,
> It cannot countervail the exchange of joy
> That one short minute gives me in her sight:
> Do thou but close our hands with holy words,
> Then love-devouring death do what he dare;
> It is enough I may but call her mine.' "

His voice rose to the challenge of the lines, rich, tender, unsullied by whatever debilitated his physical self. The laughter that followed, however, was hollow and bitter.

> " 'I am no pilot; yet, wert thou as far
> As that vast shore wash'd with the farthest sea,
> I would adventure for such merchandise.' "

Another long pause, then:

" 'Thou desperate pilot, now at once run on
The dashing rocks, thy sea-sick weary bark!
Here's to my love!' "

Another pause, so long that Helva wondered if he slept.

" 'Ah death, where is thy sting?
O Grave, thy victory?' "

Helva felt herself wince at the scorching regret, the
yearning in that emotion-laden voice. He wants to
die! He expects this venture to kill him and he wants
to die.

Helva comforted herself with a string of Kira's most
colorful oaths, wishing she knew more about the mechanics of this Beta Corvi psyche transfer. Well, if they
were, as reputed, able to stabilize isotopes, they obviously were energy-engineers of a remarkable genius.
Now, considering that the brain generated electricity, a
very primitive form of energy, so presumably the
electrical charge could be transferred from one re-
ceptacle to another. In theory, easy; in practice? There
could be a power loss, a faulty imprint in the receiver.
Someone could return halfwitted? Helva abandoned
that thought on the grounds of insufficient data. Besides, this was not her problem.

And she doubted Prane would be able to effect his
demise: not with Kurla Ster determined to keep the
mortal spark in his own husk. She knew nothing of
these Beta Corviki, but it was a convention among all
the sophisticated societies she had encountered that
sentience was not permitted to waste itself. Kira Falernova had found it excessively difficult to commit suicide.

And, if Kurla was not stupid, which she didn't appear to be despite this terrible infatuation for Prane,
she must be as aware of his death wish as of his
physical pain.

Helva's thoughts chased around, directionless. She had so few facts, including how Prane Liston could have reached such a state of decay in today's diagnostic-preventive and corrective medical climate. He was patently in his second 50 years—but soft bones? Bone marrow can be calcium-shot, phosphorus supplemented to the diet. Yet Ansra had made sly digs about drug addiction. Said his brains were soft . . . no, his head bones, Helva corrected herself . . . 'his headbones are softened by mindtrap.' Yet mindtrap was a harmless drug; mind-expanding, yes, but long and widely used by anyone who wished to retain information without loss. The adult mind loses 100,000 neurons a day. An actor couldn't afford memory loss. Was it possible that mindtrap, overused for a long period, could build up a harmful residue injurious to the bones?

Helva tapped the ship's memory banks, but there was no recorded incidence of any side-effect for mindtrap. An actor, however, playing on hundreds of planets, exposed constantly to some cosmic radiations, suffering a minor breakdown of cell-coding? A protein lock? Surely some medical engineer would have noted it, could isolate the faulty enzyme and correct?

Helva looked in on the sleepless man. He was murmuring speeches now, changing his voice as the lines went from character to character. Entranced, Helva listened through the ship's night as scene after scene poured from the Solar's lips, word perfect. Shortly before dawn, the litany ceased as sleep finally bestowed her accolade of peace.

Dawn came and went. Helva performed the routine check of all systems, ran a scan on detectors and established that there were no ships within hailing range. She was irritated . . . and relieved.

The first one to stir was Kurla. She drifted immediately to Prane's bedside. Her concern dissolved as she found him sleeping quietly, the fatigue lines smoothed from his face. Her own expression infinitely tender with love, the girl withdrew, pulled the door across, and floated over to the galley.

Davo joined her shortly. "How is he this morning?"

Defensively, Kurla started to go into medical detail.

"I'm not at all interested in your lover's internal economy . . ."

"Prane Liston is not my lover."

"Oh, hath desire outstripped performance then?"

"Davo, please!"

"Don't blush, my dear. Only teasing. However, a simple yes or no will suffice. Can Prane rehearse today? That free-fall staging is going to be difficult and he mentioned wanting to go through several scenes now when he has more time. Helva can oblige us with free-fall as we choose. Can't you, Helva?"

"Yes."

"It sounds so human," Kurla said, suppressing a little shudder.

"*She*, please, Kurla. Helva is human; aren't you, Helva?"

"Oh, you'd noticed?"

Davo laughed at the consternation on Kurla's face.

"My dear Miss Ster, surely you, a medical attendant, would have tumbled to the identity of the captain of our ship?"

"I've had a lot on my mind," she said, lifting her chin defensively. "But I apologize," she added, swinging round, "if I've offended you, Helva. . . ." Then her eyes rested on Prane's closed door and her face flooded with color.

"*You* have been the soul of discretion," Helva replied, aware of the girl's sudden confusion. "As *I* try to be," she added, so pointedly that Davo understood Kurla's blush.

"Honor among cyborgs, huh?" he asked, his eyes dancing as he added a subtle thrust of his own.

"Yes, and considerable evidence that we are emi-

nently trustworthy, loyal, courteous, honest, thoughtful, and inhumanly incorruptible."

Davo roared with laughter until Kurla, pointing toward Prane's cabin, shushed him.

"Why? I want him up and about. It ought to be good
for his soul to wake to the sound of my merry laughter."

"That sounds like a good entrance line," Prane remarked, pushing the door aside. He was smiling slightly, his shoulders erect and easy, his head high, all
trace of fatigue and weakness erased. He hadn't had
that much rest, Helva knew it, not after murmuring
through plays half the night. But he even looked
younger. "Shall we have at it, Davo?" he asked.

"You'll 'have at' nothing, Solar," Kurla said emphati-
cally, "until you've eaten."

He meekly acquiesced.

In spite of her intention to remain aloof from the
personality conflicts of this quartet, Helva watched
the rehearsal with keen interest. A script was thrust
in Kurla's hands and she was made the prompter.

"Now," Prane began crisply, "we have been given
no inkling of Corviki attitude toward personal combat,
if they have one. We don't know if they can appreciate
the archaic code which made this particular duel in-
evitable. Interpreting our social structures, our ancient
moralities, however, is not the function of this troupe.
According to the Survey Captain, the Corviki were entranced with the concept of special 'formulae' (the
crew had been watching Othello) intended purely to
waste energy in search of excitation and recombina-
tion with no mass objective." He gave an embarrassed
laugh. "There always has been an element of the population that ranks play-acting as a waste of energy.
However, there is no point in our trying to play Shakespeare as a social commentary. We shall be classicists
—pure Shakespeare as the Globe troupe would have
played it."

"For purity, then, Juliet ought to be a preadolescent boy," Davo reminded him with wry malice.

"Not that pure, Davo," Prane laughed. "I'll keep the casting arrangements as they are, I believe. We shall have enough of a problem acting in free-fall and getting used to the envelopes the Corviki will supply us. So, if we can get stage movement set in our minds now, we shall have only the problem of becoming accustomed to the new form when we reach Beta Corvi. I think of the exchange as merely another costume.

"Now Davo, as Tybalt, you enter downstage. Benvolio and Mercutio will be stage south and I, as Romeo, will approach from elliptical east."

Both men had worked in free-fall, Helva noticed, for they modified all gestures skillfully yet managed to simulate the power of a thrust, the grace of a dancing retreat. Such movements, however, required great physical effort and both were shortly sweating as they floated through their measured duel again and again to set the routine in their minds.

They worked hard, experimenting, changing, improving until they got through the duel scene twice without a flaw. Even allowing for his handicap, Helva was impressed by Prane.

Ansra drifted languidly into the main cabin and the atmosphere changed so abruptly that Helva inadvertently scanned her warnings system.

"Good morrow, good madam," Prane said jauntily. "Shall we have at the balcony scene, fair Juliet?"

"My dear Solar, you have obviously been hard at it with Davo. Are you feeling up to more?"

Prane hesitated a microsecond before he bowed and with a genuine smile replied: "You, as Juliet, are up, my dear," and he gestured with a flourish to the area where she was to play the scene, above him.

He turned then, floating to the edge of the cabin and Ansra, her jibe ignored, shrugged and projected herself upward.

"Give me Benvolio's line, please," Prane asked Kurla.

Ansra's entrance had flustered the girl and she flipped nervously through the sides.

"Act II, scene i, Kurla," Davo murmured encouragingly.

Helva dropped her voice to a tenor register:

" 'Go then; for 'tis in vain
To seek him here that means not to be found.' "

"Zounds, who was that?" cried Prane, whirling in such surprised reaction that he drifted toward the wall, absently holding himself off with one hand.

"Me," Helva said meekly in her proper voice.

"Can you change voices at will, woman?"

"Well, it's only a question of projection, you know. And since my voice is reproduced through audio units, I can select the one proper for the voice register required."

The effect of her ability on Prane, Helva noticed, was nothing to its effect on Ansra.

"How could you see to read the line?" Prane demanded, gesturing toward the script in Kurla's hands.

"I've been scanning the text from the library banks." Helva forbore to tell the long story of the childhood years during which she had been hooked on ancient movies, leading somehow naturally to Shakespeare, and opera, both light and grand. Her only hobby—and it was her own memory she was scanning.

Prane imprudently flung out both arms and had to correct against the ceiling.

"What incredible luck. Can you, would you read something else?"

"What? Auditioning a ship, Prane?" Ansra asked, her voice richly intimating that he'd gone mad.

"If I'm not wrong," Davo put in, his eyes glinting sardonically, "Helva here is also known as the ship

who sings. Surely you saw the tri-cast on her some years
back, Ansra? In fact I know you did. We were playing
the Greeks in Draconis at the time."

"If you please, Davo," Prane-the-director interrupted, gliding over to Helva's central column. "You
are the ship who sings?"

"Yes."

"Would you be kind enough to indulge me by read-
ing the Nurse's speech, Act I, scene iii, where Lady
Capulet and the Nurse discuss Juliet's marriage. Begin
'Even or odd of all days in the year' . . ."

"The nurse is to be played as an earthy type?"

"Yes, indeed, blissfully unregenerate. Her lines are
a triumph of characterization, you know: only she can
speak the ones the playwright gave her. That is, of
course, the test of true characterization."

"I thought this was a rehearsal of my scene, not a
lecture," Ansra remarked acidly.

Prane silenced her with a peremptory gesture. "The
cue is," and he altered his voice to a husky, aging
contralto, " 'A fortnight and odd days' . . ."

Helva resigned herself to an active part in this incident, and responded as Nurse Angelica.

Helva called a halt to what promised to be a round-
the-chrono affair, on the spurious grounds of some
critical computation. What had turned critical was
Ansra's temper.

Davo and Kurla had willingly read additional parts,
Davo with an insight to the minor characters that
wrung mute respect from Helva and generous thanks
from Prane. Kurla rose to the challenge of Lady Montague. Ansra's Juliet became less and less convincing.
She was "reading," not acting, certainly not reacting
to the passion, the youthful enthusiasm and tender
passion of Prane's Romeo. She was wooden. The
voice was youthful, the gestures girlish, but she resisted

every effort of Prane's to draw out of her that quality he wanted Juliet to project.

None of this was obvious from the even tone of his courteous suggestions, but it was most apparent to the others. And to Helva, Ansra's behavior was doubly inexcusable.

Once Helva had withdrawn, Kurla announced that it was time to eat a hot decent meal. She then insisted that they all get some sleep. Helva watched surreptitiously as Kurla ran a quick medical check on Prane. She, too, was amazed that the Solar was in remarkably strong vigor after such an intense and long rehearsal.

"You've got to rest, Solar Prane. I don't care what the recorder says. You can't put forth the energy you did today without replenishing it in sleep," Kurla said firmly. "*I'm* tired! And *you've* another planetfall to make."

He made a boyish grimace but lay back on the shock-mattress, his eyes closed, one hand on his chest.

Tenderly Kurla covered his long, lax body. She turned abruptly and let her motion carry her quickly from the cabin. Prane's eyes flew open and the look in his eyes was almost more than Helva could morally observe. So Kurla was indeed the sun of Prane's regard and Ansra, the envious moon, already sick and pale with grief . . .

Helva was overwhelmingly relieved that she'd be out of this affair in a scant day's time. And yet, Ansra had been indiscreet enough to hint at action more vengeful than envious. Would the fact that she now knew Helva was no automaton inhibit her plans?

The passengers began to sleep. All, that is, except Prane. He began Richard III, with Gloucester's "Now is the winter of our discontent" to Richmond's "Peace lives again: That she may long live here, God say amen!" Considering the day's proceedings Helva thought that choice of sleep-conjuring all too appropriate. If mindtrap produced such perfect recall . . .

Sometime toward dawn of that day, Helva remembered a detail, and berating herself for incredible obtuseness, contacted Regulus on the tight beam.

"Good to hear your voice, Helva," Central Com responded with marked affability.

"I distrust such geniality from you. What is being cooked up for me? Not another brawnless assignment—because I'll refuse it. I've got rights and I'll invoke 'em."

"My, we're touchy. How can you be so suspicious? And so crass?"

"So you'll know exactly how I stand. Now listen to me, is there a free accommodation, no, make it a suite . . . on the Orbital Station in the free-fall section?"

"I'll check, but why?"

"Check and answer."

"Aye-firmative."

"Great. I request that it be assigned Solar Prane and such of his company as accept. We've been running in free-fall, in preparation for their assignment and they ought not to have a readjust to full-grav."

"Good suggestion. But doesn't such an assignment tempt you, Helva?"

"Don't use that wheedling tone with me, Central."

"When you obviously have taken their welfare to heart enough to request orbital accommodations for Solar Prane?"

Helva caught herself. She mustn't sound so concerned.

"I was raised to be considerate. Just seems a shame to set back the progress they've made in free-fall adjustment."

"No problem, Helva. This Beta Corvi mission has topmost priority."

"Say, I'm curious about this psyche transfer bit . . ."

"Hold it, gal. Ask me no questions, since you've made it so plain where you stand."

"Okay, I'll stand off, but I think it's petty of you," and she closed the tight beam.

Until her passengers awoke, Helva pondered Central's comments. They wanted her for this: well, they could beg, blandish and bribe, but she was resolved to resist all bait until she was partnered.

She did not bother to inform any of her passengers of her sub-light arrangements with Central, but connected with the proper hatch at the Orbital Station as if this had been her programmed destination. Regulus IV swam beneath them, brilliant in the reflection of its primary.

"We were told we'd be landing at Regulus Base," Ansra protested as she looked into the lock of the Station. She glared threateningly at the startled lock attendant, drifting midportal.

"Free-fall?" Davo exclaimed. "I'd rather stay here."

"This is ridiculous," Ansra went on, directing herself to the confused attendant. "I demand to be taken to the Base. I demand to see the official in charge of this assignment."

"The XH-834 is scheduled to land at Base as soon as she has discharged her passengers here, Miss Colmer," the man said placatingly.

"If you will move into the main cabin, Miss Colmer, I can close the locks now," Helva said, for Prane and Kurla had pushed into the Station lock.

Ducking around Ansra, the attendant sent the luggage, piled in the lock, spinning stationward. As soon as he was clear, Helva closed her outer portal. Ansra was forced to step inside.

"Just wait till I report you, you . . . you . . ."

"Thing? Informer? Abomination? Fink?" Helva tendered helpfully.

"I'll have you decommissioned, you tin-plated bitch!"

Just then Helva applied thrust sufficient to send

Ansra, accustomed to free-fall, reeling backward into the nearby couch. And kept her there, cursing steadily and viciously, all through reentry and touchdown.

"You'll regret that insolence, too, you bodiless Bernhardt," was Ansra's parting taunt as she staggered to the passenger lift.

"Sorry you had trouble enduring standard reentry maneuvers, Miss Colmer. You were advised to remain on the Station," Helva boomed on her exterior speaker for the benefit of the vehicle waiting to take the woman the short distance to the Main Administration Complex before which Helva had landed.

"Hey, Helva, what did you do to that Colmer creature?" Central Com asked her on the private beam a little while later. "If you weren't in good odor with the powers-that-preside, you'd be in for an official reprimand and a fine. She's got some good friends in high places, you know."

"So that's how she got this assignment."

"Hey, gal, I'm on your side, but that kind of remark . . ."

"If I wanted to be nasty, I'd play back some of the honest-to-goodness, unexpurgated, uncensored deathless moments of my most recent trip through the vacuum of outer space."

"Like, for instance?"

"I said, if I *wanted* to be nasty." She cut the contact and looked around for more sympathetic company.

Crowding the Administration landing acres were no less than 20 brain ships. A veritable convention? Old home week? She spotted Amon, right up in the front row with five of her own class. When she tried to signal the VL-830, she couldn't get through. In fact, she couldn't get a line in to any of her peers: the ship-to-ship frequencies were overloaded.

Was everyone aspiring to that damned Beta Corvi

assignment? She ought to warn 'em off. She called the traffic tower to ask for another landing slot, preferably nearer the brawn barracks. There must be other ships on the 20 kilometers-square base interested in chatting with her.

"So nice to hear from you," Cencom cut in over Traffic Control. "Orders are for you to stay put, loud-mouth."

"Can I at least have some company? From the brawn barracks? Remember? I was promised a brawn *this* time. And this time I'd better get one. If you knew what this poor lone female, totally unprotected from . . ."

"I *can* promise you company," Cencom grudgingly admitted and cut off.

Helva waited, her circuits open, her passenger lift invitingly grounded. And waited. She was beginning to experience justifiable irritation when she received a boarding request. Activating the lift eagerly, she was disappointed to scan only one figure gliding up to her lock.

"You're not a brawn."

"Thanks, pal," the wiry small man said in an all-too-familiar voice.

"You're . . ."

"Niall Parollan, of Regulus, your coordinating communications officer, Planet Grade, Section Supervisor, Central Worlds BB Ship Division."

"You've got your nerve."

He grinned amiably at her, not the least bit intimidated by her booming. "You've enough for four of me, dear." He used the manual switch to close the lock and sauntered over to the couch that faced her column. His uniform was regulation, but it had been tailored to fit his short, well-proportioned body: the boots he wore were Mizar gray lizard and molded the calf of his leg.

"Make yourself at home."

"I intend to. Feel I ought to get to know you better now I'm your supervisor."

"Why?"

He gave her a wicked stare and smiled, showing very white even teeth.

"I wanted to see just why such a storm is raging over the possession of one Helva, the XH-834."

"Among brawns?" She was gratified.

"You sound hungry. Need your nutrients checked?"

"I don't trust you, Parollan," Helva announced after a pause. "There is nothing to see . . . of Helva."

"Now, there's where you're wrong, girl," and he rubbed one short-fingered, broad-palmed hand across his mouth and chin. "Yes, there is something about you . . ."

"I had a new spray job at Nekkar."

"I know. I checked accounting."

"The ingrates. Thought I got that free." Then, as he chuckled at her surprise, she added, "If you've been checking my standing, you know I'm well able to afford any penalties for refusing assignment."

"Oh ho, you bite, too," crowed Niall, rocking back and forth in an excess of delight. "Don't fool you, do I?"

"Not for a microsecond. I want a brawn, Parollan, not a snippy little mouthpiece like you."

He roared with delight.

"Now I see why." Then suddenly he was completely serious. He leaned forward, his eyes on her panel in an attitude so familiar it gave her a frightful wrench. Then he was talking and she listened.

"Item: the Beta Corvi assignment will require an unusual exercise of diplomacy on the part of both partners, as brain and brawn will be in direct contact with the Corviki throughout the mission. The shell person has the additional responsibility of direct and discretionary control over the Corviki psyche transfer mechanisms—a control which will necessitate the use of an additional synapse connection."

Helva made a whistling sound. At the least, it meant opening the titanium column, a difficult experience for any shell person: at the worst, actual penetration of the shell that would be traumatic to most.

"Ships of the two most recent classes would require no shell penetration. They were already fitted with supplemental leads, placed in the cerebral areas required by this connection, in case future modifications might be needed."

"That would leave Amon out," Helva said.

"He's out anyhow," Niall affirmed. "He never heard of Shakespeare and his brawn couldn't act his way out of a saloon brawl."

"The brawn has to act, too? Well, that obviously lets me out as I have no brawn at the moment, do I?"

"God spare me your tongue when you're really mad. Actually Chadress Turo has been called back on active duty . . ."

"Another temporary? No, absolutely not."

"For this assignment, some ships would change brawns in a flash. Blast it all, Helva," Parollan shouted, "don't be such an ass. Listen to me. You've never before been stubborn for the wrong reasons."

Helva digested that unpalatable charge in silence. "I'll listen."

"That's more like my Helva."

"I'm not *your* Helva."

"You sound like Ansra Colmer."

Helva sputtered indignantly.

"You do, throwing your weight around . . ." Niall insisted.

"She hasn't been trying to scratch Solar Prane from the mission, has she? Because if she has . . ."

"She's got very influential backing," Niall said, but

something in his attitude, a certain tenseness, a sly gleam in his eye, warned Helva.

She chuckled softly, watching the effect on him. He reacted.

"I thought so," she laughed aloud. "Her backing won't mean anything if the probability curve still favors Prane. And nothing's occurred to change that, has it?"

"Trust actors to blab all over the place," Niall growled, his features screwed up into a sour expression. "You must have stayed up all night listening to their nightmares."

"I told you there had been some real interesting lifelike dramatic interludes. Let me know if she leans too hard on Prane."

Niall's head shot up, his face cleared of disappointment.

"Look, Helva, can't you see how valuable you'd be? You're on to Ansra. Do you realize she's gone from ship to ship, sounding out brains and brawn? That *she's* recommending the properly sympathetic partnership to Chief Railly which will aid and abet the success of the mission?"

"Wouldn't put it past her. If I were you, I'd get Davo Fillanaser to cite the jeopardy clause on her. She means to upstage Romeo."

"*I* know it!" Niall exploded from the couch, pacing the cabin. "And you know it. But she does have pull and the probability profile still favors her as Juliet. We can't shake it. We *need* you!"

Pointedly, Helva said nothing.

"Prane asked if you were available."

"Is this an official notice of mission, supervisor?"

"It carries a triple bonus, Helva." He was not capitulating.

"I wouldn't care if it carried a free maintenance ticket for my operable lifetime, Parollan. I know my rights. Is this an official notice of mission?"

"You stubborn, fardling jackass of a titanium-coated

virgin!" shouted Parollan. He turned on his heel and pounded out of the cabin, slapped up the lock release and jammed down the lift control, descending without another look in her direction.

Helva glared at him, infuriated to the core by his compound insults, arrogant manners, twisted arguments, veiled blackmail and outright bribery. How he had ever got to be a supervisor she didn't know, but she had her rights and one of them was to choose her directing personnel and . . .

Someone was requesting permission to board.

"If you've come to apologize, Niall Parollan . . ."

"Apologize? Are we late or something? They just now gave us the A-O," a baritone voice shouted into her audios.

She paused long enough to distinguish half a dozen chattering voices.

"Who wants to board?" she demanded.

"She sounds mad about something," came a hoarse whisper.

"We're from brawn barracks and we'd very much like to . . . to . . ."

"Court her, that's the term, brasshead," prompted the hoarse whisperer.

"Permission granted," Helva said, trying not to sound as sour as she unaccountably felt.

Seven persons, five men and two women, crowded onto the lift, arguing and hollering about bruised feet and ribs all the way up. Helva could feel the strain on the lift mechanism, then bodies exploded into the lock as if in free-fall, all scrambling, to be the first to salute her. Helva stared down at the handsome, grinning faces; strong, tall people all eager to please her, to court her, to be her brawn.

Others arrived as the news circulated that the XH-834 was being courted. In fact, Helva sent the lift back down as soon as the newest arrival stepped into the lock. So it wasn't surprising that Kurla Ster could step into the lock without advance notice.

"Hey, don't gawk, girl. Come on in and take your chances with the rest of us," someone encouraged her.

"She's not competition, brawns," Helva sang out. "Let her through to the pilot's cabin."

Kurla raised one hand as if to protest, her face reflecting confusion and embarrassment. Before she could verbalize, she was pushed through the crowd and into the cabin.

"Nothing's happened to the Solar, Kurla?" Helva asked, the moment the door shut on the noise.

Relief washed away the uncertainty as Kurla cried, "You *do* care about him."

"I respect Solar Prane as an artist and as a human being," Helva replied, choosing her words carefully, wondering if Parollan were behind this visit.

"Then why did you refuse the assignment when he specifically asked for you?" There was a shrill note to the girl's voice, although she was trying hard to speak evenly.

"I have not refused the assignment."

Kurla's lips tightened angrily. "Then Ansra Colmer *has* been able to keep your name off."

"I don't know anything about that, Kurla. I have been approached . . . unofficially . . . and I was very flattered that Solar Prane asked for me. But I have also made it plain . . . unofficially . . . that I do not want another assignment with a temporary brawn."

"I don't understand. I thought it was interference from Colmer. That you didn't realize he wanted you. Don't you realize there's not another ship that even knows who Shakespeare was, much less quotes him on cue? And he thought you might even like to play the Nurse. He was honestly impressed with your reading on the way here. Why, you're so perfect, it's like an answer to an impossibility. And he's got to have the very best there is. It's got to be perfect . . ."

she fought to control her voice, "It's just got to be perfect."

"Because it's the end for him?"

Kurla seemed to crumple in on herself and sagged against the bulkhead, unbidden tears in her eyes.

"God spare me a woman's tears," Helva said, angry and annoyed. "So it's his swan song and you've decided that I'm the ship to sing it?"

"Please . . . if you've a gram of humanity in you . . . !" Kurla covered her tactless mouth with both hands, her eyes wide.

"Actually, about 22 kilos of me is very human, Kurla . . ."

"Oh, Helva, I'm so sorry," she stammered. "I'm so sorry. I had no right to come here. I'm sorry. I thought if I could just explain . . ."

Awkwardly she got to her feet, her muscles straining.

"I'd appreciate it if you'd forget I came here," Kurla went on in a very stiff, formal voice, fumbling for the door release. "It is always a mistake to act on impulse."

"Is it true that not one of the others knows Shakespeare?"

"*I* wouldn't demean myself with lies."

"So Ansra is making it very difficult."

The pride seemed to drain out of Kurla and she leaned her head wearily against the door for a moment, defeat showing in every curve of her slender body.

"She implies the most despicable things about him. She's said . . . never mind. But she is undermining him with the rest of the cast. And . . . and Helva, I don't trust her."

"Then have her replaced, you little idiot."

"Me? What could *I* do? I'm a medical attendant."

"Kurla, the man's dying. You can't be deluding yourself about that . . ."

"No. That's the one delusion I don't have." Something seemed to pull the girl erect then. "I just don't
want him cheated out of this last perfect performance. His acting is all he has left and he's so good at
it."

"You've influence with him, though. Get him to replace Ansra."

Kurla shook her head sadly. "He won't because he
believes that she's the best Juliet available so he'll put
up with her . . . temperament. And . . ." Kurla
hesitated, the struggle with honesty apparent in her
expressive face, "she was, when they rehearsed back
at Duhr. Then . . . she changed. Overnight. Prane
won't do anything. And she'll destroy him, Helva. I
know it. Somehow she'll destroy him."

"Not while I've got my eye on her, she won't,"
Helva replied firmly.

The speed with which Chadress Turo arrived
afterward struck Helva as suspicious, but she knew
Kurla's visit had not been planned by Parollan. And
she liked Chadress. He could not have been retired
very long, for his step was springy and an old, un-
altered shipsuit outlined a strong, muscular body. He
wore a clutch of achievement stars but no honors,
which meant he had plenty but was no braggart.

"Welcome board, Chadress Turo of Marak. It's nice
to have a partner, however briefly."

Chadress caught the caustic undertone. "Hope I'm
not the cause of your regrets?"

"No. You're the first happy face I've seen in the
last two hours."

His eyes twinkled. "You've been put into coventry
by the brains and I had to be smuggled aboard to
avoid outraged brawns. Oh, they'll all forget their
pique. They always do. However, officially, you're in
very good odor. Supervisor Parollan is taking personal credit for convincing you to accept . . ."

"The nerve of that pipsqueak . . ."

"I thought so," laughed Chadress. "Well, no matter. I'm not the only one who thought you'd be the only ship to do the job right and I've only rumors . . . and legends . . . to go by. But it's going to be a tricky mission with so much at stake, and so many explosive . . ."

"Personalities?"

Chadress laughed. "I've met many actors—I'm a classic buff myself, that's why I was called back . . ." he paused, his eyes seeing a middle distance, a slight frown on his face. "In fact, I leaped at the opportunity. Some of us should be allowed to die in harness. No matter. Here's the mission tape," and he dropped it in the slot. Before he touched the playback switch, he closed the lock and turned off all but the console audio. Then he eased into the pilot's chair and settled himself to listen.

Helva was amazed at how much of the tape's information she knew. The Nekkarese com man had had most of it correct.

A survey ship on a routine mission had intercepted pulsed energy emissions of tremendous power near Beta Corvi. They tracked the emissions to the sixth planet, a methane-ammonia giant, and assumed an orbit. Before they could prepare probes for exploration in such a corrosive atmosphere, they were contacted by the Corviki.

" 'It felt like pressure, as if a giant hand were covering my head and pressing knowledge into my brain,' " was the taped comment of the survey ship captain.

The unusual form of communication was nevertheless precise enough for the Corviki to grasp the nature of their unexpected visitors and to discover a commodity which they, unimaginably sophisticated scientifically, wanted.

" 'I guess the best analogy,' the captain of the ship went on, 'is that of the pure researcher who has devoted half a century to an intensive study of some esoteric subject. He masters it and finally has time to look around him and discovers that other things exist . . . like girls,' the captain snickered, 'and sex. He understands the theory but not the application, and he sure wants to learn.' "

Romeo and Juliet was a sample of the merchandise that had aroused the Corviki curiosity. If acceptable, the human company would teach understudies the full play, with movement adapted for the free-fall condition of Beta Corvi. Payment would be the Corviki process of stabilizing certain isotopes in the transuranian group whose power potential was unrealizable due to an exceedingly short half-life. Central Worlds badly needed such a process and the XH-834 was to ensure the success of this dramatic mission.

"Well, we'll give it the old home-world try," Helva said.

"You don't sound so sure."

"It sounds all too simple. For instance, this psyche transfer: how do we know it won't develop some unexpected snag and leave our people trapped down there in Corviki envelopes?"

"That's one reason we're equipping you with an override and a time control."

"Suppose the Corviki override me because they adore Colmer's Juliet?"

Chadress grinned at the notion, but threw the schematic picture of the transceiver circuitry onto the pilot's console. "Every eeg expert in the galaxy has had a go at these. There are no extraneous circuits, nothing that is not accounted for in the schematics. Furthermore, *we* manufactured them, not the Corviki. Now, they do specify that 7 hours is the endurance limit for our life form."

"Ahah!"

"Cool it. The transceiver has a time control, set

for the maximum of seven hours, our time, so nothing could happen."

"After the maximum period, what happens to the personality if . . ."

"Don't invent problems. We've got enough. However, I did speak to the Survey Ship Captain and he was most encouraging about the transfer. In fact, he said it was perfect for a bunch of actors. You *think* that you want to be on the surface of the planet. And you are! No pain, no strain. Simplicity itself."

"Simplicity has a habit of expanding into catastrophe!"

Chadress called her a pessimist and went on with the briefing. She thought of half a dozen factors that could alter disastrously betwixt here and Beta Corvi, the least of which was ringing in an unknown device.

The adjustment to be attached to herself was even simpler. Even ingenious, she admitted, examining the compact device under microscopic lenses. It would link several infinitesimal strands already embedded in her cerebrum: one which extended deep in the area controlling the optic nerves, for the psyche transfer was triggered by this portion of the human brain. The other two were to link cross-over reflexes that would enable her to time and to disconnect the psyche relay for the rest of the mobiles. All three synapse attachments were self-activitating and did not appear on the pilot's board.

The hookup had to be made with Helva under anesthesia, and she disliked that part intensely. It was unnerving for her to hear the chief of Regulus Base (no less) mouth the pitched syllables that triggered the panel that was the only access to her shell behind the titanium column. It seemed she hovered in an eternity of vulnerability before he touched the anesthesia release. She instinctively struggled against unconsciousness. Was that how poor 732 had felt? Or had her madness banished fear?

Helva's thought was no sooner formulated than she was conscious again. Startled, she gazed out into an empty cabin, irritated that Chief Railly dared leave her unprotected. Then she was aware that considerable time had elapsed since the chief had spoken—18 hours, 20 minutes and 32 seconds, to be precise.

"Awake again, Helva?" and Chadress stepped into her lock. "I say, they certainly timed it to the exact second. I'm to ask if you've a headache?"

"Headache? How could I? I've no pain reflexes."

Then she looked around her main cabin, where transceivers had been stowed by her couches, and wall units had been added to accommodate the additional personnel. Bunks had been added to all her cabins and another table fitted into the pilot's cabin.

"I'm a ruddy troopship."

"Indeed you are," Chadress agreed, "and the troupe is assembling."

Five men ascended in the lift and were introduced by Chadress, but she found it easier to think of them as the parts they would play. The introductions were cut short by sirens and the advent of a fleet of ground vehicles.

"Ansra's made the scene," the man who played Prince Escalus announced in a dry voice.

No one seemed sorry when Chadress refused any boarders, including Chief Railly. As he took the restriction in good part, the others had to and Ansra was reduced to waving and smiling at her admirers as she was lifted smoothly lockward.

"Here I am again, Helva," she said in a bright, glad way that certainly didn't deceive Helva.

"Welcome aboard, Miss Colmer." You feed me the cue, Helva thought to herself, and I'll read the appropriate line.

Immediately Central Com—and it wasn't Niall Parollan's voice—gave her clearance for the Orbital Station. The shuttle run was fast, and in no time Helva was at the free-fall lock.

The scene was reminiscent of the Duhr landing: Davo, Solar Prane and Kurla the central figures of a smiling cluster. But here, the whole cluster entered, all of them floating with excellent control into the cabin, pushing down to the couches and securing themselves for maneuver and acceleration. There was neither wasted time nor motion.

Prane looked so gay and alert that Helva glanced at Kurla, whose attitude would transmit a truer reflection of her patient's health. The girl was radiant, her eyes as bright as Prane's, her manner proud and confident. She managed a polite nod to Ansra, who smiled fixedly at everyone.

By contrast, Davo looked tired and thoughtful. He pushed immediately toward the sleeping accommodations and meshed himself into a bunk.

Prane hovered in front of Helva. "I want to thank you, very much, for putting aside your personal preferences to undertake this venture. Chief Railly has assured me that you will have the topmost priority when you return."

Helva did not have time to analyze why his words disturbed her, for the Orbital Station transmitted good luck and clearance. Chadress did the manual piloting —that was protocol—but Helva was so used to doing things herself it was hard to watch. Not that he was inept. Damn, damn, damn, she thought, glancing around the crowded cabin, wishing half her mind were busy on something routine, how had she let herself get talked into this?

The moment Chadress announced turnover and free-fall, Prane called a rehearsal. First he put the five men who had joined the ship planetside through the staging they had missed. They'd all worked in free-

fall and they knew their roles. All they required was
time to familiarize themselves with movements and
the Nurse's voice issuing from the wall. Ansra, however, chose to be difficult about that. She undulated
toward the director—whether to charm him or intimi-
date him was a question.

"Really, Prane, I can project any emotion required
of any capable actress, but to pretend an . . . an
abstract voice is Juliet's Nurse is the end. How can I
play to a wall? And, how may I ask, can . . . Helva
(it seemed to be difficult for Ansra to name her) ac-
quire any ease in free-fall, when I understand she has
never made any use of a body?"

"My stage directions are perfectly clear and are
printed in my circuitry. Therefore I cannot make a
mistake. That is, as long as you are where Juliet is
supposed to be," Helva answered.

No one actually laughed aloud at the putdown. Ansra
resumed her proper position, frowning, and chewing
her lip.

However, her assertion that she could project any
emotion required of any capable actress seemed to fall
short of the mark in scenes with proper actors. Her
Juliet remained wooden and inadequate. She did not
take fire from Romeo's speeches, although how she
could fail was beyond Helva's comprehension. The
man was inspired . . . and inspiring.

Relieved now for many days of the press of gravity
on his spongy bones, buoyed constantly by the success
of every other aspect of this singular production, Prane
exuded a vitality, an enthusiasm that was contagious.
He was apparently indefatigable.

As he was setting scene iv of Act I, with himself,
Mercutio, Benvolio and others doubling up as maskers
and torchbearers, Mercutio finished his speech:

". . . Come, we burn daylight, ho!"

The scene had been quick, bright exchanges, the

lighthearted nonsense of friends bound for a gay evening.

Mercutio repeated his line. Hastily, Helva remembered she doubled as prompter and found the place.

" 'Nay, that's not so,' " she read out.

Silence met this attempt, so she, too, repeated the line.

"We know the line," Prane said as this additional pause lengthened conspicuously. "Who says it?"

Helva gulped. "You do."

For a moment a terrible expression haunted his eyes. Then he burst out laughing and the terror was gone. " 'Tis always the littlest line that escapes," and he briskly cued Mercutio.

That night, as everyone slept, Prane was restless. Shamelessly, Helva turned up the volume in the cabin he shared with five other men. He was repeating scene iv over and over. Then he lay silent. Helva thought he slept, until she saw his right hand slowly creep to his belt, carefully extract a small pill from the waistband fabric of his shipsuit. With a gesture counterfeiting a random sleepy movement, the pill reached his mouth.

The secretiveness of his action, added to the intense rehearsal of that scene, gave Helva a tragic insight to the Solar. He *was* an addict, in the most horrifying degree: mindtrap, listed as harmless in the galactic pharmacopoeia, had become poisonous to him, fatal to mind and body. And he knew it. Yet more devastating to Solar Prane was loss of memory and to prevent that, he courted self-destruction.

Except for Ansra, rehearsals proceeded well. How Prane kept his temper with such deliberate obstructionism, Helva did not know. Every scene the Solara played began to sag, lose fire, drop pace. But Prane did not react. And Ansra apparently gave up trying to goad him into an action no one could condone. She took to needling Kurla, a far more vulnerable personality.

Fortunately, Nia Tubb, the Lady Capulet, shared the pilot's cabin, which was the women's room. She was wise in the ways of human relations and if she said nothing to the point, she did buffer Kurla from Ansra's hostility. She also helped Kurla in her lines, kept up a lighthearted monologue when the women were alone. But even she could see Ansra's tactics increasing the pressure on the sensitive, anxious medical attendant.

"Honey, you have any *real* trouble with Colmer, you let me help, huh?" Nia Tubb said to Kurla one morning.

"Thanks," Kurla answered with a wan smile.

"Say, just between the two of us, Prane's no addict, is he? He doesn't look like one and I've seen enough to know, but still—"

"Solar Prane developed an adverse chemical reaction to long use of mindtrap."

"I always thought mindtrap was the most harmless thing in the world. I've used it myself times without number."

"Ordinarily. But the Solar has been using it for over 70 years. A residue of the silicon content, which ought to have been flushed out of his system, has built up in his tissues. He also has a liquid retention problem and the diuretic originally prescribed combined unfavorably with the mindtrap residue, leaching potassium from his system in an unremediable process."

"What does that mean? He looks fine to me."

Kurla's voice, dispassionately clinical, was more tragic than tears.

"In low-grav conditions, in free-fall particularly, there is no strain on the skeleton and he's fine. But his bones are soft: a fall, a blow, any long period of heavy physical strain and he would . . . in effect . . .

break up. And the silicon is gradually choking his vital organs to death."

"Replace 'em!"

Kurla shook her head. Nia patted her hand sympathetically. Helva interrupted them with a rehearsal call. And that was the worst rehearsal yet. Ansra's attitude had insidiously undermined the entire cast. Everyone was off; they blew their lines, forgot stage business. When Mercutio and Paris got into a fight that was not in the script, Prane called a halt.

"We've gone stale. We'll take today off and tomorrow. Helva, break out the liquor rations. Nia and Kurla, would you be kind enough to see what surprises the galley might serve us? Helva, have you some tri-casts of interest? We need to relate to the everyday worlds that we have forgotten, immersed as we have been in ancient England."

Ansra stalked out of the main cabin, slamming the door to the women's quarters. Helva looked in to find her staring angrily into a mirror. It was disconcerting for Helva to watch her frustrated, brooding self-examination while Nia and Kurla chattered inconsequentialities in the galley.

Helva tried to be everywhere, keeping an ear out for any trouble . . . any more trouble, that is. Davo floated purposefully toward Prane. Since Helva had begun speaking only from the main cabin, she fostered the tendency for her passengers to forget she had ears and eyes everywhere in the ship.

"You must realize by now, Prane," Davo was saying, "that Ansra is determined to ruin this production. And she is succeeding admirably."

Prane regarded his friend for a long moment, a slow smile beginning. "You've a solution?"

"Let's put her off balance. Remember what we used to do on the long hauls on tour?"

"Reshuffle all the parts?"

"Exactly. Christ, we all know each other's lines and movements."

Prane began to grin mischievously. "And . . . let Helva be Juliet?"

"No, Kurla is Juliet!" Davo returned Prane's surprised stare with a dead serious dare.

"And Romeo?"

"That part need not change," Davo said evenly, then added in a light voice, "but I shall be Friar Lawrence and marry you two."

Prane waited till everyone had eaten and was relaxed with Thracian beer. The announcement met with approval, raucous and bawdy.

"I'll be Lady Capulet," Escalus announced in a squeaky falsetto.

"And I'll be Lady Montague," said Friar Lawrence in a quavering contralto, reverting to his own normal bass to add, "Always thought she was a wino."

"I'll be Escalus," Helva volunteered in a voice so like the real actor's the man dropped his tankard.

"You could be the whole damn play all by yourself," Davo vowed, his voice far more slurred than it should be on Thracian beer. "There isn't one part *you* couldn't do."

"Really? In that case, I'll be the Nurse," Ansra Colmer announced. "Then Helva can see how the part should be *played*."

"And Kurla will be Juliet," Davo cried, his eyes on Ansra. "Set the stage, oh chorus. Places, everyone. Places."

" 'Two households, both alike in dignity . . .' " Helva began promptly in a basso, sweeping everyone into the act before they had time for second thoughts.

Davo came on as Sampson, and Chadress, normally Lord Capulet, as Gregory, hamming their lines and indulging in slapstick nonsense. Balthasar rolled on, as though drunk, slurring through the establishment of conflict between the two houses. Lines were rattled off, and actors bodily moved each other into proper stage position or deliberately upstaged the speaker.

When Escalus-Lady Capulet glided on in the company of Nurse Angelica, Ansra, with deliberate malice, dispensed with fun and *played* her part as she had not played Juliet. And somehow twisted her lines as Nurse to mean something entirely different. Her exit line: "Go girl, seek happy nights to happy days," was barbed enough to make Escalus falter.

But then Juliet met Romeo at the feast, and Ansra's spitefulness backfired. For Prane was a different, tenderer Romeo, his voice trembled not with fatigue but with newfound love, gentle, protective, eager. And Kurla, her eyes equally discovering her lover, was Juliet: breathless, shy, daring, and precious. She blushed shyly as she said,

"For saints have hands that pilgrims' hands do touch,
And palm to palm is holy palmers' kiss."

She turned her hands palms down on Romeo's, as he had so often directed Ansra only to have her mistime the words and action as to make them meaningless.

Romeo raised Juliet's hands on his, and the ardor in his eyes, the answering joy in hers, made that little scene so tender that everyone was spellbound.

" 'Thus from my lips, by thine, my sin is purg'd' " said Romeo in so soft a voice it seemed a faint echo, but it hung clearly until his lips met Juliet's in a kiss that was a devout an avowal as a shout.

Her role forgotten completely, Ansra flung herself forward at the two still embraced and lost to their surroundings. And the proximity alarms twanged. They had arrived at their destination.

"Now," Chadress said to the actors, all seated in the main cabin, hastily cleared of all its party debris, "the transceivers were fitted to your head sizes so they will be quite comfortable. You all heard the reports from those survey ship members who used the first device. You know the transfer process is painless and easy. You think yourself on the surface and there you are."

"How can you think yourself on a surface you've never seen?" Nia demanded, grimacing at the transceiver she was holding.

"The nearest analogue would be the undersea scapes on Terra in the Carribean area, or the water world in Aldebaran. Or Vega IV. Imagine yourselves surrounded by seaweeds, all shapes and colors. Yes, the survey people repeatedly emphasized the enormous importance of color. The Corviki resemble a marine animal in the class hydrozoa, sort of a large sac-like body with a complex collection of tendrils that may be nerve endings."

"Gawd, what a costume!" Nia Tubb muttered, shuddering.

"It'll fit, I'm told." Chadress grinned at her. "Now, Helva is our fail-safe. She's equipped with an automatic return relay. We've been warned not to remain too long in the Corviki environment."

"Why?" Ansra demanded in a bored voice.

"The Corviki undoubtedly have good reason, but they did not say what. Now, Prane?"

The Solar rose, looked around at the entire cast. "We all know the importance of this unlikely exchange of Shakespeare for power. The Bard has been translated into every conceivable language, alien and humanoid, and somehow the essence of his plays has been understood by the most exotic, the most barbaric, the most sophisticated. There is no reason to suppose that Will Shakespeare hasn't got something to say to the Corviki . . . if we do the job wholeheartedly . . . or whatever our Corviki envelopes use for that Organ.

"Ladies and gentlemen, curtain!" He sat down and donned his transceiver, settling back in the couch and relaxing completely. In a few seconds a light glowed across the rim of the transceiver.

"If that's all there is to it," Nia Tubb said, and pulled hers down on her head.

The others imitated her more or less simultaneously until only Chadress and Helva remained on board.

"Check Prane," Helva said.

"He's all right as far as I can see. I'll see you down there, Helva."

And he was gone. Helva had the uncanny notion that the new synapse leads were burning hot. But that was impossible. She willed herself to descend. On the heels of the thought that this was the first time *she* had been outside a shell in her life, came a terrifying surge of primitive fear and then . . .

Transfer!

Her first indication of the difference involved pressure . . . an enveloping pressure. But the Corviki had said they would provide empty envelopes for the cast to occupy. She was enveloped and the envelope was also enveloped. She could "feel" it all around. She undulated experimentally, hoping to rid herself of this sense of being covered. It was somehow unclean to feel all along every part of her. And yet, even as she felt loose, she was at the same time compressed. Not gravity pressure, but something *in* which she was and was moving. Well, movement was not a new skill for her: this was, then, just a form of motion. She wriggled again and things that were part of "her" floated up from beneath her. She could not look at them because they floated away when she tried. Hmm. She could see every part of her ship-self from one scanner or another. How limiting mobility was. Well, she'd look around as far as she was able. And stared down, down, in an unlimited perspective until finally her sight distinguished a burbling, burping mass

of ochre eruptions that she recognized as "ground."
Above and around her fronds swayed, exhaled and
inhaled in a full spectrum of colors unbelievably varied
and varying: colors which in some cases had "sound"
and "smell" as part of their value. Only "smell" was
also a novel sensation to Helva, who had utilized
gauges all her life instead of the olfactory sense.

"Adapting, Helva?" a familiar presence dominated
her mind. Instinctively she turned toward the 'sound'
that wasn't sound as she had previously known it,
but a patterned interruption of the pressures around
her.

"It's odd to feel physical sensations," she replied.

"It would be, for you."

"How do you feel, Chadress?" For the presence was
indisputably her brawn.

"Velvet, soft, deep, a very pleasurable tactile sensation, I assure you. And a sense of unlimited power."
Chadress was impressed. "Of being young and new
again." Here the dominant quality of his thought was
incredulous and self-amused. "They have evidently
lent us brand-new, guaranteed-unsullied shells."

"I wonder where they get them from."

A new dominance approached them and this entity
was recognized by both as being a true Corviki. The
presence was very dense and Chadress and Helva
both received an undeniable feeling of great age and
wisdom, of a unique application of basic energy.

"I am your Manager," he introduced himself. "The
others are all contained. We may proceed with this
expression of energy."

"That which we call a rose by any other name
would smell as sweet," thought Helva as they propelled
themselves toward a sphere-shaped area, surrounded
by unanchored lumps of a dead black substance, framed
by enormous breathing fronds. And suddenly, she
could recognize everyone, despite their apparently

homogeneous shape, by the slight variation of color tone and pressure weight.

Prane came on as dense as Manager, Helva discovered. She began to equate density with age or wisdom. Subjectively, she wondered how she "felt" to others. Then Prane called her as chorus to open the rehearsal.

For a frantic moment, she wondered how she could possibly project "chorus" without the audio equipment available on the ship. She had an intense desire to retreat back to her own shell again. But Prane was Director and one obeyed Director.

" 'Two households, both alike in dignity,' " and somehow her dominance enlarged, darkened, and she was more than herself.

Then Sampson and Gregory emerged from behind fronds and their dominance was shallow, light, tenuous as if inconsequential. In a fashion the cast managed to condense or dissipate themselves through the scenes until by Act IV, the new medium and the difference or exposition no longer seemed strange.

It was almost physically painful to be wrenched by the time control back into the ship and discover that they were, sadly, only flesh and blood. No one said much. They ate a great deal quickly, and then went to bed.

Helva, unfortunately, was wide awake and, for the first time in her conscious life, envied the others for the gentle oblivion of sleep. She tried not to think of the experiential effect of mobility on her conditioning. She disciplined herself by running a full scan outside. Not because anything might have changed but just to make sure all was as before. They were in orbit, black space topside, but the amorphous boiling cloud of diffuse colors, shot with brilliant lights, loomed below. She ran a check on her systems and discovered something a little unnerving in her engine compartment.

There was something blocking her readings there, yet the systems were all green on the boards. She could not "feel" power, although there was no evidence of its absence: it was simply unavailable to her. As she pondered the implications of this, she heard a faint susurrus. She snatched at the diversion and traced it: Prane at his litany.

" 'If by your art, my dearest father, you have
  Put the wild waters in this roar, allay them. . . .' "

She listened avidly until the sleepy voice trailed into silence after

" 'As you from crimes would pardon'd be.
    Let your indulgence set me free.' "

They picked up the staging the next "day" where they had left off. Helva had the feeling none of the Corviki had left the "stage" or were even aware that the troupe had been away. Did they control time as well as energy? Was time, as one Alpheccan theoretician maintained, merely another emission of energy?

Her perceptions were more acute today. She had control over her envelope and the sensory data it constantly received. And while the others were beginning to act, Ansra was consciously damping down.

Manager approached Ansra, in front of all, just before time was up.

"There is no logical reason to withhold energy. Conservation is not the aim of this experiment. We are assessing the effects of this form of energy expulsion on the pressure-senses and dominance factors. You inhibit this experiment. Therefore, lose energy as the equative factors require."

"Or?"

A ripple of pressure and color answered Ansra's ultimatum.

"The envelope will be permanently emptied . . ."

"I will not go back to that perverted seascape to be insulted and degraded in public," Ansra declared.

She was rather magnificent, Helva thought, even if she left her audience unmoved.

"That is sufficient, Ansra Colmer," Prane said quietly, rising from the couch, his voice glacial, his eyes stony, his attitude unbending. "You have made your personal preferences and private opinions known to each and every member of the cast. However, there is more at stake than personal differences and everyone here has been exceedingly forebearing with your whimsies and little schemes. You *will* go back tomorrow and you will, as you were advised by the Manager, lose energy as the equative factors require."

"Who's going to make me?" Ansra struck a pose with that challenge.

"Any one of us, honey," Nia Tubb replied, forestalling Chadress and Davo, who began to rise from their seats. "Any one of us would be glad to make you. In fact, you might find when we got through with you here that it would be a relief to get into that Corviki envelope."

"You wouldn't dare!"

Helva wondered whether Ansra, having taken a stand, was too hardheaded to retreat, or unable to believe that one of her standing could be violable. Fortunately, she was also a person who could not tolerate physical pain and a half-dozen open handed blows from Nia were an effective proof and promise.

"Oh, no you don't, honey," Nia cried, grabbing Ansra's arm as the sobbing woman headed for the cabin. "You're not moving from my side—because I don't trust you out of my sight. Now you sit down and you'll eat and you'll behave. And tomorrow you'll be the best Juliet that's ever trod air."

That scene, on top of the psychological exhaustion of rehearsing on Beta Corvi, drained everyone's reserve. Chadress and Kurla passed around liquor bulbs and a high-protein soup. As soon as they ate, people drifted off to their bunks and meshed in.

"Keep Nia and Ansra under observation, Helva, will you?" Chadress suggested.

There's something different about him, Helva realized, a new depth, oddly Corvikian.

"Do you think she will play now?" Helva heard Kurla asking Prane. The two were the last awake, and seemed unable to separate.

"Her color was that of an anger-fear composite. . . ." Prane stopped short, staring down at Kurla.

"You're thinking Corviki," she laughed, her eyes dancing. "It's contagious, isn't it? Like assuming the characteristics of the part you're playing? See, even a rank amateur like me picks up tricks of the trade!"

"You transfer into a very solid, warm presence on Corvi, my dear."

The laughter caught in her throat and her eyes were filled with a haunted yearning. They seemed to be a breath away from a kiss when Prane, a garbled sound issuing from his throat, whirled away down the corridor.

Ansra lost energy the next rehearsal with such good will they were able to run completely through the play. Prane was so pleased with the result he informed the Manager that they could give the first complete performance.

"My energy group is excited to experience the total pressure dominances of these envelopes," the Manager replied, emanating the lavender-purples Helva equated with pleasure in Corviki. "Your next entry here is convenient?"

Prane agreed heartily.

"If this emission is satisfactory," Chadress asked, shading his dominance with the sharply controlled waste of deference to a superior force, "will Corviki entities then undertake a transfer of our patterns so we may fulfill our contract with you?"

"Affirmative. For it is evident that there is a loss of ego-entity superior to the programmed minimum. Entropy could exceed basic energy requirements."

Helva felt she'd better analyze that statement the moment she returned to herself. It sounded . . . ominous . . . to Helva, but not to her imprinted self in the Corviki envelope. Such a split of personality could be dangerous indeed.

Once back on the ship, it was easier to spot those who were psychologically twisting their orientation. They tended to express themselves in Corviki terms, as Prane and Chadress had the night before. The only one who seemed impervious was Ansra, but then, Ansra was so wrapped up in her personal grievances, she had no energy . . . there I go, moaned Helva . . . for objective experiences.

Opening night on Beta Corviki was a white-hot, frenetic triumph as far as Corviki acceptance of this form of energy loss was concerned. Beyond the stand of fronds were masses of Corviki, pulsing, throbbing as they absorbed the cast's emission, to all appearances starved for this form of energy.

Helva could feel her Corviki envelope swell to incredible dimension as the feedback resulted in a thermal reaction, giving her an unlimited mass to energize to a high excitation level. Yet she was also aware that the Corviki audience understood the conflict of the two warring energy-groups, of the desire of the two new, but not shallow, entities to combine into a new force group, of the energy-stoking of herself as the Nurse, of the brilliant light of beta particles exchanged by the two new entities, swearing neuron coalitions and, finally, forced to expend the vital energy of their cores to bring the warring groups to the realization that coexistence was possible on their energy level.

As the Prince summed up the entropy death of the two, novas of approval exploded outside the fronded area. And Helva, gross with feedback, found herself racing to emit into the nearest drained entity some ergs of that pressure, in a self-sacrifice that was ecstatic. All around her, the atmosphere crackled, popped, boomed and thundered with the resultant explosions as immeasurable positive forces recombined and all the previously expended energy was reabsorbed.

Then, indeed, did Helva bless the surgeons. Bless and curse them for hauling her inexorably back from such glorious intercourse. She dazedly recalled her scattered wits as warning lights and signals penetrated the coruscating impressions and forced her to be aware of imminent danger.

Lax figures lay, lifeless puppets with no more sign of vitality than the slight rise and fall of chests.

Scared, Helva tripped the transceivers. Lights reluctantly faded on the transceivers and still no one stirred. It seemed an eternity to Helva before Ansra moaned.

"Ansra. Ansra," Helva called in an insistent, hard voice, hoping to penetrate the woman's trancelike state. "Ansra. Ansra."

"Wha . . . what?"

"Get to the galley. Get stimulant K, in the blue i.v. spray."

It was like moving a robot. She kept droning her orders, relentlessly forcing Ansra to obey. The woman's eyes blinked, her body jerked as Helva encouraged, ordered, demanded the necessary actions. Finally she got Ansra's hands around the right i.v., and got the uncoordinated body to depress the dermospray against her arm. The stimulant took effect.

"Oh migod, oh migod," Ansra muttered hoarsely. "Oh migod."

"Ansra. Give them all injections. Move, woman, move."

The actress was still little better than an automaton, so Helva took advantage of her will-lessness to make her give Kurla and Prane the first injections. Then Chadress. It was a stunned group who returned to their former bodies.

"I don't think I can go back there," Escalus told Prane in a hoarse tremulo. He put both hands to his temples, where the transceiver had left a red band. "Never thought to see the day when I couldn't face an audience because they *liked* me too much. But man, that place is . . . is," his eyes widened with a terror he mastered. "I almost said, pure entropy." And he laughed. "But *that's* what's wrong with it all."

Prane, looking as drained and haunted as the others, managed a weak smile.

"There is no question that we have been overwhelmed by an unpredicted reaction. At this moment," and he paused to emphasize the phrase, "I would find a return engagement inconceivable. No, no discussion now. We need to convert mass—in the parlance of our hosts—into much-needed energy and to conserve our emissions. But I want to say how very, very proud I am of you all."

It was as well, Helva knew, for the cast could not have accepted, in their present enervation, the devastating truth of their captivity.

The silence of the ship was unbroken, even by Prane's nightly litany. Helva, too, found herself close to the verge of unconsciousness, too fatigued to worry about the problems of the morrow.

The next day brought no visible change. Everyone was still enervated. Kurla turned professional and roused those seeking oblivion in slumber to take high-protein meals and massive therapeutic i.v. sprays.

Toward the evening of that day, Helva got Chadress alone in the galley for a conference.

"We'll have to put it off as long as we can, Helva.

These people are drained dry. I know," and he shook his head slowly. "How're you doing?"

Helva temporized. "I always maintained shell people are as human as anyone mobile. I know it now. I'll find it extremely difficult to go back to Beta Corvi myself. Only I *know* we have no choice."

"What do you mean, Helva?" Chadress didn't have enough energy left to be more than mildly curious.

"They're wondering where we are right now. They have the understudies lined up and raring to learn."

Chadress mustered a defeated groan.

"Helva, how can we ask anyone here to undertake that?"

"As I said, Chadress, we have no choice."

"I don't follow you."

"There is a little block on any lead into my power sources. I couldn't even dodge a meteor if I had to."

Chadress dropped his head into his hands, his whole body shuddering. "Helva, I *can't* go back. I can't. I'd . . ."

"You don't have to go back. Not right now. Lord, you don't even have the energy to put on a transceiver," she said, deliberately misunderstanding him. "It's up to me."

"What's up to you?" Prane asked, drifting into the galley.

"I'm going down to explain our absence."

"On the contrary," Prane objected, trying to straighten his shoulders but all he managed was a direction-less lurch against the warming units. "I'm the director. I should explain our inability to fulfill our contract."

Chaddress groaned in distress.

"You're out on your feet, Prane. Chadress, too. I'm going. That's final. Chadress, we'll discuss this further when I get back," she ordered. "Chadress?" she prompted until he nodded acquiescence.

Pain assailed Helva's mind in a brief flicker of thought as she reentered the Corviki envelope. The myriad tactile sensations from her trailing appendages indicated the presence of several strong pressure-dominances. How was she going to explain human frailty to these masters of pure energy?

The atmosphere, however, was unusually free of energy emissions. Manager, dark and full and rich, discreetly contained his mass of pressure-dominances. The others, ranged beyond him at a courteous distance, must be the understudies, she thought. If a Corviki had compassionate levels in his consciousness, surely the Manager was activating them, for he was patient as Helva struggled to present the explanatory equation, pointing out the unresolvable fractions. He replied with a show of depletion that could only be an apology that the unprecedented feedback and the production of an unstable reaction mass had resulted in such entropy for the visitors. However, they had themselves as cause.

Nevertheless, Manager sternly informed Helva, a new condition of immense significance had developed. Every single energy group around this thermal core insisted on obtaining the formulae which could repeat those unique emissions. The benefits of such expulsion would rejuvenate static energy groups once considered lost beyond reactivation. The formulae must be passed on. No matter would be considered too precious in the exchange.

Helva, feeling she was emitting desperate energies, repeated the impossibility.

Some arrangement would have to be effected, the Manager insisted. There was one unit—he drew the equation of sound that meant Juliet—which had shown an admirable control of intrinsic energy. Let it return and deliver the formulae. Otherwise . . . the Manager swayed his tentacles in an unnerving approximation of a human shrug.

For a long interval Helva lacked the moral courage to indicate her return. She tried to think how this simple mission had turned into such a catastrophe. Ruthlessly she reviewed the elements of this impasse, trying to find a solution. There *had* to be one.

How cosmically ironic that Ansra Colmer, so bent on ruining them, was the only personality with sufficient egocentricity to survive the experience. But would she save them all?

"I'm not out of my mind, even if you all are," was Ansra's immediate response. "Nothing . . . not even if you beat me to death . . . could make me go back to that . . . that . . . gas factory. I've done all my contract called for."

"Actually you haven't, Ansra," Davo replied wearily, "not that any of us are likely to take you to task for it at Guild. But those contracts read that, if the Corviki accept our dramatic presentation as payment for their techniques, we must instruct Corviki understudies."

"Go back? Just to teach a Corviki to play Juliet?" Ansra laughed, shrilly, semi-hysterical. She whirled on Prane. "I told them at Regulus that you'd fail. And you have! I'm glad, *glad*, *GLAD!*"

Her hatred washed like a visible tide over sensibilities already abraded and tender. Still laughing, she careened off the walls on her way to the cabin, collapsing like a limp doll in front of the mirror, alternately laughing and staring at her reflection.

"She's gone stark raving mad," Nia stated in a flat voice.

"I don't think so, unless we're all mad right now," Davo replied judiciously.

"Well, we can't just sit here and let her spite us," Nia exclaimed, rousing to indignation. "She's just got to do her part."

"The show must go on?" Escalus asked sarcastically. "Not this one."

"I apologize to everyone," Prane began, rising to his feet. "Ansra's grievance is with me. You shall not be the victims of it."

"Christ, Prane, spare us that role," Davo exploded.

"No role, the solution is simple," the Solar went on, his voice and manner so matter-of-fact that the accusation of heroics was void. "As director, I know every single line in this play. In fact, I have complete recall of some 212 ancient, medieval, classical, atomic, and modern dramas."

"You'd die under the strain," Kurla cried, throwing her arms around him.

He disengaged himself, smiling tenderly at her.

"I'm dying anyway, my dear. I'd prefer a good exit line."

"Next week *East Lynne*," roared Helva, successfully shocking everyone alert with her mocking laughter. Prane was deeply hurt, which Helva found a trifle healthier than heroic self-sacrifice. "Now will everyone *calm down*! All is not lost because Ansra Colmer is a vicious, vengeful bitch. In the first place, Solar Prane, we don't want the Corviki possessed of our entire bankroll in one mass cathartic purge. One play, *Romeo and Juliet*, which has rolled 'em up by the fronds, is all we contracted for. And we shall give it to them and then accelerate out of their sphere of influence as fast as I can blow my jets. I shall strongly, urgently recommend that we do not darken their dominance again until our bright boys figure out how to cushion our fragile psyches against Corviki feedback.

"And, Solar Prane, you are not the only person on board with perfect recall. I know this may sound fatuous but I, too—probably Davo as well, possibly our Escalus—know every bloody line of R & J, too. All three of us are physically and emotionally better able than you to go back down to Beta Corvi . . ."

"*Listen to me*," she bellowed when everyone began to protest. She shifted to the voice that signified a broad smile and hammed it: "*This is Your Captain speaking!*" And as they broke into laughter, became dead serious. "I, Helva, have the final responsibility for this mission and for everyone on board the ship."

"I know all of *Romeo and Juliet*, too. Used to play Juliet, you know, when I was in my first hundred," Nia said quietly, before Helva could continue. "And you've forgotten something, Helva. A very essential point. It's *performances*, on Beta Corvi, not rehearsals, which rock us. I feel sure I could cope with a rehearsal situation, with the customary halts and breaks needed to teach understudies. We don't even have to rehearse the full seven hours. Not if these Corviki want the plays so bad. We can call the tune." Then her expression changed and she glanced toward the women's cabin, where Ansra was laughing softly. "And I'll be goddamned if I'll let that bitch close the most successful show I've ever been in."

Escalus roared with laughter and embraced Nia in a mighty hug.

"By the toenails of the seven saints of Scorpius, neither will I!"

"I'm game, too," Benvolio agreed, "and bugger her!" he added with a rude gesture in Ansra's direction.

"Look, Helva, get the Corviki to give us another day's rest," Chadress said. "Then we'll all go down and finish the job. The show must go on!"

"Who'll do Juliet?" Davo asked and then answered his own question by pointing directly at Kurla. "You'll do Juliet."

"Oh, no. Not me!"

"Why not, my sweet young love?" asked Prane, pulling her hands from her cheeks and kissing her tenderly before them all. "You're more Juliet than she at her best."

"I'm worried about only one thing," Escalus said then. "I don't like her—here—with us—there," and his forefinger punctuated his words with stabs in the proper directions.

"A very good point," Davo agreed with a whistle.

"No problem," Helva assured them. "Miss Colmer is . . . resting, I believe the professional term is. I shall encourage it." And she proceeded to flood the pilot's cabin with sleepy gas.

The Manager signaled acceptance, emitting relief that the problem had a solution. Helva sent everyone off to bed after a protein-rich meal. Kurla and Nia preferred to bunk on the couches despite the fact that Helva had cleared the gas from the cabin. Kurla agreed to administer a timed sedative to Ansra to keep her unconscious while there was no one in the ship.

The cast voted to limit the first rehearsal to 4 hours. However, all apprehensions vanished when it became evident to the troupe that the understudies were very discreet with energy emissions. In fact, back at the ship again, there was a mood close to hysterical relief.

"Those Corviki are the quickest studies I've ever worked with. Tell 'em once and they just don't forget," Escalus exclaimed.

"Yes, they are holding back, aren't they," Davo agreed. "But will they know how much to emit, to make the show come alive? I mean, there's that old difference between amateur and pro."

"Good point, Davo," Prane said, "and one I discussed with Manager. I talked over unconserved energy levels with him and he assured me that he had taken measurements during our performance so that they will know when to emit energy to produce the proper reactions. He has great dominance, that man, great dominance."

"And a fine sense of level integrities, too," Chadress added, nodding thoughtfully.

"You sound more Corviki than human," Nia said in her droll way.

Prane and Chadress looked at her, their expressions puzzled.

"Well, you do," Kurla agreed.

"Imitation is the sincerest form of flattery, you know," Prane said into the silence, but, to Helva, his joviality sounded forced.

The second rehearsal went so well that Prane decided only one, slightly longer additional session would complete the contract.

"Let's get it over with then," Escalus said. "There's something seductive about that freak-out place that gets to you. I've a hard time thinking human."

Escalus was right, Helva thought. She found it all too easy to think in Corvikian terms. And Prane and Chadress seemed to have moved theatre semantics into another frame of reference entirely. She'd heard them discussing staging in terms of excitation phases, shell movements, particle emissions, subshell directionals until she wondered if they were talking theatre or nuclear physics.

She kept an eye on Prane, anyhow. Kurla was, too, but playing Juliet to Prane's Romeo was overloading her circuits sufficiently to cloud her discretionary . . . Helva caught herself up sharply. The sooner they all got away from here, the better.

She watched Kurla administer an additional sedative to Ansra. The woman had been kept unconscious for 40 hours. Five more wouldn't hurt her. It had certainly improved the ship's atmosphere.

She told Kurla that she'd be down directly and then checked all circuitry on the ship. Once the Corviki removed that power block they could leave, but she wanted no last-minute delays.

Prane was offstage when she got down, dominating with his understudy. She found hers and then was swept into scene ii of the fourth act.

The Corviki had more trouble this cycle controlling their suppressed energy. It occurred to Helva that Davo need not have worried that the dramatic content would be lacking. Remove all the instructors with their frail spirits, and the Corviki would deliver every bit of excitation required by the formulae.

Helva had to expend effort now to control excitement. Prane did, too, for as he and his understudy, the two Balthasars beside them, waited to enter the churchyard for Romeo's death scene, he seemed to be leaking energy.

"The time controls are fixed?" he asked nervously. "They cannot be altered?"

He was on before Helva could answer.

The rehearsal was soon over. The Manager had to exert tremendous control over his spontaneous emissions as he complimented the actors. He announced that the information on isotope stabilization had been sent to the ship in a specially prepared container, and that the ship's power was unblocked. He kept emitting on such a broad band that Helva felt the insidious tug of entropy and resolutely made her farewells.

Transferring back, it took her a moment—a moment of regret that seemed an eternity—to get her bearings. She detected the container neatly secured in her engine room, violently radioactive as yet, so it had better stay where it was.

Someone groaned in the dimly lit cabin. Dimly lit? But she hadn't lowered the lights!

She brought up every light in the ship, scanning the pilot's cabin for Ansra. The bed was empty. How had she thrown off the drug? Helva did a searching scan and found Ansra, crouched down by Prane's body. In her hands were the wires that led to the transceivers on Prane and Kurla.

"Ansra, that's the same as murder!" Helva roared, trying with sheer volume to stun the woman. With the determination of vengeance, Ansra ripped the helmets from their users and tried to tear the units apart.

Even as Ansra was acting, Helva triggered the return on the transceivers, desperately hoping that she'd forestall Ansra's intention. It seemed so long, with the woman's harsh panting as metronome, until transceiver lights winked out across the rim of the helmets. On one, the light remained. On Chadress.

"Davo! Davo!" Helva shouted.

The actor, shaking his head as the urgency of her voice roused him, responded dazedly. Then he saw Ansra, saw what she was doing and launched himself at her. Davo's thrust pinned her against the far wall as other members of the cast began to revive.

"Escalus, help Davo with that crazy woman," Helva ordered, for Ansra was twisting and screaming, beating at Davo with maddened strength. "Benvolio, come on, man. Snap out of it. Check Chadress. How's his pulse?"

Benvolio leaned to the limp body beside him. "Too slow, I think. It's so . . . so faint."

"I've got to get back to Corvi. Someone—Nia, you're awake. Find two usable transceivers in the mess Ansra made of them and put 'em on Prane and Kurla. I've got to get them back here."

"Wait, Helva." She heard Davo call as she was in the act of transferring.

The Manager was beside her. And so were the shells that were undeniably Prane, Kurla, and Chadress. Their pressure dominances were overwhelming.

"Stay with us, Helva. Stay with us. It's a new life, brand new, with all the power in the universe to control. Why go back to a sterile life in an immobile envelope? Stay with us."

Too tempted, too terrified to listen further, Helva retreated to the safety of her ship, the sanctuary of the only security she knew.

"*Helva!*" Davo's voice rang in all her ears.

"I'm back," she murmured.

"Thank God. I was afraid you'd stay with them."

"You knew they'd stay?"

"Even without Ansra's help," Davo admitted. Beyond him Nia nodded.

"It's the answer for Kurla and Prane, you know," Nia said. "Hell, they can combine energies now," and her laugh was mirthless.

"But Chadress?"

"Shock you, huh, that a brawn would defect?" Davo asked sympathetically. "But he wouldn't be a brawn much longer, would he, Helva?"

"And what if I had stayed?"

"Well," Davo admitted, "Chadress didn't think you could, but he did think you should."

"It was a case of being where I am needed, Davo. And sometimes you have to help by *not* doing anything, I guess," she added, more to herself. She looked then toward the four breathing but lifeless bodies. "*Four?*" she cried aloud, stunned to identify Ansra, laid beside the others. "What did you do? How could you do it?"

"Easy," Nia replied, shrugging negligently. "A case of the punishment fitting the crime. Besides, the Corviki are better qualified to deal with unstable energies than we are, Helva. Can't we leave now?"

"Manager said the exchange had been made," Escalus said. "Have they unblocked your power?"

"Yes," Helva sighed, unwilling to act yet.

"Helva," Davo murmured gently, his hand palm down on the titanium column, "Helva, the play was the thing, wherein to catch the conscience."

As she wearily fed the return voyage tape into the computer, his words echoed in her mind like a gentle absolution.

With an exquisite sense of reprieve, Helva watched official debriefing experts disperse to their waiting vehicles that clustered in the floodlights at the base of the XH-834 like energy motes . . . Helva censored that analogy. Night-piercing lights blinked on, jabbed in crisscross webs as the groundcars turned and wheeled. All momentarily were parallel, outlining the darkened lower stories of Regulus Base tower. Not all the vehicles made for this structure, Helva noted. Some darted beyond, out of the Base complex, into the distant metropolis.

Shell-people were presumably inexhaustible, but Helva felt drained and depressed. She was not sure which experience had been the worse: coping with Beta Corvi or with the repetitive questioning of the affair by singleminded specialists. She could appreciate why Prane had made use of mindtrap to retard neuron loss. Had she no memory banks to scan, she might cheerfully have forgotten much of what had happened. Too bad she couldn't.

Helva sighed. Not, Helva, the XH-834, sleek BB ship of Central Worlds Medical Service, but Helva, the woman.

They encase us in titanium shells, place the shells in titanium bulkheads and consider us invulnerable. Physical injury is the least of the harmful accidents that this universe inflicts on its inhabitants; it is soonest mended.

Lights began to appear in the Base Tower and Helva was perversely delighted. So, others would have a sleepless night tonight. They deserve it, unsettling her fragile resolution of the Beta Corvi affair with their barrage of questions. How powerful was the Corvi community? How large were the individual entities? How long did she believe the human/Corviki shells that contained Prane, Kurla, Chadress, and Ansra would retain their previous loyalties and memories? How soon could, should a second expedition attempt to broach their atmosphere? What other mediums of exchange would Helva recommend, assuming Prane's encyclopedia of drama was bled from him? And why did she feel that the Corviki environment was so dangerous to the human mind? Could she explain the dangers? Could she recommend preventive measures to be used in preconditioning?

There was no consolation in the fact that every other member of the mission was also being closely interrogated, prodded and probed, physically as well as mentally. At least she was spared that, although the shell medics had run an acidity test and checked the intake on the nutrients that sustained her. There had been a rise in the protein flow, which was deemed consonant with the unusual activity required of her.

The Base computers were going to get a workout tonight, but she didn't want to have to think at all. Not about the Corviki, at any rate, or the four humans who had opted to remain in Corviki shells, to exchange and lose energy in the new sub-orbital . . .

"I don't want to think at all," Helva said aloud.

Restlessly she scanned outside, her glance reaching briefly the lighted windows in the brawn barracks. She felt no desire to place a call there. She hadn't the requisite flexibility to enjoy contact with new personalities, usually such a reviving and stimulating experience for her. She didn't want, either, to be alone tonight.

"This time I get a brawn before I move a centimeter from this base," she vowed.

The Service cemetery where Jennan lay buried was mercifully lost in darkness kilometers across the huge Base field, but she began to feel that distance psychologically diminishing.

Rather than dwell on that closed chapter of her life, she masochistically reviewed the last few hours. Had she really given them all the information available to her? Was she subconsciously withholding a single important fact or minor observation? Had she really analyzed the schizophrenic trauma of the human mind in the Corvi shell? Had she . . .

A groundcar braked to a rocking drop at the base and someone activated the passenger lift, which she had not withdrawn when the last of the debriefing group had left.

"Who the hell . . ."

"Parollan!" a sharp voice reassured her in the Supervisor's curt way.

As her Service Supervisor, Niall Parollan had naturally been present during debriefing. He had kept to the role of arbiter, speaking only when the experts had got excited or too insistent on points that Helva was unable to clarify. She had been grateful as well as impressed by his unexpectedly deft handling of the incidents. Evidently Parollan enjoyed considerable prestige in spite of his blunt manners. Was he returning for a private session?

He stepped into the airlock, feet spread, arms dangling at his side. He was glaring at her column with unexpected belligerence.

"Now what have I done?" Helva asked, masking a sudden apprehension.

As he broke the pose and swaggered forward, Helva wondered if he had been drinking heavily.

"I claim refuge, milady," he replied, bowing with exaggerated flourishes.

"And a cup of coffee?"

"You're out of it. Those fardling circuit-clowns drank it all up. But you're off bounds and incommunicado 'sfar as Cencom knows—my orders, m'love —so you're the safest place for *me* to be."

"You're not in trouble over the Beta Corvi . . ."

"Trouble?" and he sat down on the couch facing her column, suddenly collapsing limply back against the cushions. "Hell no. Not my Helva gal. Not Niall Parollan, Supervisor extraordinary. But *we* are," and a wild sweep of his arm suggested galactic rather than service parameters. "Well, you're not to be bothered, and I'm not to be bothered, and by morning, maybe the ol' brains'll be ready for more draining and dredging and . . ." his voice ground down to a whisper.

Helva thought he had gone to sleep, but then she saw that he was regarding her through narrowed eyes.

"Did *anyone* remember to tell you how far you exceeded optimimum expectation? Did the Chief remember to mention you've got two more commendations on your distinguished record? And a whopping bonus!" He pounded the couch in emphasis. "You'll Pay-off if you keep up this rate." Then his voice softened. "Did I remember to thank you, Helva, for pulling off a lousy, fardling, stinking job you got conned into . . ."

"Not by you, Parollan. . . ."

"Ha!" Niall Parollan arched his body to let out that burst of laughter before he sank again into the cushions. "Well, you did a great job, gal. I don't think another ship could have pulled it off."

"Maybe another ship would have brought all her passengers back."

"Of all the noisome fardles, Helva," and Parollan sat straight up, "I don't need that kind of irrational thinking from *you!* Prane and Kurla had their own reasons for transition; so did Chadress. All three profited. As for Ansra Colmer, best place for that bitch. Outsmarted herself for once. There is true justice in the universe, and the Corviki never heard of Hammurabi!"

He lay back again, lacing his fingers behind his head.

"I like to see 'em sweat, those nardy bastards in Procedures," he chuckled.

"Over the bodies? Wouldn't decent burial be indicated by now?"

"Why? The bodies are still clinically alive, Helva. *Your* body is clinically dead," he added with utter disregard for the tacit strictures on that subject in the presence of a shell-person. "And neither you nor I, nor anyone else on this Base tonight thinks *you're* a zombie. What does constitute death, Helva? The lack of mind, or soul, or what-have-you? Or the lack of independent motion? You're mobile enough, my pet, and you can't move a muscle."

"You're drunk, Niall Parollan."

"Oh, no! Parollan's a long way from drunk. I'm just hanging loose, gal, hanging loose." He sat up in a single movement that denied any impairment of motor control. "Ethically, socially, you delivered four corpses to that Fleet ship outside Beta Corvi. Four mechanically functioning but empty husks. And their original inhabitants, owners, what-have-you, won't be back in 'em."

He was on his feet, striding toward Helva. "There's your chance, gal. Opt out . . . opt out into Kurla's body: it's the youngest. Or Ansra's. Or Chadress' for that matter, if you'd like a change of pace."

For one blinding second of whirling possibilities, Helva considered the staggering proposal. As she had fleetingly considered remaining in the Corvi shell. Had she really presented an unbiased report to the specialists?

"Presuming, of course, that I want to be a mobile human. Remember, Parollan," she managed to answer in a reasonable voice, "I've just *been* in another body. I find I prefer myself."

Parollan was staring at her with an inscrutable intentness. He put one hand out to stroke the smooth metal on the exact spot where the seam closed access to her inner shell.

"Well put, Helva, well put." He turned and walked to the galley. He was dialing for soup, not a stimulant, Helva noticed with relief. He sat down again in the main cabin before he broke the heat seal. The wisp of escaping steam seemed to mesmerize him, for he shook his head as the pop of the released top broke the semitrance.

"I didn't think you'd go it," he remarked in a casual tone.

"Why did you ask then? Testing, Supervisor?"

He glanced up, chuckling at the purring tone in her voice.

"Not you, m'gal . . ."

"And I am not your gal . . ."

". . . Irrelevant!" and he took a careful sip of the hot soup.

"Then why did you ask?" she insisted.

He shrugged. "Seemed like a once-in-a-lifetime chance to get you out of that titanium chastity belt."

Laughter burst from Helva. "I've been out. On Corvi."

"Tried it once and didn't like it?"

"Movement? Freedom?" she asked, deliberately ignoring the double meaning expressed in the cocked eyebrow and malicious grin on Parollan's face.

"*Physical* movement," he qualified, his manner wary. "*Physical* freedom."

"Define 'physical.' As this ship, I have more physical power, more physical freedom, than you ever will know. I think, I feel, I breathe. My heart beats, blood does flow through my veins, my lungs do work: not as yours, but they are functioning."

"So are the hearts and veins and lungs of those four—four nothings in the life support room of Base Hospital. But *they* are dead."

"Am I?"

"Are you?"

"You're drunk, Parollan," she accused in a flat, cold voice.

"I'm not drunk, Helva. I'm discussing a deep moral issue with you and you evade me."

"Evade Niall Parollan? Or Supervisor Parollan?"

"Niall Parollan."

"Why are you discussing this deep moral issue with Helva, Niall Parollan?"

Unexpectedly he shrugged and leaned back, his

shoulders sagging as he lapped his fingers around the soup cup and regarded its contents moodily.

"Passes time," he said finally. "We both have time on our hands tonight. Time that must be passed some way or other. Silly to waste *our* valuable time (and he gave a sardonic laugh) in small talk. Might just as well discuss a deep moral issue which, I might point out, you dumped into our laps. Which no one's going to resolve anyway. You should've made the Corvi clear their garbage before you cleared their fartful atmosphere. Say, *did* you smell that stuff they breathe?"

Helva found herself answering his question while another part of her rapidly churning mind wondered at his remarkable behavior.

"I, Helva, have no olfactory sense, so I, Helva, wouldn't have noticed how the Corviki atmosphere 'smelled'. None of the others mentioned it, so I assume that, for Corvi entities, the atmospheric odor was unexceptional."

"Aha!" The thin forefinger jabbed at her accusingly. "You don't have that physical ability."

"Nor am I sure that I want it . . . except to smell coffee, which everyone says smells particularly pleasant."

"Remember to order some in the morning."

"Order's already on file with Commissary," Helva said sweetly.

"That's my gal."

"I'm not your gal. And, at the risk of being a bore, why are you here, Niall Parollan?"

"I don't want to be bothered by those fardling specs," he muttered, jerking a thumb over his shoulder in the direction of the Base Tower, "and I would be if they could reach me. They can't here because Cencom is not allowed to admit any calls to you, Helva XH-834, until 0800 because you, Helva *m'gal,* have had enough of them for one revolution. Haven't you?" His question crackled in the air. "Don't deny it," he advised when she didn't answer immediately. "I know you well enough . . . oh, I know you, gal, like no other man ever has . . . and you were so close to telling them to stuff it, you were so close to . . ." his voice trailed off briefly. "This assignment was a lot rougher on you than you'll ever admit."

She said nothing.

He nodded and took another mouthful of soup.

"You aren't drunk," she said.

"I told you that." He grinned at her.

"I hadn't realized," she went on in a light tone to hide the fact that she was deeply touched by his unexpected empathy, "that ship-sitting was a function of a Supervisor."

He waggled a lean finger expressively. "We have wide discretionary lattitude."

"And am I really incommunicado until 0800 or were you merely keeping me from meeting personable brawns?"

"Hell no," he explained, his eyebrows arching in protest. "That's absolute fact you can check out. *You* can call out, you know. It's just no one can call in. And . . ."

"You're here to divert me from calling the brawns."

"That woman's got brawns on the brain!" he exploded. "Go ahead," he urged, "call the brawns in. Rouse the whole barracks. We'll have a swinging party . . ." He was halfway to the console.

"Why are *you* here?"

"Hey, moderate your voice, gal. I'm here because you're the safest place for *me* to be." He turned back to her again, grinning wickedly. "Sure you don't want to call the brawn barracks?"

"Positive. Why are *you* escaping?"

"Because," and he dropped down onto the couch again, making himself quite comfortable. "I've had it with their nardy questions and suspicions and . . ."

"Suspicions?" Helva pounced on the word.

Niall made a crude noise. "*They* (and his fingers flicked in the direction of the Tower's lit windows) got fardling damned theories about schizoid brains and blocks and that kind of drift."

"About me?"

Again the expressive rude noise. "I know you, gal, and so does Railly and we're taking none of that crap about *you*."

"Thanks."

"Don't get snide with me, Helva," and Parollan's voice turned hard. "I'll make you work your ass off for the Service. I'll make you take assignments you don't want because they're good for you and the Service . . ."

"Good for me? Like the Corvi affair?"

"Yes, damn your eyes, good for *you*, Helva. For the woman inside that armor plate!"

"I thought you were urging me to come out of my armor plate . . . into Kurla's body."

Parollan was still. His angry eyes seemed to bore through the column into her shell. Abruptly he relaxed and leaned back again, apparently at ease, but Helva noticed the small contraction of jaw muscles.

"Yes, I was, wasn't I?" he said mildly. With a sigh, he swiveled his feet up on the couch and yawned in an exaggerated fashion. "You know, I've never heard you sing. Would you oblige?"

"To keep you awake? Or would you prefer a lullaby?"

Niall Parollan yawned again, laced his fingers behind his head, crossed his neatly booted ankles and stared up at the ceiling.

"Dealer's choice."

Surprisingly, Helva felt like singing.

The Ship
Who Dissembled

"Brain ships don't disappear," Helva said in what she hoped was a firm, no-argument tone.

Teron stuck his chin out in a way that caused him to appear a neckless Neanderthal. This mannerism had passed from amusing through annoying to unendurable.

"You heard Central," Teron replied at his most didactic. "They do disappear, because they have disappeared."

"The fact of disappearance is inconsistent with shell psychology," Helva said, barely managing to restrain herself from shouting at top volume. She had the feeling that she might force him to understand by overwhelming him with sound alone. She knew this was basically illogical, but in trying to cope with Teron over the past galactic year, she found she reacted more and more on an emotional rather than a reasonable level.

This partnership was clearly intolerable—she would even go so far as to say, degrading—and she would allow it to continue no longer than it took them to finish this assignment and return to Regulus Base.

Helva had had enough of Teron. She did not care two feathers in a jet-vent if the conclusion wasn't mutual. It had been difficult for her to admit she had found herself in a situation she couldn't adjust to, but she and Teron were clearly incompatible. She would just have to admit to an error of judgment and correct it. It was the only sensible course of action.

Helva groaned inwardly. He was contagious. She was talking more and more as he did.

"Your loyalty is commendable, if, in this instance, misplaced," Teron was saying pompously. "The facts are there. Four brain-controlled ships engaged on Central Worlds commissions have disappeared without trace, their accompanying pilots with them. Fact: a ship can alter its tape, a pilot cannot. Fact: the ships have failed to appear at a scheduled port-of-call. Fact: the ships have failed to appear in the adjacent sectors of space nearest their previous or projected ports-of-call. Therefore, they have disappeared. The ships must have altered the projected journey for no known reason. Therefore the ships are unreliable organisms. This conclusion follows the presented data and is unalterable. Any rational intelligence must admit the validity of that conclusion."

He gave her that irritating smirk she had originally thought a sweet smile.

Helva counted slowly to 1,000 by 10s. When she spoke again, her voice was under perfect control.

"The presented data is incomplete. It lacks motivation. There is no reason for those four ships to have disappeared for their own purposes. They weren't even badly indebted. Indeed, the DR was within 3 standard years of solvency." Just as I am, she thought. "Therefore, and on the basis of privileged information available to *me* . . ." she came as close as makes no never mind to spitting out the pronoun, ". . . your conclusion is unacceptable."

"I cannot see what privileged information, if you actually have any," Teron awarded her a patronizing smile, "could change my conclusion, since Central has also reached it."

There, Helva thought to herself, he had managed to drag in old infallible authority and that is supposed to stop me in my tapes.

It was useless to argue with him anyway. He was, as Niall Parollan had once accused her of being, stubborn for the wrong reasons. He was also pigheaded, dogmatic, insensitive, regulation-hedged and so narrowly oriented as to prevent any vestige of imagination or intuitive thinking from coloring his mental processes for a microsecond.

She oughtn't to have thought of Niall Parollan. It did her temper no good. That officious little pipsqueak had paid her another of his unsolicited, unofficial visits to argue her out of choosing the Acthionite.

"He passed his brawn training on theory credits. He's been slated for garbage runs, not *you!*" Niall Parollan had cried, pacing her main cabin.

"And *you* are not the person who will be his partner. His profile-tape looks extremely compatible to me."

"Use your wits, girl. Just look at him. He's all muscle and no heart, too perfectly good looking to be credible. Christ, he's . . . he's an android, complete with metal brainworks, programmed in a rarified atmosphere. He'll drive you batty."

"He's a reliable, well-balanced, well-read, well-adjusted . . ."

"And you're a spiteful, tin-plated virgin," said Parollan and for the second time in their acquaintance, he charged out of her cabin without a backward look.

Now Helva had to admit Niall Parollan had been demoralizingly accurate about Brawn Teron of Acthion. The only kind thing that could be said about Teron, in Helva's estimation, was that he was a complete change from any other partner she had had, temporarily or permanently.

And if he called her an unreliable organism once more, she would blow the lock on him.

However, Teron considered he had silenced her with the last telling remark. He seated himself at his pilot control board, flexed his fingers as he always did, and then ran his precious and omnipotent data through the computer, checking their journey tape. It was obvious he was out to thwart any irrational desire Helva might have to change their journey and make them disappear.

Teron worked methodically and slowly, his broad brow unwrinkled, his wide-cheeked face serene, his brown eyes never straying from the task at hand.

How, under the suns of heaven, did I ever have the incredible lack of insight to pick him? Helva wondered, the adrenalin level in her shell still high. I must have been out of my ever-loving, capsulated mind. Maybe my nutrient fluid is going acid. When I get back to Regulus, I am going to demand an endocrine check. Something is wrong with me.

No, no, no. Helva contradicted herself. There is nothing wrong with me that getting rid of Teron won't cure. He's got me doubting my sanity and I *know* I'm sane or I wouldn't be this ship.

Remember that, Helva, she told herself. It's quite possible that, before this trip ends, he'll have persuaded you you're a menace to Central Worlds Autonomy because your intelligence is so unreliable the safest thing for the known world is for you to opt out. Him and his assumption that a brain ship must be an unreliable organism because they/she/he (never it, please) could digest data, ignore the irrelevant, and proceed on seemingly illogical courses to logical and highly successful ends. Such as the tangle she and Kira had got into on Alioth.

And to quote particulars, she, Helva, had already been unreliable several times in her short career as a brain ship. Teron had been 'kind enough' to point out these deviations to her, as well as a far more logical course of action under all the same conditions, and he had admonished her never to act outside cut orders while he, Teron of Acthion, was her brawn partner. She was to do nothing, repeat, *nothing*, without clearing first with him and then with Central. An intelligent organism was known by its ability to follow orders without deviation.

"And you actually mean," Helva had remarked laughingly the first time Teron had made this solemn pronouncement—she had still had her sense of humor in those days— ". . . that, if our orders require me to enter an atmosphere my subsequent investigations proved was corrosive to my hull and would result in our deaths, I should follow such orders . . . to the death, that is."

"Irresponsible orders are not given Central Worlds Ships," Teron replied reprovingly.

"Half a league, half a league
Half a league onward . . ."

"I do not understand what half leagues have to do with the principle under discussion," he said coldly.

"I was trying to make a subtle point. I will rephrase."

"In a concise, therefore comprehensible, manner, if you please."

"Orders can be cut without foreknowledge of unavailable but highly relevant facts. Such as the before-mentioned corrosive atmospheres . . ."

"Hypothetical . . ."

". . . but valid as a case in point. We do, you must admit, often approach relatively unexplored star systems. Therefore, it is entirely possible, not merely hypothetical, that precut orders can require an intelligent and mature reevaluation which may require what appears to be insubordinate alteration of those same orders and/or rank disobedience to those before-mentioned orders."

Teron had shaken his head, not sadly, because Helva

was certain he had experienced no deep *human* emotions in his life, but reprovingly.

"I know now why Central Worlds insist on a human pilot as commander of the brain-controlled ships. They are necessary, so necessary when an unreliable organism is nominally in control of so powerful an instrument as this ship."

Helva had sputtered in astonishment at his misconception. She had been about to point out that the pilot control board did not override her. *She* had the override on the pilot.

"There will come a day," Teron had continued inexorably, "when such poor expedients are no longer necessary. Automatic operations will be perfected to such a fine degree, human brains will no longer be needed."

"They use *human beings*," Helva had replied, pronouncing each syllable distinctly.

"Ah, yes, human beings. Fallible creatures at best, we are, subject to so many pressures, so frail a barque for so great a task." Teron tended to go in for homiletics at the drop of a gauge. "To err is human, to forgive divine." He sighed. "And when this human element, so prone to error, is eliminated, when automation is perfected—ah, there, Helva, is the operative word—when it is *perfected*, there will be no more need for such stopgap techniques as Central Worlds must presently employ. When that perfection is achieved, ships will be truly reliable." He patted the computer-console patronizingly.

Helva had stifled a monosyllablic comment. Historical and incontrovertible arguments welled up from her schooling and conditioning years. These were based, she abruptly realized, on incidents that unfortunately tended to support his peculiar theory of unreliability—however sane the outcome. In each instance, the brain ships had acted by ignoring or revising previous orders as the unusual circumstances they encountered required them to do. By Teron's unswerving logic, intelligence itself—whether shell or mobile—is unreliable. Helva could not see him ever admitting that intelligent conclusions are not always logical.

And right now, every scrap of intelligence, instinct, training, conditioning, and reason told Helva that brain ships do not just *disappear*. Not four in a row. Not four in less than a Regulan month. One in 100 years, yes, that was possible, logical and probable. But there was always some hint, some deducible reason. Like the 732—psychotic with grief on Alioth.

Why had she allowed Kira to leave her when that assignment was over? Kira would have been quite of Helva's mind in this matter, but Helva did not see the faintest hope of convincing Teron that multiple disappearances were so preposterous. Because it involved some intuition, of which Teron had none.

How had this didacticism of his escaped Psychprobe? And another thing she had noticed about him, whether he would ever admit it consciously or not, the very concept of cyborgs like Helva was repugnant to Teron. A brawn was very much aware, if the majority of Central World's populations were not, that behind the ship's titanium bulkhead reposed a shell, containing an inert—but—complete human body.

If only Teron weren't so thoroughly irritating, she could almost feel sorry for him. And before he had antagonized her, she had actually understood this drive to perfection that motivated every thought and action. Teron was psychotically afraid of error, of making any mistake because mistake implied failure and failure was inadmissible. If he made no mistakes, he would never be guilty of failure and would be a success.

Well, Helva mused, I'm not afraid of making a mistake and I'm not afraid of admitting failure. And I sure made one with Teron. When he starts mistrusting shell people, he is not good to me or Central Worlds. Well, *I* won't be vindictive. I'll request a change and take the fine. It won't set me too far back in the red. And with a new partner and a couple of good assignments, I'll still Pay-off. But Teron goes off my deck!

The decision of divorce, now subvocalized, made her feel much better.

When Teron woke the next "day," he checked, as he always did, every gauge, dial and meter, forward and aft. This practice took him most of the morning. A similar rundown would have taken Helva 10 minutes at the outside. By custom and by any other brawn but Teron, the check was left to the brain partner. Wearily Helva had to read back to Teron her findings, which he corroborated with his own.

"Shipshape and bristol fashion," he commented as he always did when the results tallied . . . as they always did. Then he seated himself at the pilot console awaiting touchdown on Tania Borealis.

As the TH-834 had had planetfalls on Durrell, Tania Borealis' fourth planet before, the spaceport was familiar with Teron; familiar with and contemptuous to the point of addressing all remarks to Helva rather than to her brawn. If this complimented Helva, it made Teron harder to deal with later. He responded by being twice as officious and pompous with the port officials and the Health Service Captain to whom their cargo of rare drugs had been assigned. A certain amount of extra precaution was required, considering the nature and potency of the drugs, but it was offensive of Teron to tight-beam back to Central Worlds for a replica of Captain Brandt's ID Cube before turning over the invaluable packet to him.

To make matters worse, Niall Parollan, being Section Supervisor, had had to take the call, and Helva caught all the nuances in his carefully official words.

Helva seethed inwardly. It would have to be Parollan. But she had the heretofore unexperienced urge to burst outward from her shell in all directions. Parollan would be unbearably righteous no matter when she filed intent to change brawns. There were three more stops, one at Tania Australis and the two Alula counterparts, before she would touch down at Regulus Base. Better let Niall Parollan have his laugh now so he'd be over it by the time she did ditch Teron.

So, girding herself for Parollan's smug reception, Helva flashed a private signal for him to keep the tight beam open. Teron, slave that he was to protocol, would see Captain Brandt off the ship, to the waiting landcar. She'd have a chance to file her intention then.

"Tower to the TH-834. Permission to board you requested by the Antiolathan Xixon," said Durrell Tower.

"Permission refused," Helva said without so much as a glance in Teron's direction.

"Pilot Teron speaking," the brawn interjected forcefully, striding to the console and opening the local channel direct. "What is the purpose of this request?"

"Don't know. The gentlemen are on their way by groundcar."

Teron disconnected and glanced out the open airlock. Brandt's car was just passing the oncoming vehicle midfield.

"You have no right to issue orders independently, Helva, when the request has been properly stated."

"Have you ever heard of an Antiolathan Xixon?" Helva demanded. "And isn't this a restricted mission?"

"I am perfectly aware of the nature of our mission and I have never heard of an Antiolathan Xixon. That doesn't mean there isn't one. And, as it sounds religious and one of our prime Service directives is to be respectful to any and all religious orders, we should receive him."

"True enough. But may I remind Pilot Teron that I am his senior in service by some years and that I have access to memory banks, mechanical memory

banks, less prone to *lapsus memoriae* than the human
mind? And there is no Xixon."

"The request was issued properly," Teron repeated.

"Shouldn't *we* consult Central first?"

"There are some actions that are indicated without
recourse to official sanction."

"Oh really?"

The groundcar had arrived and the Xixon-people
had dutifully requested permission to board. Their arrival meant no chance for Helva to speak privately
with Central. She was doubly infuriated by Teron's
childish insistence on seeing whoever these Xixon were.
She knew perfectly well, if *she* had countermanded
his order, he would have been in the right of it to call
her down. But since *he* had taken the initiative, naturally
it was all in order.

The four men stepped on board, two in plain gray
tunics, stepping smartly inside the lock as though the
vanguard of a great dignitary. Sidearms hung from
their belts and both wore curious cylindrical whistles
on neckchains. The third man, gray of hair but
vigorous, obsequiously ushered in the fourth, a white-
haired man of imposing stature in a long, gray-black
robe. He fingered a whistle, larger than the guards,
but similar in design, as if it were some sacred talis-
man.

There was something not at all reassuring, Helva
noted, in that obsequious performance. For the gray-
haired man, in the action of ushering, was missing
no single detail of the cabin's appointments. Just as
he switched his direction to put him beside Teron,
who was still at the control console, the old man
reached the titanium bulkhead behind which Helva
resided. The maneuvers were almost completed when
something in Helva's mind went wild with alarm.

"Teron, they're imposters," she cried, remembering
with sudden hope that the tight beam to Central
Worlds was still open.

The white-haired man lost all trace of formal dignity and, mouthing syllables in a frightful cadence, stabbed a finger towards her column.

Helva, in the brief moment before she lost consciousness, saw the two guards blowing on their whistles, the piercing notes sonically jamming the ship's circuitry. She saw Teron slump to the floor of the cabin, felled by the gray-haired man. Then the anesthetic gas the old man had released into her shell overwhelmed her.

My circuits are out of order, Helva mused . . . and then returned to acute awareness.

She saw nothing. She heard nothing. Not so much as a whisper of sound. Not so much as a tiny beam of light.

Helva fought a primeval wave of terror that all but washed her into insanity.

I think, so I live, she told herself with all the force of her will. I can think and I can remember, rationally, calmly, what has happened, what can have happened.

The horror of complete isolation from sound and light was a micrometer away from utter domination of her ego. Coldly, dispassionately, Helva reviewed that final, flashing scene of treachery. The entrance of the four men, the arrangement of the two guards and their whistle-ornaments. A supersonic blast patterned to interfere with her circuitry, to paralyze her defense against the unauthorized activation of her emergency panel. The maneuvering of the third man to overpower Teron.

Now, Helva continued inexorably, this attack was engineered to overcome brawn and brain simultaneously. Only someone intimately connected with the Central Worlds would have access to the information needed to vanquish both mobile and immobile units. The release syllables, and the proper pitch and cadence at which they must be spoken, were highly guarded secrets, usually kept separate. For anyone to have known this information was shocking.

Helva's mind leaped to an obvious, but still startling conclusion. She knew now how the four brain ships had "disappeared." They had unquestionably been shanghaied in much the same way she had been. But why? She wondered. And where were the others? Incommunicado like herself? Or driven mad by . . .

I refuse to consider that possibility for myself or any other shell personality, Helva told herself firmly.

Constructive thought, fierce concentration, will relieve the present tedium.

The first ship to disappear was the FT-687. They had also been on a drug run, picking up raw material, though, not distributing it. So had the RD-751 and the PF-699. This line of thought bore possibilities.

The drugs that she had been delivering were available only through application to Central Worlds and were delivered in minute quantities by special teams. A 100cc ampul of Menkalite could poison the water of an entire planet, rendering its population mindless slaves. A granule of the same drug diluted in a massive protein suspension base would inoculate the inhabitants of several star systems against the virulent encephalitis plagues. Tucanite, a psychedelic compound, was invaluable for psychotherapy in catatonic and autistic cases, since it heightened perceptions and awareness of environment. The frail elders of Tucan had revived waning psychic powers with its use. Deadly as these drugs might be in one form, they were essential to millions in another and must be available. The damoclean sword of use and abuse forever swung perilously over the collective head of mankind.

Not even a shell-person was sacred from the machinations of a disturbed mind.

Disturbed mind? Helva's thoughts ground down. Where was that idiot brawn of hers right now? Him and his Neanderthal attributes—his muscles would be very useful. She felt a distinct pleasure within herself as she recalled his being clouted wickedly by the third man. She hoped he was bruised, beaten, and bloodied. But at least he could see and hear without mechanical assistance . . .

Helva felt every crevass of her mind quivering with the effects of sense deprivation. How long could she keep her mind channeled away from . . .

Two households, both alike in dignity . . .

I attempt from Love's fever to fly . . .

Fly, I cannot see. Fly?

The quality of mercy is not strained . . .

It droppeth as the gentle rain from . . .

No, not heaven. Portia will do me no good. The Bard has played *me* false when I have been his sturdy advocate on other shores.

In Injia's sunny clime where I used to spend my time . . . Time I have too much of or not enough. Could it be that I am suspended midway between time and madness?"

There once was a bishop from Chichester

Who made all the saints in their niches stir . . .

I had a niche once only I was moved out, not by a bishop, but a Xixon.

I should sit on a Xixon or fix on a Xixon or nix on a Xixon or . . .

I cannot move. I cannot see. I cannot hear . . .

Howlonghowlonghowlonghowlong? HOW LONG?

When in the course of human events, it becomes necessary for one country to dissolve the . . . I'M dissolving.

There is nothing I can think of in all space and time that does not bring me right back to . . .

SOUND

A scraping metallic sound. But a SOUND upon her aural circuits. Like a hot iron in her brain, a fiery

brand of sanity after the dense, thick, solid, infinite
inquiet soundlessness. She screamed, but having no
connections except the aural, screamed soundlessly.

Something was thundering:

"I have reconnected your sound system!"

Helva toned the volume rapidly down to an acceptable level. The voice was harsh, whining, nasal, unpleasant, but the sense divinely welcome.

"You have been disconnected from your ship function."

The words made no immediate sense. She was
listening to the glory of sound and the sensation of
noise was unbelievable agony. It took a moment for
those syllables to reform themselves into comprehensible tones.

"You have been connected to a limited audio-visual
circuit to permit you to retain your sanity. Any abuse
of this courtesy will result in further . . ." a nasty
laugh accompanied the threat, ". . . if not permanent,
deprivation."

Unexpectedly sight returned, an evil benison, because of the object in her lens. She could not suppress
the scream.

"This is your idea of cooperation?" demanded the
strident voice and a huge cavern, spiked with great
ivory tusks, opened directly in front of her, pink and
red and slimy white.

She adjusted vision hastily, putting the face into
normal proportions. It was not a pleasant face even
at proper size. It belonged to the man, no longer dis-
guised as old, who had styled himself the Antiolathan
Xixon.

"Cooperation?" Helva asked, confused.

"Yes, your cooperation or nothing," and the Xixon
moved his hand to one side of her limited vision, wrapping his fingers around input leads.

"No. I'll go mad," Helva cried, alarmed, frightened.

"Mad?" and her tormentor laughed obscenely.

"You've plenty of company. But you shan't go mad . . . not yet. I have a use for *you*."

A finger dominated her lens like a suspended projectile.

"No, no, fool, not like that!" her captor shrieked and dashed off to one side of her screen.

Desperately assembling her wits, Helva tuned up her hearing, sharpened her sight focus. She was facing a small audio-visual amplification panel into which her leads and those of . . . yes . . . she could count 12 other . . . input lines were plugged. She had only one line of vision, straight ahead. Directly in front of her, before the panel, were two shells, trailing fine wires like fairy hair from their blunt tops. Within those shells existed two of her peers. There should be two more. Beside me? She had a peripheral glimpse of more wires. Yes, beside me.

Carefully, she drew against the power in the amplifier. A very limited capacity. To her left, whence the Xixon thing had gone, was the beginning of a complex interstellar communications unit from the look of it and the few dial readings she could see.

Xixon returned, smiling a mocking, smug smile at her.

"So you are the ship who sings. The Helva obscenity. May I present your fellow obscenities. Of course, Foro's company is limited to groans and howls. We kept him in the dark too long," and the Xixon howled with pure spite. "Delia's not much better, true, but she will speak if spoken to. Tagi and Merl had learned not to talk unless I address them. So shall you. For I have always wanted my own zoo of obscenities and I have them all in you. And you, my latest guest, will cheer my leisure hours with your incomparable voice. Will you not?"

Helva said nothing. She was instantly plunged into utter dark, utter soundlessness.

"He is mad himself. He is doing this to terrify me. I

refuse to be terrified by a madman. I will wait. I will
be calm. He has a use for me so he will not wait too
long before giving me sight and sound again or he will
defeat his purpose. I will wait. I will be calm. I will
soon have sight and sound again. I will wait. I will be
calm but soon, oh soon. . . .

"There now, my pretty awful, you've had time to re-
consider my generosity."

Helva had indeed. She limited her capitulation to a
monosyllable. The blessedness of sight and sound could
not quite erase the endless hours of deprivation, yet
she knew, from the chronometer on the panel board,
that he had shut her off for a scant few minutes. It
was frightening to be dependent on this vile beast.

She refined her vision, scanning his eyes closely.
There was a faint but unmistakable tinge of blue to his
skin tone that tagged him as either a native of Rho
Puppis' three habitable worlds or a Tucanite addict.
The latter seemed the more likely. Well, she had been
carrying Tucanite and she knew the RD had, also.

"Feel like singing now?" His laugh was demoniac.

"Sir?" said a tentative and servile voice to her left.
The Xixon turned, frowning at the interruption.

"Well?"

"The cargo of the 834 contained no Menkalite."

"None!" Her captor whirled back to Helva, his eyes
blazing. "Where did you squander it?"

"At Tania Australis," she replied, purposefully
keeping her voice low.

"Speak up," he screamed at her.

"I'm using all the power you've allowed me. That
amplifier doesn't produce much."

"It's not supposed to," the Xixon said irritably,
his eyes restlessly darting around the room. Suddenly
there was his finger obscuring all other objects from
her vision. "Tell me, which ship is to deliver Menkalite next?"

"I don't know."

"Speak up."

"I feel that I am shouting already."

"You're not. You're whispering."

"Is this better?"

"Well, I can hear you. Now, tell me, which ship is next to deliver Menkalite?"

"I don't know."

"Will you 'don't know' in darkness?" His laugh echoed hollowly in her skull as he plunged her back into nothingness.

She forced herself to count slowly, second speed, so that she had some reference to time.

He did not keep her out very long. She wanted to scream simply to fill her mind with sound, yet she managed to keep her voice very low.

"Isn't it any better?" he demanded, scowling suspiciously. "Took that Foro obscenity off completely."

Helva steeled herself against the compassion she felt. She comforted herself with the knowledge that Foro had already been mindless.

"For speech, it is sufficient," she said, raising her volume just slightly. She could not use that ploy again for it would cost Merl or Tagi or Delia what fragile grip they had on sanity.

"Hmmph. Well, now, see that it does."

He disappeared.

Helva heightened her listening volume. She could hear at least 10 different movement patterns beyond her extremely limited vision. From the reverberations of sound, they were in some large but low-ceilinged natural rock cavern. Now, if the main communications panel, part of which was visible to her, was a standard planetary model, if there were not too many chambers beyond this one to diffuse the sound, and if all the madman's personnel were nearby, she might just be able to do something.

He wanted her to sing, did he?

She waited and she kept calm.

Presently he returned, absently rubbing his shoulder. Helva increased magnification and noticed the traces of the subcutaneous blue. He used Tucanite, then.

A chair was produced from somewhere for him and he settled himself. Another disembodied hand provided a table on which a dish of choice foods was set.

"Sing, my pretty obscenity, sing," the mad Xixon commanded, reaching languorously above his head toward her input leads.

Helva complied. She began in the middle of her range, using the most sensuous songs she could remember, augmenting them subtly in bass reflex but keeping the volume tantalizingly low so that he had to crouch forward to hear her.

It got on his nerves and when he peevishly reached out to snatch all but her leads from the board, she begged him not to deprive her peers of sense.

"Surely, sir, you could not, when all you need do is augment my power just slightly from the main board. Even without their very minute power draw on this amplifier, I could not possibly Reticulate a croon, for instance."

He sat up straight, his eyes flashing with anticipation.

"You can Reticulate the mating croons?"

"Of course," she replied with mild surprise.

He frowned at her, torn between a desire to hear those renowned exotic songs and a very real concern to limit a shell's ability. He was deep in the thrall of the Tucanite now, his senses eager for further stimulation, and the lure of the Reticulan croons was too much for him.

He did, however, call over and consult with a fawning technician, who blinked constantly and had a severe tic in one cheek. Fascinated, Helva magnified until she was able to see each muscle fiber jerk.

She plunged into dark soundlessness and then, suddenly, felt renewed with the sense of real power against her leads.

"You have ample power now, singer," he told her, his expression vicious with anticipation. "Perform or you will regret it. And do not try any shell games on me, for I have had them seal off all the other circuits on this amplifier. Sing, shipless one, sing for your sight and sound."

She waited until his laughter died. Even a Reticulan croon could not be heard . . . or be effective . . . above the cackling.

She took an easy one, double-voicing it, treble and counter, testing how much power she could get. It would be enough. And the echo of her lilting croon came back, bouncingly, to reassure her that this installation was not large and was set in natural stone caverns. Very good.

She cut in the overtones, gradually adding bass frequencies but subtly so they seemed just part of the Reticulan croon at first. Even with his heightened sensibilities, he wouldn't realize what she was doing. She augmented the inaudible frequencies.

Her croon was of a particularly compelling variation and she heard, under her singing—if one would permit Reticulan croons such a dignified title—the stealthy advance of his slaves and co-workers, lured close by the irresistible siren's sounds.

She gathered herself and then pumped pure sonic hell into the triple note.

It got him first, heightened as he had been by the Tucanite. It got him dead, his brain irretrievably scrambled from the massive dose of sonic fury. It got the others in the cavern, too. She could hear their shrieks of despair over the weird composite sound she had created, as they fainted.

The overload shortcircuited several panels in the master board, showering the unconscious and the dead with blinding sparks. Helva threw in what breakers she could to keep her own now-reduced circuit open. Even she felt the backlash of that supersonic blast. Her nerve ends tingled, her "ears" rang and she felt extremely enervated.

"I'll bet I've developed a *very* acid condition in my nutrients," she told herself with graveyard humor.

The great room was silent except for hoarse breathing and hissing wires.

"Delia? Answer me. It's Helva."

"Who is Helva? I have no access to memory banks."

"Tagi, can you hear me?"

"Yes." A flat, mechanical affirmative.

"Merl, can you hear me?"

"You're loud."

Helva stared straight ahead at the dead body that had tortured them so cruelly. Oh, for a pair of hands!

Revenge on an inert husk was illogical.

Now what do I do? she wondered. At that point, she remembered that she had been about to divorce Teron. *And the tight beam had been left open!* Parollan wasn't the kind to sit on his hands. WHERE WAS HE?

"There you are, Helva, back at the old stand," the ST-1 Captain said, patting her column paternally.

She scanned to make certain the release plate was locked back into seamless congruity with the rest of the column.

"Your new cadence-syllable release was tuned into the metal and Chief Railly is the only one who knows it," the Captain assured her.

"And the independent audio and visual relays are attached to the spare synapses of my shell?"

"Good idea, that, Helva. May make it a standard procedure."

"But mine are hooked up?"

"Yes, yours are hooked up. Seems like a case of

asking for clearance when the ship was blasted off, this precaution after the fact, but . . ."

"Have you ever been sense-deprived, Captain?"

He shuddered and his eyes darkened. None of the Fleet or Brain-Brawn Ship personnel who penetrated the Xixon's asteroid headquarters would be likely to forget the pitiable condition of the shell-people—the amplified human beings who had once been considered invulnerable.

"Tagi, Merl, and Delia will recover. Delia'll be back in service in a year or so," the Captain said quietly. Then he sighed, for he, too, couldn't bring himself to name Foro. "You people are needed, you know." He leaned forward so suddenly toward her panel that Helva gasped. "Easy, Helva." And he slid his hand down the column. "Nope. Can't even feel the seam. You're all secure."

He carefully gathered up the delicate instruments of his profession, wrapping them in soft surgi-foam.

"How're the brawns?" she asked idly, as she stretched out along her rewired extensions, shrugging into her ship skin.

"Well, Delia's Rife will pull out of Menkalite addiction. He'd had only the one dose. They've still to track down the other two ships, but I expect all the brawns'll survive." His expression altered abruptly as if he had caught an unpleasant smell. "Why did you have your tight beam channel open, Helva? When we got that brawn of yours out of his padded cell, he was furious that you could disregard proper procedure in such a fashion." The Captain managed to sound like Teron for a moment. "Why, if you hadn't, and Cencom hadn't heard the whole damned thing. . . . How come you left the channel open?"

"I'd rather not say, but since you've met Teron, you might do a little guessing."

"Huh? Well, whatever the reason, it saved your life."

"It took 'em long enough."

The Captain laughed at her sour complaint. "Don't forget, you'd been cleared, so your kidnappers just lifted off Durrell before your supervisor could stop 'em. But Parollan sure scorched the ears of every operator in frequency range getting Fleet ships after you. At that, with a whole sector to comb, and the drug runners using this asteroid off Borealis as a hideout, too close to Durrell to be even a probability, it took a little time."

"That Xixon thing was smart-mad, hiding right out in sight."

"Well, he had a high intelligence factor," the captain admitted. "After all, he made it into brawn training 20-odd years ago."

That had been an unnerving development, Helva reflected. If he'd actually qualified and then developed neural maladjustments . . . He had taken enough Tucanite to break the deconditioning mind blocks— another matter that was going to be reevaluated by Central Worlds as a result of this incident—and had managed to insinuate himself into maintenance crews on Regulus Base, laying the groundwork for his operation by the judicious use of addictive drugs on key employees. Then, using Central World brains ships with drugged brawns under his control, he could have landed anywhere, including Regulus Base.

"I'll be off now," the Captain said, saluting her respectfully. "Let your own brawn take over now."

"Not if I can help it," Helva replied.

Whatever bond of loyalty she had once had for Teron had dissolved as surely as she had been parted from her security. Teron, having decided that he was hopelessly incarcerated, had stolidly composed himself to await the worst with calm dignity . . . as any logical man ought to do.

On anyone else's tapes (including the Captain's, to judge by the expression on his face), such logic was cowardice; and that was Helva's unalterable conclu-

sion. Although she would grant that his behavior had
certainly been consistent.

Delia's Rife, on the other hand, had *tried* to break
out. He had clawed a foothold in the padded fabric
of his cell, lacerating hands and feet in the attempt to
reach the ceiling access hatch. Dizzy from a Menkalite injection—confused and weak from starvation intended to allow the Menkalite to work unhindered in
his system—he had actually crawled as far as the airlock when the rescue group had arrived.

Helva let the ST-1 down the personnel lift and ran
a thorough but hasty flip-check of herself, scanners,
sensory meters, power-pile drive chamber, inventory.
It was like revisiting a forgotten treasury of minor
miracles. Helva wondered if she had ever before appreciated the versatility incorporated in her ship body,
had really valued the power she had at her disposi-
tion, or cherished the ingenuity of her engineers. Oh,
it was good to be back together again.

"Helva?" a low voice spoke tentatively. "Are you
alone now?" It was Central Worlds on the tight beam.

"Yes. The ST-1 has just left. You can probably reach
him . . ."

"Shove him," and then Helva realized that the hoarse
voice must belong to Niall Parollan. "I just wanted to
know you were back where you belong. You're sure
you're all right, Helva?"

Niall Parollan laryngitic with concern? Helva was
flattered and surprised, considering his uncomplimen-
tary description hurled at her at their last parting.

"I'm intact again if that's what you mean, Parollan," she replied in droll good humor.

She could have sworn she heard a sigh over the
tight beam.

"That's my girl," Parollan laughed, so it must have
been a wheeze she'd heard. "Of course," and he cleared
his throat, "if you hadn't had your synapses scrambled
on Beta Corvi, you'd've listened to me when I tried

to tell you that that simple simian Acthionite was a regulation-bound brass . . ."

"Not brass, Niall," Helva interrupted sharply, "not brass. Brass is a metal and Teron has none."

"Oh ho ho, so you admit I was right about him?"

" 'To err is human . . .' "

"Thank God!"

Just then Teron requested permission to board.

"I'll see you later, Helva. I couldn't stomach . . ."

"Don't go, Parollan . . ."

"Helva, my own true love, I've been glued to this tight beam for three days for your sake and the stimu-tabs have worn off. I'm dead in the seat!"

"Prop your eyelids open for a few moments more, Niall. This'll be official," she told Parollan as she activated the personnel lift for Teron. She felt a cold dislike replace the bantering friendliness she had been enjoying.

Big as life and disgustingly Neanderthal, her brawn strode into the main control room, saluting with scant ceremony toward her bulkhead. Strode? He swaggered, Helva thought angrily, looking not the least bit worse for his absence.

Teron rubbed his hands together, sat himself down in the pilot's chair, flexed his fingers before he poised them, very businesslike, over the computer keyboard.

"I'll just run a thorough checkdown to be sure no damage was done." His words were neither request nor order.

"Just like that, huh?" Helva asked in a dangerously quiet voice.

Teron frowned and swiveled round in the chair toward her panel.

"Our schedule has been interrupted enough with this mishap."

"Mishap?"

"Modulate your tone, Helva. You can't expect to use those tricks on me."

"I can't expect what?"

"Now," he began placatingly, jerking his chin down, "I take into consideration you've been under a strain recently. You should have insisted that I oversee that ST-1 Captain during that installation. You might have sustained some circuit damage, you know."

"How kind of you to consider that possibility," she said. That was it!

"You could scarcely be harmed, physically, contained as you are in pure titanium," he said and swung back to the console.

"Teron of Acthion, all I can say at this point is that it's a damned good thing for you that I am contained behind pure titanium. Because if I were mobile, I would kick you down that shaft so fast . . ."

"What has possessed you?"

For once, sheer blank illogical amazement flashed across Teron's face.

"Get out! Get off my deck! Get out of my sight. Get OUT!" Helva roared, pouring on volume with each word, with no regard for the tender structure of the human ear.

With sheer sound she drove him, hands clapped to the sides of his head, off the deck, down the side of the 834 as fast as she could escalate the lift.

"Take me for granted, will you? Unreliable organism, am I? Illogical, irresponsible, and inhuman . . ." Helva bellowed after him in a planet-sized shout. And then she burst out laughing, as she realized that such emotional behavior on her part was the only way she could have routed the over-logical Teron of Acthion.

"Did you hear that, Niall Parollan?" she asked in a reasonable but nevertheless exultant tone. "Niall? Hey, Cencom, you on the tight beam . . . answer me?"

From the open channel came the shuddering discord of a massive adenoidal snore.

"Niall?" The sleeper wheezed on, oblivious, until

Helva chuckled at this additional evidence of human frailty.

She asked and received clearance from the asteroid's half-ruined spaceport. She was going to have a long chat with Chief Railly when she returned.

Her penalty for "divorcing" Teron would be a speck against the finder's fee for four shanghaied BB ships. And there ought to be a Federation bonus for aid in the apprehension of drug runners. Totaled, if true justice was giving her half a chance, the rewards might just make her a free ship, out of debt, truly her own mistress. The thought was enough to set her singing.

The
Partnered Ship

Hurtling through space at speeds no unprotected human could tolerate, Helva contemplated the delightful knowledge that she had paid off her indebtedness to Central Worlds Brain-Brawn Ship Service. She was her own mistress. Free. And free to choose, at long last, a partner, a brawn, a mobile human to companion her wherever she chose to wander. She was no longer limited to those sterling souls, fresh and eager from Academy training, fully indoctrinated in Central Worlds' ethos, conditioned to a set way of thinking and acting, molded according to predetermined physical, intellectual, spiritual, psychological requisites, and *not* what she had in mind. She could pick anyone now. She could . . .

Well, now, come to think of it, she couldn't. Brawns, for all their shortcomings, were not ordinary technicians, cranked out by the thousands from specialists' programs on every planet. They were especially trained and educated to function in an unusual partnership. She could not pick out an agreeable personality and find him deadheading on that charm. Even on short contracts, with an industrial or planetary agency, she'd have to rely to a certain degree on a brawn with sense, integrity, and a certain breadth of education, or she'd get royally rooked, industrially and systematically. And besides, she wanted a permanent partner, not another transient. She wanted companionship, an intelligent, sympathetic friend: not a passive employee.

Another factor limited her field further. Many otherwise well-adjusted citizens of a complex, civilized galaxy were revolted or superstitiously terrified at the thought of a human being entombed in a bulkhead, connected to the operational circuitry of a powerful space ship. The neurosis could even extend to personalities like Teron, who deluded themselves that a shell person was really not human, was actually a highly sophisticated computer.

Very few people she had met, Helva admitted sadly, thought of her as Helva, a person, a thinking, feeling, rational, intelligent, eminently human being.

Jennan had. Theoda, except for that one brief instance of rapport, had been too immersed in her lifelong expiation to entertain a personal reaction to Helva, the human. And, although Kira Falernova had been with her over 3 years, neither of them had let the friendship develop into a deep attachment.

In fact, the only mobile human who appeared to regard Helva as Helva was Niall Parollan. And for all Helva knew, he had merely developed an effective way of handling his BB ship subordinates by alternately praising and insulting them in that highly personal, stimulating way.

And yet, he had stayed on the tight beam for 3 days, nursing that tenuous trace of her whereabouts. He could just as easily have delegated the duty to a regular com man. That he hadn't done so absolved him of her previous grievances.

She hoped someone had discovered him asleep at the control panel. He must have been in a deuced uncomfortable position to snore that way. Helva chuckled to herself. Too bad he wasn't bigger. He'd've made a good brawn. And yet, he was passed over, while someone like that nardy idiot, Teron, tall, brawny enough to look at, not only got into training but completed the rigorous course. He must have done it . . . as Niall had acidly suggested . . . on theory credits. Perhaps Central Worlds had better reevaluate their image requirements as a result of this Borealis fiasco. What heavy-worlders like Parollan lacked in stature, they made up in mass . . . and pure cussedness.

"Fardles," Helva said in unaccustomed profanity. The word echoed satisfactorily through the empty cabins. "I wonder if he stayed awake long enough to record my divorce."

She didn't like to contemplate Niall's remarks anent ditching Teron. She could practically hear his rasping voice reminding her that he'd tried to talk her out of Teron.

"For a smart ship, you can be a dumb broad!"

Well, it hadn't been a complete disaster: she'd have that to counter Parollan's scorn. In fact, if Teron *hadn't* been such an irritating dolt, the Xixon creature would never have got into the main cabin; she and Teron wouldn't have been overwhelmed and she wouldn't have made enough in bonuses and rewards to Pay-off so soon.

That was such a comforting thought. To accomplish Pay-off so early on in her career; to reach the goal all BB ships dreamed of. So, now what? She needed a brawn, one of her exceeding careful choice, and she needed another goal, a point, a destination. Maybe one would supply the other. Or vice versa?

"I could go to the Horsehead Nebula," she said aloud for the sound of it.

And the sound triggered a carefully suppressed memory: Jennan leaning against the console, grinning at her, his eyes alight with affection and humor . . .

"If they ever take us off the milkruns, we'll make a stab at the Nebula, huh?"

She was off the milkruns, but Jennan lay dead in

Regulus Base cemetery, all their wild, happy schemes entombed with him. The challenge of such a flight, unaccompanied, was as empty as her ship self.

Horsehead Nebula, indeed! To divert her trend of thought, she ran a rapid calculation. Oh, she could make it, for all her present material dependence on man. Her pile was fresh, though she wished someone would rattle a few brains and develop an energy source that would utilize the full potential of the f.t.l. principle. It was like having two high gears in a powerful ground car that couldn't be used because they'd burn up all available fuel in a few milliseconds. As it was, she could reach the Horsehead . . . in a 100 standard years, at her present top speed.

And then what? You needed someone to celebrate a victory with, to extole a notable achievement, or any triumph was empty. If there was no goad to progress, advance was sterile. You needed a goal, or there was no point to anything.

Now Helva could understand why older class ships suddenly opted out for no discernible reason. And she wondered why Pay-off had seemed so enviable a state. Here she was. And where was she? Shell-people like Amon and Treel, so determined to get here, would never believe that it was the act of paying off that really mattered.

The ship-to-ship band bleeped through her gloomy reflections.

"Helva, this is 422!"

"Silvia!"

"From you I'll accept the name. Rumor is that you've reached Pay-off."

"According to my computations I have!"

"What's the matter with you, then? That's not the end of the world. It's the beginning."

"Of what?"

"Say, that Borealis sense-deprivation hit you hard."

"No, no, really. I'm all right. I just don't like solitude."

"You don't appreciate being well off," Silvia went on in her cynical way. "I'd've thought you'd be glad to be rid of that asinine Teron. He reminded me so much of that half-lobed . . . well, never mind him. Helva, you're going to have to watch your step. You've Paid-off in less than 10 standard years. That's too soon. Much too soon for Central Worlds to be willing to let you off their hook."

"I'm not so sure I'm off," Helva replied.

"What do you mean? Listen," and Silvia's voice sounded fierce, "if there's any funny taping on you, you call in the Mutant Monitors or the Society for Preservation of the Rights of Intelligent Minorities. That'd be Amiking and Rocco on Regulus. Amiking's SPRIM, got the fancy uniform, but it's Rocco who has the brains. You get them in on any discussions. Demand a recalculation of all costs from the day they shelled you out of your cradle."

"Silvia, there's not going to be any trouble about the Pay-off figures. I'm clear. I'm sure of it."

"Then what's the problem?"

"What do I do *now*?"

Silvia spluttered for a moment. "Don't you realize," she demanded angrily, "that industrial complexes, not to mention planetary unions, will pay you any figure you name? For any time you'll spare them? Of course, you do have to watch yourself with private industry. They play dirty. Before you touch down at Regulus, you call Broley. A city shell-person *always* knows who's ready to bid and who you can trust. Particularly Broley. He'll get you a good contract!"

"And a good brawn?"

"Are you on that wheeze again, Helva?" Silvia was disgusted. "Change around. Grab the kind of technician you need for an assignment, then drop him. I'd've thought you'd had quite enough of brawns for a while."

"Quite enough brawns, yes. I just want one who'll stay a while. If only Jennan . . ."

"If only . . . 'If' converts no energy and has no credit. You don't seem to realize, Helva, you're a top BB ship. You'll have brawns begging to board you. Take your pick. Sure, you and Jennan made a fine team. His death was a piece of rotten luck. But he is dead. Let him rest in peace. Find yourself another guy, someone up to your calibre: not another blunt-brained bastard like the one you shouted off your deck."

Helva was startled that Silvia had already heard about that.

"And if you've got to have a partner, grab one young, train him up right. The Academy ruins more than it improves. You ought to know by now what you don't want in a partner. Teach him what he ought to know. Don't wait for the impossible! Engineer it. And look out for Railly's conniving. He's going to try to keep you on the roster or I haven't been around this Service for 400 years."

"Why have you been around for 400 years, Silvia?"

There was such a long silence Helva wondered if they'd gone beyond contact range.

"I don't ask myself that any more, Helva. I used to when I was your age and Pay-off seemed close. Then we ran afoul of a meteor swarm off Saadalsund and . . . well, there's usually something interesting to do for Central Worlds. I've had good partners and bad ones, too." Her voice wavered now from attenuation. "Be careful, Helva. Don't sell yourself cheap."

The contact broke then but the comfort of Silvia's astringent concern overshadowed the substance of her warning for a time.

To reassure herself, Helva ran through the computations again, starting with the fearful debts of her early infancy and childhood. The pituitary adjustments so that her body would not outgrow the final capsule and the delicate brain surgery that made Helva the ship had been, as always, expensive. However, since there could be no "slaves" or "indentured" servants within Central Worlds Autonomy, committees and organizations of dedicated citizens decreed that a salary scale, a bonus-and-awards system, should provide incentive and remuneration for shell people in every occupation.

Now Helva could see that the subtle, massive conditioning she'd received in her formative years was double-edged. It made her happy as a shell-person, it had dedicated her to her life in Service, and it made Pay-off a mockery. What else could a BB ship do but continue as she had started . . . in Service? The same must apply to shell people trained to manage ships, mining planets or industrial complexes. And yet there was compensation.

The memory of Jennan rose to plague her again—to plague and console. Those had been marvelous years; short but full of a glowing wonder of self-discovery and joint exploration. They'd been eager for the challenge of each new mission to be faced together. They'd taken a perverse pride in her sobriquet. And Jennan had had to defend them both against the ridicule of other brawns until the JH-834 had been admired and respected as the Ship Who Sang. Jennan had been unique. But surely there would be another man with other qualities to recommend him.

She wondered if she had unconsciously chosen Teron because he had been the antithesis of her first brawn. Well, Silvia was right: she ought to find a reasonable compromise, train him up as a proper brawn. Train him up to consider her a person, not a ship or an emotionally responsive computer.

She was Paid-off. She could take time to look around, to let Broley find a reliable, independent contract.

Idly she wondered how long it had taken the FG-602 to contract with the Alpheccan Confederacy. He'd Paid-off just before her birth. She'd met him once with Jennan, but both he and his partner affected an amused, detached superciliousness that had been offensive.

She could, she supposed, broadcast an advertisement right now. She began to feel better. Action, that was what she'd needed. But perhaps it would be smarter to report in to Regulus Base, make sure all was in order. It was only sensible to keep on good terms with Central Worlds. She'd need their technicians and maintenance sheds for any overhauls.

She found she had slowed somewhat and added thrust, confidently speeding back to Regulus. She began to cast up a list of qualities that she wanted in a partner, and the traits to avoid. So pleasant were her meditations that it seemed no time at all before she had to request landing instructions from Cencom.

"Why, Helva, as I live and breathe," Niall Parollan answered her.

"Catch up on your beauty sleep?"

"Both."

"Both?"

"Caught up with beauty and sleep!"

"She didn't mind your snoring?"

"*They* were too exhausted to hear and much too grateful to comment, m'gal."

"I am not your gal."

"The endearment is considered an accolade by many."

"How do you arrange that delusion?"

Niall chuckled maliciously. "I pick *my* partners carefully, not just for the symmetry of their features and the density of their skulls."

"All right, Parollan. You've counted coup. By the way, I trust you stayed awake long enough to register Teron's dismissal?"

"Oh, yes, and took even greater pleasure in posting the penalty to your account."

"I can afford it."

"I know," and there was an unexpected grimness in his voice. "Put your lazy tail down on Pad No. 3, Administrative Landing. An official welcoming committee has been waiting for you."

"You mean, an emancipation delegation."

Cencom was silent.

Well, she'd got off lightly at Parollan's hands. She'd miss him. His caustic manner had been stimulating, and whatever his motives, he had been there at the end of the tight beam. Independence would have its own compensations. Wouldn't it?

As she jockeyed with finicky precision onto the No. 3 pad, she experienced another jolt of uncertainty. Every conscious hour of the last 10 years had been devoted to Central Worlds. She had "belonged" in that Service and had not been aware of her indebtedness to them. Well, she was just going to have to make some drastic reorientations in her thinking. Change was necessary to growth and maturity.

She was about to send a peremptory signal to Cencom to get a move on when she saw the group emerging from the Base Tower. Niall Parollan was dwarfed by the other three tall men. She recognized the burly figure of Chief Railly: fitting and due her achievement. The other two men she identified as Commander Breslaw of Engineering and Admiral Dobrinon of Xeno Relations. This wasn't a standard graduation line-up. Silvia might be right about Central not letting her off their hook. She ought to have called Double M or SPRIM. Or Broley. She could hardly blast off now. She'd fry the quartet of notables.

So she lowered the passenger lift and cannily turned up her audio units. However, none of the visitors made any comments until they reached the lock. Then they only played the precedence routine.

However, after Niall Parollan had politely ushered
the Chief from the lift, he stared at Helva's column
with a definitely possessive air. As he stepped into the
lock and tossed off the customary salute, it was as if
he had proclaimed her his exclusive property.

His audacity staggered her. It wasn't Railly she
must guard against: it was this liter-sized, heavy-
world machiavelli, Parollan!

Dobrinon noticed the Supervisor's salute.

"Gentlemen, our manners," and, bringing his boot-
heels smartly together, he accorded her the proper
ceremony.

Service had such archaic traditions, Helva mused;
like saluting a ship on boarding. Or did they salute
her as a ranking officer? Probably not. Salutes between
persons had to be reciprocal. She'd train her new
brain to salute. Sentimental about the Service?

"And our profound gratitude, Helva," Chief Railly
was saying, holding his own salute an overlong moment. "Your superb courage and resourcefulness at
Borealis are already Service legends. A triumph of
mind over immobility. We're proud, very proud, to
have had you on our roster."

Helva caught the past tense and wondered again at
Parollan's attitude.

"You know Dobrinon of Xeno and Breslaw of Engineering, of course," the Chief went on, so smoothly
passing by the adroit admission that Helva wondered
if she had heard aright. And why were these two here
if she were, by tacit admission, an independent.

"Yes, we've met," she admitted so drily the Chief
chuckled.

He gestured for the others to take seats, his deference of moments before giving way to the next
order of business. Helva scanned the delegation warily.
Parollan gave her a quick, sideways grin before he
settled himself on the couch, one arm draped negligently along the back.

"As if he meant to stay a while," Helva thought sourly.

"I don't know if the directive reached you in transit, Helva," the Chief said, "but those audio-visual modifications you suggested are going to be built into every new shell. Never again will one of our people have to suffer sense-deprivation. Can't imagine why such a contingency wasn't provided for long ago."

Breslaw cleared his throat and pulled at his left ear, managing not to look at anyone as he replied. "Units exist in prematuring shells, Railly, and used to be transferred at final encapsulation of ship-designated personnel until the 4th Class. In that century, modifications to the inner shell made direct linkage to the ship's facilities and seemed to make an auxiliary system redundant."

Railly frowned. "Sometimes these apparent archaic traditions passed along in Service do have their place in our modern context."

"Unfortunately, the shell people kidnapped by Xixon were all of later classes."

"Yes, indeed, that was unfortunate, Breslaw. In your case, Helva," the Chief went on briskly, "there will be no charge for the modification. That puts you right close to Pay-off . . ." he held up his hand, smiling benignly as Helva started to interrupt, ". . . probably over and to spare. I think there's no question that you'll get full finders' fee and the reward for the apprehension of federal offenders. That comes in from Central Bureau of the Federation." Railly had taken to pacing the length of the cabin. Helva couldn't decide if he had a guilty conscience or was gathering mental take-off speed. In either case it augured ill for her.

"Therefore, Helva, Regulus Base must consider you a free agent," he announced in stentorous tones, smiling again to contradict apparent reluctance. "We're proud of your record, Helva. Very proud." He dropped his voice to a confidential aside. "All space-drek to the contrary, we wish all the BB ships could perform at such efficiency and remove themselves from our fiscal autonomy. Be quite an achievement to run the Service in the black. However, pending the confirmation of those rewards, Regulus Base is required to consider you unavailable for a new assignment of any duration."

"And you had one in mind for me."

"Yes, we did have one in mind," Railly admitted with twinkling eyes and the paternal smile. He glanced expectantly toward Parollan.

"Rather pointless to waste your valuable time, Chief, discussing it then, isn't it?" Helva asked just as Parollan got to his feet.

"Why, I don't think the Chief would ever consider you a waste of his time, Helva," Parollan said, his eyes mocking, challenging her. "Of course, if you've made other plans on the way back from Borealis, it was real courteous of you to check in here and say goodbye." He turned on his heel and started purposefully for the lock. "Drop in again sometime."

"Just a minute, Parollan," Railly said.

The Chief managed to control his expression but Breslaw looked close to panic and Dobrinon's smile had frozen in alarm. Whatever they had had in mind for her must be mighty big. She didn't trust any ploy of Parollan's but these other two were keen, solid, honorable specialists. It wouldn't hurt to listen.

Parollan got to the lock, turned to give her a hearty wave.

"Parollan!"

He halted, hand on the left rail, his face expressing only polite attention. He wasn't giving anything away.

"What had you cooked up, Parollan?"

"I? I'd *cooked up* nothing."

Helva ignored Dobrinon's startled exclamation.

"We had," Parollan admitted after a glance at the

Chief, "discussed another assignment for the TH-834 after that spectacular drug-run. Naturally that mission has been aborted due to circumstances beyond our control."

Helva chuckled to herself. He hadn't let her off lightly on the matter of Teron after all. He'd needle her for the next 25 years for that mistake . . .

"As a matter of purely academic interest—until those rewards are posted to me—would you deign to discuss this aborted mission?"

"No harm in discussing it, certainly," he agreed as he sauntered back into the cabin, "while we wait for confirmation from Federation." He settled his wiry body into a comfortable position before he continued. "It had originally been planned to assign the TH-834 to the projected Beta Corvi mission."

"Beta Corvi?" Helva suppressed the flicker of alarm. Then she laughed out loud. "Teron of Acthion in a Corviki shell, coping with the environment?"

Niall regarded her sardonically for a moment. "You yourself made the point that Ansra Colmer, a true egocentric, singleminded, stubborn, and pragmatic as hell, suffered the least personality trauma from the phenomena of the Corviki transfer. Teron was so well endowed with the same sterling attributes that it was obvious he'd . . ."

" . . . Not last a minute as a personality on Beta Corvi, and you know it, Niall Parollan. That man was incapable of coping with such anomalies." Parollan's tactics infuriated her. Why, what he had suggested was nothing short of bald murder. And he'd talked Railly into the scheme? Had they both wanted to get rid of Teron?

"Now, really, Helva," Railly said, stepping forward as if separating two antagonists, "I was never in favor of Teron as your brawn, if you'll forgive the reminder . . ."

"*You* were right, Chief," Helva said in so sweet and contrite a tone that Parollan snorted his disgust.

". . . And sorry to be, I assure you. However, no harm appears to have resulted."

"Except that Helva's now a free agent," Parollan said in a completely expressionless voice.

"Exactly," Railly continued with unexpected enthusiasm. "And, unless Helva has other plans in mind, perhaps we all can make her see the advantage of undertaking this new mission in spite of her changed status."

There was an odd half-smile on Parollan's face as he returned his Chief's intense stare.

"Yes, perhaps we can," the Supervisor said with a hearty lack of enthusiasm.

Helva saw Dobrinon give him a quizzical look and Breslaw was plainly startled. Something was going amiss with their sales pitch?

"Well then, Helva," Railly started off determinedly, "*have* you any plans in mind?"

"She's had no time to advertise," Niall said abruptly. "She made no planetary calls on the return trip here. And I doubt that even the most assiduous of our known informers has had time to discover that the XH-834 has Paid-off. It so rarely occurs this early in service."

"I'll answer for myself, thank you, Parollan."

The others were staring at their colleague with blank astonishment. The atmosphere in the cabin had become strained. Helva was at a loss to figure out why Parollan was deliberately disrupting the mood Railly was attempting to create. Trust him to have an ulterior motive—but what?

"So my enterprising supervisor planned to have me go back to Beta Corvi? That somewhat explains Admiral Dobrinon's presence. And you, Commander Breslaw? Or is Engineering bidding against Xeno for my services?"

"We were hoping to combine forces, Helva," Dobrinon answered after an uncomfortable pause.

Someone has missed his cue, Helva thought.

"It seemed appropriate," Breslaw said, breaking his silence, "that you should be the first ship to benefit from the discoveries resulting from the Beta Corvi data you brought back."

If Engineering had used the stabilizing key for unstable isotopes . . .

"Just how would I have benefited?" Helva asked casually. She kept one eye on Parollan. He was adept at titillation. She wouldn't put it past him to have staged this whole thing, including his own apparent disinterest, to arouse her to indiscretion. Of course, she'd want an improved f.t.l. drive!

"When we began to study the basic theories," Breslaw was saying, "we could see an immediate application to our present f.t.l. system. You're surely aware, Helva, that the potential of the f.t.l. principle is vastly beyond present performance. The problem has been an energy source that could tolerate the demands full f.t.l. speed requires. The Corviki data makes intergalactic travel possible in this decade. This year!"

Intergalactic travel? Helva's excitement matched Breslaw's. Between which galaxies? This one and . . . the Horsehead Nebula?

"Yes, intergalactic distances traversed in a fraction of present estimates," Railly said, as if he sensed they had her attention. "Imagine it, Helva, unlimited power, literally inexhaustible power, to take you to the edge of the galaxies visible from the rim of the Milky Way. Beyond any space now known to man." Railly spoke urgently, firing her desire. "Power to make those f.t.l. drive components work efficiently for the first time since they were designed. All we've lacked has been a constant fuel source to stand up to the drain of energy required. And you've the chance to

explore unknown space. You can chart new star systems, open up whole galaxies for Central Worlds."

That reminder brought her out of those stars.

"Interesting. Very interesting. The f.t.l. always has
been a case of having a good cart and no draft animals
strong enough. However, if this radical new development stemmed from the Corviki data, why is another
mission necessary?"

Railly gestured to Breslaw, who began whipping
out cube-graphs and computer tapes, which he arranged nervously on her console.

"With the Corviki data for stabilizing unstable isotopes, we were able to make use of that form of waste
energy, not just for the fractional seconds of half-life
before the AMUs deteriorated, but for as long as that
power was needed. Imagine it, Helva," said Breslaw's
eyes, glowing with wonder, "the power of an exploding
star, always equal to that of the exploding star at its
highest energy level."

The cabin seemed to darken at his words. It was
an exploding star—operating at its highest energy level
—Ravel's sun, that had burned Jennan to death as
she had frantically tried to outrun its fantastic energy.
But to have such a power . . . *enslaved to her requirements?*

She *had* to have it. An inner nova to expiate the
crime of the outer. Hammurabian justice at its purest!
She forced herself to listen to Breslaw's explanations.

"Admittedly, Helva, there are tremendous subtleties
involved which, I readily confess, no one in my team
is scientifically sophisticated enough to appreciate. It's
almost as if the Corvi were discussing personal intimacies rather than sub-particular facts, but the result
is a fantastic-discipline of nucleonic forces.

"As you'll notice, Helva," and he pointed to the
first cube and tapped the equations into the ship's
computer, "the isotopes are permitted to radiate energy
in cycles, but instead of a decrease in the energy

available as deterioration occurs, the energy level remains constant. By varying the number of cycles initiated per second, or millisecond for that matter," and Breslaw beamed with paternal fondness for the abilities of his development, "the f.t.l. drive receives the power it requires to exceed the speed of light by any multiple required. To traverse a given distance, in a given length of time, the original f.t.l. equations supply the rate of cycle variation needed!"

With an unexpectedly dramatic flourish for such a pragmatic man, Breslaw tapped out a set of voyage requirements.

"If you have to get to, say, Mirfak, in 2 standard days, you can, now. Instead of taking . . . oh, how long?"

"Four weeks." Helva supplied the answer absently, more intent on following the print-in of the profoundly interesting equations.

"Four weeks then. Well, you can see the advantages."

And then Helva understood what necessitated the new mission to Beta Corvi.

"One would scarcely try to release that kind of energy within a solar system without knowing the subjective and objective effects. What disadvantages have you observed?" she asked. "Are these computations based on experiment, or sheer theory?"

Doubt and concern dampened Breslaw's ardor. "We have tested the CV energy source, Cycle Variant. We took every possible precaution, used a very slow cyclage rate. It was impossible," he said, grimacing, "to keep the experimental vessel in range of the testing instrumentation . . ."

"The vehicle was manned, or BB?"

"Manned." Breslaw's answer was just audible.

"The effect of such acceleration on the personnel was fatal?"

"Not that we know of." Breslaw glanced sharply at Railly, who had been talking in a low voice to Parollan. Before Helva could turn up her audio, the two separated, Railly joining Dobrinon on the couch, leaving Parollan alone, opposite them. Niall's face was inscrutably polite, his eyes guarded.

"Well, why don't you know?"

"The vessel has not returned. The estimated time of arrival is 9 years standard. It has been sighted returning on normal drive. Their last intercepted communication indicated we must proceed with immense caution in the use of this power source."

"Evidently. I'd also hazard a heavy hand was on the CV switch to get that far out of com range. You should have used a BB ship with no fragile brawns to clutter up the test run."

"There was also a suggestion that we may have misused the Beta Corvi data," Breslaw went on, nodding thoughtfully at her observation. "You can easily extrapolate the destructive potential of the CV factor. We must be sure we have not perverted the data and unleashed uncontrollable or unstable emissions that might have cosmic repercussions." Breslaw looked toward her, worried and hopeful.

That could be some pile to put rods in, Helva mused, although she hoped they wouldn't have to damp that reactor. Intergalactic travel! The test ship flung *9 years* away from known space!

"First, I am gratified by the confidence you have in me, gentlemen," she said after a long moment. "However, I cannot help wondering if you selected me because, being Paid-off—in theory, that is—I am therefore most expendable, constituting no embarrassing debit loss on the fiscal records."

Only Parollan appreciated her levity and he laughed with uninhibited delight.

"Your facetious attitude is ill-timed, Helva," Railly remonstrated. "You are the least expendable of our ship personnel. I fail to see, Parollan, the humor in such an outrageous suggestion." There was no mistaking the anger behind his reprimand.

"In that case," Helva said, "you're a low species of extortionist."

"What?" Railly bellowed, diverted from Niall.

"You know perfectly well, Chief Railly, that I'd want to possess such a drive once I knew of its existence. I'd certainly want to remain in Central Worlds Service to get it!"

Parollan sobered instantly, staring at her.

"Thta's the game, isn't it?" Helva demanded, her voice cold because she was talking to Parollan and he knew it now. He kept staring at her, the muscles in his jaw twitching.

"Frankly, yes," Railly answered when it was obvious Parollan would not. "And there's not much time for you to decide."

"How so?"

Some subtle change in Railly's face roused her to a bitter anger. So this was how Central Worlds treated their BB ships. She *should* have called in Double M and SPRIM. She should have got in touch with Broley. Let Central Worlds fight its own fires.

"Central Worlds is bound by Federation directives, Helva, directives controlled and promulgated by the peoples of the civilized galaxy. There is no latitude on some of those strictures. You are under your original obligation to Central Worlds until those additional bonuses come through from Federation. After that, an entirely different set of directives controls the kind of authority, the type of contract, the wording and restrictions of the clauses, the payments and prerogatives of any further dealings we have with a BB ship. If we operated any other way, Helva," Railly went on implacably, "we would have the humanities' guardians scanning our tapes, sitting on our shoulders, hindering our operations. You have proved to be an extremely capable contractee. The Service needs you. Our need

has, so far, been to your benefit. You have been given
extraordinary opportunities to achieve Pay-off early
in your career. We felt you might consider that at this
time, when we are offering you the chance to be the
first BB ship with a fully realized f.t.l. drive."

"If apologizes are in order, kindly accept them. I
did not realize that contract terms changed after Pay-
off was achieved. However, you can scarcely blame
me for wanting to understand all the factors involved
in what was only to be a discussion, pending confirmation of those rewards.

"Inherent in Commander Breslaw's explanation is
the possibility that I could blow myself into a nova . . ."

"I protest," Breslaw jumped to his feet. "You can
see that the theory is valid! It has been tested . . ."

"And scared you into taking the precaution of checking against perversion of data. I like my skin, gentlemen. I prefer it in one piece."

"Your shell is solid titanium," Breslaw said heatedly,
"impervious to . . ."

"The full power of an exploding sun in my guts?"
Helva snapped. "I've already suffered from the heat
of a nova, Breslaw. And this solid titanium shell of
mine has proved to be no sanctuary against injury . . .
and the perversions of man."

Breslaw sank to the couch, utterly deflated. Of the
others, only Parollan suffered neither embarrassment
nor chagrin. He had jerked his head toward her column, at her rebuttal. His lips were set in too bitter a
line even for the cynical supervisor. For a moment,
his eyes were unguarded, reflecting a physical pain
and an expression Helva had seen once before—in
the eyes of a dying man.

It was he who broke the silence, speaking in a heavy,
tried voice.

"There's been no attempt to mask the danger involved, Helva. And we've tried to make an unwieldly
forest of restrictions work for you. It would be more

advantageous for you to extend the original contract than to enter a completely new one. You can check your files on that if you doubt me. We can amend some of the old clauses. We cannot change any of the new. Now have the courtesy to hear us out and then a simple yes or no is all that's required."

He sounded indifferent to that decision now, and she couldn't understand why.

Dobrinon cleared his throat and walked slowly toward her column as if gathering his disrupted thoughts.

"The projected mission to Beta Corvi had multiple purposes, Helva, every one needing abilities, talents, and background that pointed inexorably to you. I'll explain those that relate to my sphere of activity.

"I believe we could condition future observers to withstand the psychological disorientation of Corviki transfers, if we had some idea of the change taking place in the human psyche that has been retained in the Corviki entity. Yes, this is asking for a double portion of your soul's flesh, Helva, but I have an altruistic reason for asking *you* to return there. Parollan and I are both positive that if you could return and reassure yourself as to the integration . . . or disintegration, of the personalities of Solar Prane, Kurla Ster, Chadress and Ansra Colmer in their Corviki environment, you might be able to resolve the sense of guilt and failure that resulted from the outcome of the first mission.

"You are the best qualified, if not the only person capable of recognizing the immigrants." Dobrinon gave a faint smile at his description. It was apt, Helva thought, trying not to admit how the notion of a return scared—and tempted—her. "Now, Davo Fillanaser has volunteered to return. But, frankly, his psyche profile indicates a deep trauma. I suspect that he would . . . ah, immigrate, too."

"Very unsettling, I assure you," Helva said. She didn't like the mental picture of Davo Fillanaser's body stretched out, uninhabited, on a couch. But, if Prane and Kurla and Chadress were content as Corviki . . . Helva forced her mind away. "Well, it's obvious we are going to need Corviki help if we are to play with their toys without damaging the entire galaxy. I assume my psyche profile was run through and you feel you can trust me to return?"

"Yes." Dobrinon's answer was prompt and firm.

"Even after the Borealis sense-deprivation?"

"I'd hazard the guess that the Corviki experience helped you during that episode."

"Shrewd of you, Dobrinon. We are all, are we not, the sum of our experiences. Which brings me to a sordid subject. I assume, Commander Breslaw, that the CV factor will be installed in my drive chambers before I undertake a return to Beta Corvi?"

"Yes, that would be a necessity. How else could they assess our application of their data?"

"And the cost of such an installation?"

Breslaw glanced nervously at Railly. The Chief inclined his head. "We can't determine the exact cost: the experimental vessel was rebuilt several times. Shielding is reinforced: structural members doubled, a new alloy on the hull. Well, I'd estimate in the neighborhood of 500,000 galactic credits."

He had the grace to look appalled, Helva noticed, although the staggering cost left her relatively unmoved. After all, she'd paid off more than that already.

"That would be if I contracted immediately?"

"Yes."

"And about twice that if the old contract lapsed?"

"I expect so." Breslaw closed his folders disconsolately as if he had now abandoned all hope of this project. This kind of pessimism irritated Helva immeasurably.

"However, Helva, if you extend the old contract,

we are in a position to flex any conditions that bind a person of your proved abilities," Railly said smoothly.

"Don't pressure me, Railly. I haven't considered all the angles from *my* point of view."

That was not true. She had made up her mind. She'd make Railly flex those conditions that bound a person of her proved ability until SPRIM and Double M could hear regulations cracking.

Parollan had certainly cooked up a real tight orbit for her. And she'd bet her next bonus that he knew exactly what an effect Breslaw's description of that power source would have on her. He didn't miss a trick, that one. He'd've seen the justice of enslaving a nova to her bidding after what Ravel's sun had done to Jennan. And he certainly had pointed out that guilt-resolution gimmick to Dobrinon. Well, she'd show this egotistical, self-assured, domineering, machiavellian refugee from a heavy-world . . . Helva brought her polemic to an abrupt halt. And stared down at Parollan.

His face was drawn into dark lines of strain and exhaustion. There was no trace in the slumped shoulders of the arrogant manipulator who called her bluff by being ready to walk out before he'd even started. There was no malicious gleam in the back of the unguarded eyes apathetically turned on her column. He must know he'd won! And, sure of her interest, was he regretting his machinations? He certainly looked as if he regretted something from somewhere in his ill-starred past.

Fine time to feel sorry for Niall Parollan! She must keep firmly in mind that they wanted her very badly indeed, for some pretty substantial reasons, and they were going to have to pay for her.

"I assume that the probability curve is high in my favor?" she broke the silence to ask.

Railly nodded.

"As I mentioned," Dobrinon said quickly, "you are

the most likely person to identify the immigrants if there is any trace of their previous personality in the Corviki entities."

"You don't think there will be?"

Dobrinon shrugged. "How can one gauge the depth of transfer with totally alien structure and psychology? As a human, I prefer to think some vestige of the humanoid remains. I recommend, however, that your initial contact be extremely brief. That is," he amended discreetly, "if you decide to undertake this mission. Under no circumstances would you be asked to jeopardize yourself in the search for others."

"The primary goal of the mission is to obtain the Corviki evaluation of the CV data," Breslaw spoke up. He glanced anxiously at Dobrinon, who shrugged his acquiescence to the priority.

Oh, she had them now.

"I should very much like to have that drive if it's feasible," Helva said. Why on earth should Parollan flinch? Were they hiding something after all?

"My personal faith in you has been vindicated," Railly declared, his usual jovial self.

"But you're going to have to agree to a few stipulations of mine or there is no point in proceeding further."

"You've never been unreasonable, Helva, and I do have authority to stretch a few regulations in your favor."

"You'd better listen to my conditions before you make any promises, Railly," Helva said drily. "I'm not about to mortgage my soul for 25 years or so, paying off 500,000 credits, on the supposition that the CV drive will be vetted by the Corviki and that I'll resolve a few dangling traumas in the process.

"This extension of my old contract will be void if the CV drive is not feasible. You can junk the modifications to my hull, I'll pay for the cost of the alloy coating, and you'll just have to write the rest off as experimental loss. That's what it'll be."

There was a hurried conference between Railly and Breslaw, with Railly reluctantly giving in to the engineer's persuasions.

"All right."

"Second, I can use my own judgment on the advisability of contacting the human immigrants on Corvi, with no penalty for not completing all phases of the planned mission."

"I think Dobrinon made that contingency clear."

"Third, the matter of a brawn partner . . ."

"You have certainly proved that you can operate better without a brawn," Railly interrupted her, all cooperation. Parollan made an inarticulate sound in his throat. "You had something to say, Supervisor?"

"May I finish?" Helva demanded acidly. "Parollan, at least, is well aware of my continuous demands for a permanent brawn. I do *not* like to operate alone. I detest it."

"It would be most inadvisable," Dobrinon put in anxiously.

"I will not undertake this mission at all without the brawn of my choice!" she said, raising her voice above the others.

"I heartily concur, Railly. This Corviki psyche exchange has tremendous emotional kickback. Parollan and I feel strongly . . ." but when Dobrinon glanced toward the Supervisor for confirmation, he got no response at all and hurriedly continued, ". . . that it is imperative for Helva to be sustained by a strong, empathic brawn as a buffer to the trauma of the experience."

"The whole discussion can be terminated right now, Railly, if my conditions are not met. They are, as your experts agree, reasonable."

Railly acquiesced, but his smile had disappeared.

"Good. My final condition also hinges on the success of the drive. You have set me 500,000 credits to pay off. Acceptable. However, with the CV utilizing the full potential of the f.t.l. drive, I will be able to get from here to there in next to no time at all. I'd be working my tail off for you. I hardly think the old scale of salary and bonuses would apply to the new level of mobility."

Railly began to protest, volubly, mentioning the possibility that Breslaw's estimate of 500,000 was conservative, but he was willing to accept that fee.

"Pure extortion," she interrupted him. "For that matter, am I expected to absorb the cost of any expensive adjustments that the Corviki might recommend? I've got to consider that, too, as well as service to a completely new power source. No, Railly, I'm sure that Double M and SPRIM might very well consider that the old rate of pay will need some adjustment upward to compensate for my increased efficiency."

"She'll be the fastest thing in the galaxy," Breslaw said.

"Whose side are you on, Breslaw?"

"In this case, Helva's," the engineer replied, unintimidated.

"I'm only asking a reasonable one-third increase: surely not excessive for such a loyal employee of Central Worlds. I'm sure you'll contrive to get your money's worth out of me, if I know how you operate?"

"How *I* operate?" Railly swung around to glare pointedly at Parollan.

"Parollan operates his section under *your* orders, Chief," Helva said, "and the dictates of expediency."

She was sorry she said it the moment the words were out. Parollan's withdrawal was obvious to the others now. He—not the Chief—had initiated this project. He had neatly layered the odds against her refusing it. She couldn't imagine what was wrong with him now. He had simply dropped out of the arguments, ignored the discussions, was totally immersed in that private struggle.

She was sorry for him. She hated him. She needed him. And she was about to get him. She couldn't beat him but she could join him.

"Do you agree to my conditions, Railly, or don't you? Take 'em or leave 'em."

Dobrinon and Breslaw added their entreaties and Helva didn't really need to hear Railly's growl of consent to know that he'd had no real alternative either.

She'd say this for Railly, he was a good loser. For a long moment after he called the revisions in to the Base computer and made them official, he stood with his head down, staring at the pilot's console. When he turned back, his face was impassive.

"I was warned you might drive a stiff bargain, Helva." He flicked a glance at Parollan. "I didn't think a BB ship would ever outguess me. But you're goddamned right," he added, his eyes flashing, "when you say that I'll work your tail off while you're still a Central Worlds ship."

"Fair enough."

"Now, Breslaw's going to want you at the maintenance docks to lay in the CV drive. You'll retain all standard equipment until the Beta Corvi vet the new drive. And yes, that's included in the 500,000. Dobrinon has a stack of results on his analysis of the Beta Corvi trauma for you to print into your banks."

"It's as much Niall's work as mine," Dobrinon said, again trying to draw the silent man into the discussion. "He had several astute correlations to make from the debriefing and psych tapes of the others on that mission that have helped my staff formulate such preliminary conclusions as we've been able to make."

"Yes, yes, Parollan's very helpful," Railly muttered. "So there's just the proper brawn left to be discussed. Right now . . ."

"Hold it," Helva interrupted him. "I thought I made it clear that I will only undertake the Beta Corvi run with the partner of my choice. Whether that man continues after Beta Corvi is not at issue."

Railly turned to her, his eyes wary. "Yes, we'd agreed to that. But you also said you wanted a permanent brawn."

"I do. But I won't go to Beta Corvi unless Parollan goes with me."

She ignored Railly's explosive protest and the astonished exclamations and congratulations from Dobrinon and Breslaw. Her eyes, her mind, her being were focused on Niall.

The wiry little man turned, his eyes seeking the exact spot on the column parallel to her head.

"This is a bad time for jokes, Helva."

"I'm not joking, m'boy."

"By all that's holy, Parollan, Helva's a genius," Dobrinon cried delightedly, clapping the unresisting shoulder. "And she's called your bluff."

"Indeed she has. You've always boasted you could outbrawn any man in the Service," Railly said in a dry, cool voice. There'd been no vindictiveness in Helva's nomination, but there was in Railly's prompt ratification. "A little field work will make you a better supervisor."

"I think Helva çan rectify that fluctuating gravity problem that bugged the test ship," Breslaw assured Parollan. "And there's always the shockweb for added protection."

Abruptly they left. Niall Parollan remained, troubled and dazed, reacting not at all in any of the ways she could understand.

"You've got to be joking, Helva," he said, his voice cracking despite an obvious effort to control himself.

"Why? You know more about brawning than anyone in Service. You know the Corviki problem backward and forward, and you undoubtedly researched Breslaw's equations thoroughly before . . ."

"Of course I did," and the control was gone. His

words tumbled out harsh and bitter. "Do you think I'd let you walk into something I hadn't checked thoroughly? But I rigged this farce. *I* did! Not Railly. I talked him into it. And Breslaw and Dobrinon, too, once I saw the possibility of hooking you."

"That was obvious!"

"You didn't have a chance, Helva, because I knew every button to push on you and when. And I did, gods help me, I did!"

"You are undoubtedly the most unscrupulous supervisor in the Service," she agreed, countering his scathing self-contempt with unruffled humor. "And that was a fardling underhanded trick you just served me."

"You're not even listening to me, you stupid tin-plated witch. Can't you understand what I did to you? I *made* you stay in the Service!"

"No. I elected to stay. On my conditions."

Niall stared wildly at her, his eyes dark with the conflict that was tearing him apart. All arrogance, all self-confidence had been stripped from him. This was too violent a reaction to finding himself momentarily outmaneuvered.

"Your conditions? Your conditions! Now there's another real fine example of cosmic justice," and he laughed hoarsely at an irony only he could see.

"Maybe you'd better let me in on that joke, Niall. I could use a laugh, even if it's on me."

There were tears in his eyes now and he held his clenched fists rigid against his thighs.

"I rigged all this, Helva, because I, Niall Parollan, could not let you leave Central Worlds Service. Oh, yes. I put every mission your way that would help you Pay-off. And when you actually had, I found I couldn't tolerate the prospect. So I set up all those clever nardy ploys to keep you in. Only when I saw you reacting just as I'd planned you should, I knew I'd used my position for the most despicable act in a long series of clever, shrewd, despicable manipulations. And

I couldn't stop what I'd started. I couldn't even think of a way to get you out of the mess. Then you—Helva —want me, Parollan, for your brawn." His laugh was a cry of anguish.

"That doesn't change my option, Parollan," she said forcefully. She had to override that horrible laughing. "I want you for brawn as selfishly as you want me in Service. And it'll be safer to have you my brawn than my Supervisor. There isn't much else for me to do anyway but stay with Central Worlds," she added in a gentler voice. "You did make it possible for me to stay on my terms, because they fardling well know that I'm the only ship to do this job. I want you as brawn, Niall Parollan, because you are clever, devious, despicable, unscrupulous, and demanding. Because you do know the right buttons to push on me. You're not much on looks and size, but I've been that road. I'll trust you to bring me back out of anything . . . even Beta Corvi."

"*Trust* me?" It was a scream starting from his guts. His body was shaking with effort. "Why, you fool, you freak-out, half-grown, wirehaired retard of a ro- mantic, tin-assed fool. You trust me? Don't you realize that I know every single thing there is to know about you. I even had a chromosonal extrap made so I'd know what you *look* like. And I know the release syl- lables they coded into your panel not seven days ago! Trust me? I'm the last person you can trust. Choose me as brawn? God!"

Helva was staggered by his disclosure. Parollan had a brawn fixation on her? She wanted to sing halle- lujahs, she wanted to scream with rage. She was exalted and full of panic. But she knew what to do. She'd better. A brawn's irrational desire to see the face of his "brain" partner was scarcely uncommon when there was a deep emotional attachment between partners. It was usually thwarted by the difficulty of removing the access panel. If Niall had those guarded syllables . . .

She had to deal with this fixation, one way or the other.

"That's why I can't be your brawn, Helva," Niall said in a broken voice. "And don't give me that assywarble about fixations are common and cured. I know the release syllables. And one day, it'd be too much for Niall boy. I'd have to open that coffin they've sealed you in. I'd have to look at your beautiful face, touch that god-lovely smile, and hold you . . ."

He'd moved, fighting the drive of his body every inch, until he was eaglespread against her column, his cheek pressed against the cold metal, his fingertips white with the effort to penetrate the unyielding surface. One hand slid slowly toward the access panel. Yet his face was oddly clear, serene, almost happy, his eyes closed as if he already held her against him.

"Then say the syllables," she cried passionately. "Open the panel, breach the shell, stare at my face and hold my twisted body. It would be better for me to die at your hands than remain an inviolate virgin without you!"

With an inarticulate cry, he jumped back as if the metal had burned him. His face was contorted in a terrible grimace.

"If you didn't then, Niall, you never will," she said, keeping her voice gentle and soothing, suppressing the unexpected longing that threatened to rob her of sanity.

"God, Helva. No!"

He whirled, running to the lock, jamming down the controls on the lift. He jumped from it before it reached ground level, and disappeared into the Tower.

And I can only wait, Helva thought bitterly. He's got to make this decision himself. He's got to want to come back because *he's* sure he can trust himself. My implicit trust in him is irrelevant. *He* must be the initiator, the manipulator, the schemer.

Why didn't I slam the lock shut? Why didn't I keep him here until he realized that he's all right now —that the critical moment had come and gone? All his defenses had been down: he'll never be that vulnerable again, either to himself or me. He's got to see that when he gets himself under control.

Surely he'll be back soon, all arrogance, jaunty, swaggering with self-assurance. If the fixation is so deep, he'll have to come back. He couldn't stay away. Only—a Niall Parollan could . . . if one Niall Parollan decided that was what he had to do. He's that kind of man. He can rationalize away all the deceitful, collusive, unprincipled things he does, dismiss them from his mind once they'd accomplished their purpose. But set him up against pressure on his deepest integrity, touch him in the core of reluctant goodness and honesty, and Niall Parollan could make the noble gesture, the uncharacteristic sacrificial act. And foul them both up for the rest of their lives!

Should she call Railly? He'd act instanter. On what? Niall had gone into the Tower. To think, consider, decide; she sincerely hoped, to come back. After what they'd put Railly through, she'd better not roil him unnecessarily. Particularly against Niall.

And Helva was stuck again, waiting, with her lock wide open and the lift ground level, immobilized.

He'd said she was beautiful. When had he had an extrapolation made from her chromosome pattern? It cost a fortune to make even a solido. Before Beta Corvi? Or at Borealis? Oh, gods, had he got hold of her medical records? No, that would have revolted a man with Niall's predilection for the nubile. She felt like giggling; wasn't *she* nubile, and young? Of course, the easy knowing way in which he inferred startling sexual prowess might be delusive. No, small men were often compensated for their lack of stature by another more generous endowment. And the appetite to fit. But her face was beautiful, he'd said. Even if it was only by way of an artificial extrapolation, it pleased her. He was unlikely to use that adjective lightly. She would have to be beautiful for him to say she was.

The concept of being beautiful was both reassuring and disturbing. Shell-people were conditioned not to think of their personal appearance, never saw any repros of themselves. These, too, were high security secrets. Evidently nothing was secret or sacred to the determined. Niall had managed to get the new release syllables, supposedly known only to Chief Railly and hypno-locked in to that mind as an added precaution.

She was beautiful. Niall had said so. Where was he?

'Men have died, and worms have eaten them, But not for love.'

She giggled unexpectedly at the ridiculous line that floated into her mind. Men had dared more for beauty, however, particularly beauty unattainable, than for any other single motivation.

For legendary Helen's beauty had Troy fallen. For the beauty of gold and gems others had risked life, superstition, and freedom. For the beauty of knowledge men had strained and died. For the beauty of a principle a host of fanatics of every moral persuasion had perished.

She didn't want Niall dying for her—beautiful or not. She wanted him at the pilot's console!

A channel opened.

"Yes?"

"What a charming welcome," a familiar voice replied.

It was not Niall's and her surge of relief died. "Who is it?"

"What an insulting change, my dear."

"Oh, hello, Broley. I was . . . expecting another call. But I'm always glad to hear from you." It was impolitic to antagonize a city shell-person, particularly when it was Broley, and especially right now. She might need his help.

"You sounded so glad! And I sincerely trust that your anticipated caller is not a rival."

"Rival?"

"Yes, yes," and a touch of asperity crept into Broley's voice. Helva brought herself up sharp. Broley wouldn't be so affable unless he wanted something. "I understand," and his voice was suave again, "that you've reached Pay-off."

"Trust you to find that out."

"Ah, then, you haven't made any commitments yet?"

"Sorry, Broley. I extended my Central Worlds contract."

"You extended? With Central Worlds?" Broley's voice was an appalled whisper. "And I always thought you were a keen one. For the love of printed circuits, why did you have to do such an irrational, acid-headed, sour-phased, debasing thing like that? Don't you realize that I have four industrials and two planets lined up ready to bid themselves out of a decade of profits to get a 6 month contract with a BB ship like you? Whatever possessed you to do it? I'm stunned! I'd better check my own acid-level. You've put me off with your folly. I'm speechless!"

Somehow Broley's exacerbations revived her. The grasping, greedy, gossiping, cynical city shell person reinforced her previous decision. There probably were six bidders waiting to cut each other's financial throats for her, but she was certain that she wouldn't enjoy working their contracts, whatever they were. There'd be all the unpleasantness with the losers. Despite every shortcoming, Central Worlds at least worked for the good of the total Federation, not for the aggrandizement of one isolated star system, or a mercenary monopoly.

"Broley? Speechless?" Helva asked with a creditable laugh. "You don't sound it."

"Parollan conned you, didn't he?" Broley countered quickly.

Helva could almost see his mind correlating bits and pieces of eavesdropped comments and private assumptions to reach that conclusion. But how much had he guessed? How much was actual knowledge? She knew Broley prided himself on anticipating events. It made him an extraordinarily capable city manager. The sprawling Regulus metropolis, immense, complicated, catering to a dozen sub-races as well as the huge humanoid population, operated smoothly without transportation slowdowns, work crises or material shortages—all under Broley's supervision. But he always had a circuit open for trouble and rumor. He loved trouble, and said it kept him young; but he relished rumor and was not above spreading some of his own simply to keep amused.

"Parollan's my supervisor," she replied airily, "but I'd a few changes of my own."

"You did bargain, then?"

"Yes, I did and, to restore myself to your good opinion, if they don't produce, the extension is void."

"I do feel better. You wouldn't care to name the conditions?"

"Bored, Broley?"

"*I've* your best interest at heart, Helva. You're one of my favorite people, ever since that first brawn of yours fought five fleet bullies to a pulp because they laughed at your singing."

Just like Broley to remind her of Jennan. And right now. Well, he'd learn the conditions anyhow so she'd better tell him and keep him friendly.

"The CV drive," he bellowed at the first mention. "You are out of your mind, Helva! I'll just keep those industrials around for you, my dear." He sounded very smug.

"The CV's that hazardous?"

"Oh, my dear Helva, they cannot have been honest

with you. Didn't you hear what happened to the test ship?"

"Nine years out, I'm told, but you know perfectly well that a shell-person is far better equipped to handle delicate circuitry than any mobile . . ."

"Balls," Broley interrupted her. "I never get time for a decent chat but something has to go wrong."

She was grateful to whatever emergency had interrupted them. A little of Broley's cynicism went a long way. When she'd been in service as long as he, would she be as misogynistic and sour? Or as impassive as Silvia, living through years of quiet desperation on the off-chance that there might be a moment of beauty, of love, tomorrow?

Where was Niall? He must have calmed down enough to think straight by now. Hours had passed since he left. He must have realized that theirs could be a brilliant partnership, rich and full! He was wasted as a supervisor. Why, they'd pay off the CV debt in contract time, if not sooner, with both of them working to that end. Then she wouldn't worry about being independent. No one could harm her with Niall as brawn. If Niall would be her brawn . . .

She glanced outside hopefully, surprised that the quick equatorial darkness had closed down on Regulus Base. Lights were few in the Tower, shining only at duty stations and odd offices. She remembered she'd turned on only the lift audios when she'd landed. Now, as she turned on others, she heard muted metal sounds from the distant maintenance shops and the measured tread of the ceremonial sentry, parading the front of the Tower.

Another of the Service's archaic whimsies, Helva thought, knowing that highly specialized sensors around the Base could detect the mere passage of a night insect, identify and destroy it if noxious before the human guardian could react to a more visible or audible invasion. But the sentry's about-face clatter was comforting. She did not feel so alone. Some old traditions did have a special place for which there was no modern substitute. Like . . . Damn Broley! Why had he mentioned Jennan?

Broley could locate Niall for her. But he'd want to know the details. And he was unlikely to be sympathetic to her need. According to Broley, shell-people ought to be autonomous as well as self-sufficient.

She hastily answered the strident call signal.

"Well, Parollan may not have conned you into all he planned, but he's certainly celebrating something!" Broley was at his churlish best. "And he started off by tangling up 15 air-cushion vehicles, and three mass transporters and that sheared off two transmitter masts. Why he wasn't killed I don't know, but there wasn't a scratch on him or the three females with him. Fortunately, no one was more than shaken in the other cars, but he's been fined a stiff 1000 credits for such irresponsible behavior. And he had the nerve to laugh. If he weren't a Service Supervisor with plenty of pull, he'd've been sent down to cool off for a few months. And it's all your fault. I'll be glad to see you go. Oh, fardles! He's at the *Vanishing Point*. And now I have to drag on emergency monitors to ensure order there! If he thinks he can get away with two civil misdemeanors in one night, he's vastly mistaken. I will not have my city disrupted by Parollan's egregious escapades."

Having vented his spleen, he broke the connection.

Parollan was trying to kill himself? She could understand the Vanishing Point visit—the house was notorious for the variety and ingenuity of its entertainments. Most planets had several such establishments, particularly in spaceport cities, and most brawns were regular customers.

It was too unsettling to contemplate his activities there. She devoutly wished that shell-people were allowed the surcease of sleep. They ought to have some way to dispense with mental activity, some refuge from unbearable thoughts. Disobediently her mind ranged back to the Vanishing Point House and its reputation.

" 'Two households, alike in dignity . . .' " she began in a resolute voice that echoed through the empty cabins. She wondered: would the Solar Prane/Corviki understand her gratitude for this pastime?

A channel opened and it was no surprise to hear Broley's sharp voice. But he sounded puzzled, not irritated.

"Did you get Niall Parollan discharged for cornering you into that extension?"

"No, I did not."

"Just asking. I simply can't imagine why he's acting the way he is. It just isn't like the Parollan *I* know."

"What's he doing?" The question was out before Helva could reflect.

"He *was* doing his usual. Now he seems to have lost what little sense all that strong drink left him. In fact the monitors were all set to close in, when he calls the House jeweler, buys all the girls a bauble, 'to remember him by,' he says. And he goes home. Alone, what's more. And you'll never guess what he's doing now."

"Not unless you tell me."

"He's got an effects-buyer in and he is selling off his furnishings, his paintings, his artifacts, his tapes. He spent a fortune on that collection and he won't get half of it back. He's sold his aircar. *And* he's selling his wardrobe."

Helva tried to quench the sudden hope this news generated. A symbolic rejection of a closed part of his life? Why? Niall knew that brawns kept a home in some port of call. Why should he sell off? Not unless . . . She refused to consider the alternative.

"You would have heard," Broley was saying, "if he and Railly had had another one of their fights?"

"I haven't heard a word from Cencom all night."

"You'll remember Broley, won't you, if you do?"

"Yes, Broley, I'll remember you."

Could the girls and the drinking and the V-P House, the farewell jewels, all be part of a bachelor night out?

Caesar and Cleopatra occupied her until dawn, until the technicians and computermen poured back into the Base complex to divert her.

An urgent beep from Cencom and then Railly was on the line, bellowing.

"What'n'ell does Parollan mean, handing in a resignation? What're you up to now, Helva? Let me speak to him. Now!"

"He's not aboard."

"Not aboard? Where is he?"

"I don't know."

"And I suppose you also don't know that Parollan left a resignation on my desk to foul up my morning? That he cited Paragraph 5, subarticle D? I'll say he's suffering from mental aberration. He's *out* of his mind. If you two think you can put something else over on the Service after that performance yesterday . . ." Railly's angry ranting trailed off. "All right, Helva," he began again in a patient voice, "what happened after we cleared out? I thought the whole matter was settled. Parollan was the brawn of your choice, and you two would handle the Beta Corvi mission as outlined. So . . . what happened?"

"A partnership is formed by the mutual consent of both parties," Helva replied, speaking slowly and carefully.

There'd been a dangerous edge to Railly's voice, an unspoken threat, and the astounding implication that she *and* Niall had prearranged yesterday's events.

Then that was why Niall had resigned, trying to stay one jump ahead of Railly—who would certainly have tried to coerce him back on board. So Niall Parollan

had made his decision. That was why he'd sold
everything off: to have money enough to get away
from Regulus, beyond Railly's authority.

It was very difficult to think clearly. And she must
keep her wits for Niall's sake. If that was what he had
to do, she wouldn't let anything hinder him.

"I am aware of that definition of partnership, Helva," Railly said acidly. "And?"

"Niall was not agreeable to the partnership."

"Now see here, Helva. No more garbage. Niall
Parollan begged to join the Service 12 years ago when
he found out he was too damned short to be a brawn.
Since he made supervisor, he's been telling brawns
how to manage their missions, their brains, and their
lives. You can't tell me that when Niall Parollan got a
ship to the point where she'd opt him as brawn, he'd
sheer off?

"Well I'll tell you, XH-834, he's going to make that
Beta Corvi mission, or he'll be in irons for the rest
of his life."

Irons? Helva thought wildly. Another Service hold-
over? How ridiculous of Railly to think he could "iron"
Niall Parollan!

Calm down and think! Railly would soon find out
Niall had sold everything. She'd better lift . . .

The shrill keen of overworked aircars roused her.
She ran an automatic check and saw a full squad de-
ploying at her base. Round one to Railly.

"Broley," she began as soon as she got through,
"you've got to warn Parollan. Railly's after him and
out for blood."

"Really?" Broley was delighted. "Parollan's on his
way to the spaceport now. He got an under-the-
counter ticket from the effects-buyer. I just found out."

"When's liftoff?"

"At 0900 but . . ."

"Warn Parollan that Railly's out to stop him. He's

mounted a guard at my base, so I'm stalemated, and the next place he'll close off is the spaceport."

"Helva, really! Parollan is Service . . ."

"Not any more. Remember? He resigned. That's why Railly wants to keep him on Regulus."

"But, if Parollan has tendered his resignation, Railly has no authority to stop him."

"Broley, you? Naive? That extension with Railly is void unless Parollan goes as my brawn on the Beta Corvi mission."

"Railly will stop him," Broley agreed, and then realized what Helva had admitted. "You tried to con Parollan into being your brawn?" Broley had a laugh like a dying amphibian, probably from lack of use, Helva thought, but at least he was not annoyed by the choice information she'd withheld. "My dear girl! You are fabulous, absolutely fabulous. Why, that man's pure stud. He'd never lock himself away in a brawn's celibacy . . . Great heaving gods, maybe he would! He sent those girls away last night."

"Listen to me, Broley. Warn Niall *now* that Railly is out to secure his hide for that contract."

"Easy, dearie. If Parollan stays missing, the contract's void?"

"Yes, yes."

"And then you'd be free to listen to my bidders?" She'd half expected that bargain, so she agreed.

"Railly's a bad enemy, Helva."

"He can do nothing to me without Parollan. And if he tries, I'll call in Double M and SPRIM."

"Them!" Broley was contemptuous.

"They have their uses, like right now."

"But my bidders will have first chance?"

"I agreed, didn't I? Now warn Parollan. And then forget where you called him."

"He's in a public cab, but I'm to remember which one, with all I have on my mind, managing this city?" Broley was chuckling as he broke the connection.

"Lock himself away in celibacy." That was what Broley had said. But Niall had called her beautiful. There had been such desire in his voice, in the wiry body straining against the metal barrier. He'd wanted to look at her, to hold her. . . .

That long night after she'd returned from Beta Corvi, he'd come to keep her company. He must have been obsessed with her then. And that was why he'd suggested that she take Kurla's empty body. How could she have been so dense not to realize what prompted that bizarre conversation!

Her body that could not function as a body, inhabited by a soul that was all too human. And Kurla's body, that was only flesh, nubile, tactile, beautiful— soul-less.

She could have been tangible for him, to be used by him, able to experience herself that ultimate gift of self . . .

Maybe, if Kurla's body had not been appropriated . . .

No! *No.* Resolutely she rejected such devastating thoughts. Broley would keep his word. He'd warn Niall. The rest was up to the man. She was sure he could keep free long enough for Railly to cool off. He had plenty of money. You can always buy safety.

But Railly was a bad enemy. Broley had been right about that. However, an unwilling BB ship is an unmovable object. Even if Railly could catch Niall, she'd only refuse him admittance. She wanted no reluctant brawn.

Reluctant? Hmm, yes, that was the key word. How droll that the first man she'd wanted as brawn since Jennan died should prove reluctant. *We lose perspective, we shell-people. We forget that not everyone is eager to share our destiny.*

But Niall had wanted to be a brawn! When he couldn't qualify physically, he had raised himself to supervise a whole section of brawns. And then she had to come along, coy and stubborn, and force him to throw away everything he'd achieved, rank, prestige, luxury.

"Broley?"

"Now what?"

"You warned him?"

"I said I would. And I did. I also made a few pointed remarks about his behavior and a warning of my own about future embroilments."

Oh, no, she groaned inwardly, Broley preaching to Niall in his state of mind?

"Where's Parollan now?"

"I can't tell what I don't know."

"You must have some idea."

"None, but you'll be the first to hear when I have. In the meantime, you'd better check your acid level, dear!" Broley signed off with that snide advice.

She had to get in touch with Niall. She'd work with another brawn, if he would stay on as supervisor. She couldn't allow him to sacrifice everything on her account.

She scanned outside anxiously. The area was heavy with small craft traffic. Railly was mounting an intensive search. If Broley wouldn't help, how could she find Niall?

Well, there was another way to accomplish the same end. And it was patent that Railly's objective was to proceed with the Beta Corvi thing. All right, then . . .

Before she could open a channel, a signal came through from the Tower. Railly advised her with stiff formality to open her com screen. The picture cleared to show Railly, shoulders thrown back, eyes straight ahead and unfocused, sitting at a littered desk, an aide hovering fearfully in the background. There were two other men in the room; the older one with a sad face wore the SPRIM uniform of green and gold. The other man was younger, with a taciturn expression in his shrewd eyes. He looked completely at ease and idly tapped the elegant boot of his crossed leg.

"Captain Amiking of SPRIM and Mr. Rocco of Double M are here in answer to a complaint registered on your behalf, XH-834." Railly's voice was as grim as his expression.

"Yes, our informant says you have enough credits from your last assignment, Helva, to Pay-off, " Rocco smoothly interjected, appearing not to notice that Railly hadn't finished his prefacing remark.

"Some Federation credits are still pending," Helva replied, conceiving it politic to be truthful, particularly if it would leaven Railly's anger.

"The credits are in but . . ." Railly began.

"Then the original financial obligation incurred by the XH-834 has been satisfied?" Amiking asked in a gentle voice.

"Yes, however . . ."

"The contingent of servicemen clustered so congenially on the landing pad occupied by Helva are there, then, to protect her from the importunities of independent bidders?" Rocco asked.

Railly compressed his lips into a very thin line as he stared coldly back at the Double M representative.

"Otherwise it looks very much like a form of moral restraint, for Helva could certainly not remove herself, if she so desired, without charring them. Which a BB ship cannot do. They ought to withdraw. Immediately."

"This is a Service Base, Mr. Rocco . . ."

"Immediately, Chief Railly, or Captain Amiking and I will be forced to suspect coercion." The Double M agent smiled indolently but his voice, too, had a cold, hard sound.

Railly barked at his aide, who fumbled with the com-unit. Almost instantly the men on her landing site began to disperse.

"Have they left, Helva?"

"Yes, Mr. Rocco. But you must understand that I extended my Central Worlds contract."

"So I'd heard," Rocco remarked, his eyes glittering as he turned politely to her. "Which makes a guard totally uncalled for. However, I'd also heard that one of the conditions of the extension specifically requested by you cannot now be filled through circumstances beyond your control. Therefore, that contract is invalid . . ."

"That contract is not invalid until Central Worlds has failed to fulfill that condition!" Railly said, emphasizing his words with an angry fist on the desk.

"Which they cannot do," Rocco countered with equal emphasis. "Niall Parollan was the brawn of your choice, isn't that correct, Helva?"

"Yes, but . ."

"He has resigned from the Service and is no longer available . . ."

"Niall Parollan will be on board the XH-834 by nightfall," Railly bellowed, rising to his feet to tower over the others. "That condition will be met and the contracted assignment will proceed."

"*If* you can find Niall Parollan," Rocco amended.

"Gentlemen, this is ridiculous," Helva said, raising her voice to be heard. "Yes, I wanted Niall Parollan as my partner. I am sorry that he could not oblige me. I deeply regret that he felt it necessary to resign from the Service to emphasize that reluctance. But I would not coerce him into accepting an onerous duty . . . Hound him. I'd rather discuss another brawn assignment."

"Why you fickle-minded, double-crossing, wire-haired retard of a tin-assed martyr," a rasping voice roared from her main corridor. "You'll discuss another brawn assignment?"

Niall Parollan stood by the open drive-room hatch, his torn mechanics overall grimed, his angry face scratched and smeared.

"Don't try to fool me, Helva, that's Parollan," Railly yelled from the comscreen.

"It is, and I deal with him first, Railly!" Helva cried. She cut the connection, slammed the lock shut, activated the tamperproof field on her hull. She was going to thrash this out right now. "What do I mean by discussing another brawn assignment? What alternative do you leave me, you drunken, womanizing, liter-sized knave! How else can I get Railly to lift the search and let you go free?"

"Free? Who's free? The moment I leave you alone you're ready to sell yourself right back into slavery! Of all the stupid, half brained, short-sighted, fardling foolish . . ."

"Foolish?" Helva sputtered with rage and indignation. "Look at you, selling off 7 years' hard work and rank because you're too damned bed-happy to go on one lousy mission for me. Force me to mortgage my soul for the second time in 2 days . . ."

"Rocco and Amiking got here, didn't they? They were to see Railly before he got out of bed to be sure you'd go free. Next thing I know that queen gossip Broley is telling me there's a full search on and . . ." His agitated recital broke off. He gritted his teeth, his eyes flashing so angrily Helva knew that Broley's sermon had been read in pure vitriol. "Rocco and Amiking are with Railly now, aren't they?" he asked with considerably less vehemence.

"Yes, they are." She matched her tone to his, too relieved to have him safely aboard to prolong a quarrel. "And you'd better have a sound explanation for Railly in nothing flat, because there's a no-nonsense penetration team assembling on the pad. And Railly knows my release syllables, too."

Niall didn't need that reminder as he heard the penetration team clank against the outer hull.

"You fool, you could have been all clear," he murmured, more desperate now than angry.

"Just the Beta Corvi mission, Niall. That's what he wants."

Niall jerked his head up. "I don't think it's that simple even for Railly."

"If the CV drive's good, I'm ahead of the game," she said. "If it's bust, then I'm free and so are you!"

"Free?" Niall repeated softly but there was an odd grin on his tired face. He put one hand out, gently stroked the panel, sensitive fingertips finding and running along the all but invisible seam of her quarters. "I'm no more free than you are, Helva. But, as the gods are my witness, I tried to get you out of this fardling foul contract I cooked up." Deliberately he jammed one fist against the column, breaking the skin and bloodying his hand.

"Stop it, Parollan. If we couldn't settle a piddling 500,000 debt in less than 10 years, we're not the team I think we are!"

He had cocked his fist to strike again, but he stepped back, staring at her, eyes wide with surprise and hope.

"You know, you're right. Absolutely right."

"Of course I am. And if you've got to exact penance, get the hell on the com and persuade Railly to call off that penetration team!"

He was already at the console, banging for vision, forgetting that Helva would do it faster for him.

"What'n'hell's going on out there, Railly? Damnall, can't a brawn leave his ship alone on a Service Base, for chrissake, without finding her subjected to some asinine indignity? I thought that nardy Beta Corvi flap had top priority! Where are the specs? Where are Breslaw's models? I need Dobrinon's files. How in hell can we lift off in 5 days unless you move those lazy techs!"

"Parollan," Railly began with a full spleen to unload, "you're under arrest. You're fined. You're . . ."

"I resigned, remember, Railly?" Niall roared back, gathering fresh impetus. "You have no authority to fine or arrest or order *me* anywhere. I'm a citizen of Central Worlds, acting as mobile partner to the Helva-834. She contracted a mission with you, stipulating in Paragraph 6, Section 1, that she would have free choice of aforesaid partner, to wit, one Niall Parollan. There was nothing taped about the rank or status of said Niall Parollan. And if you think you can make something of it, my resignation is time-stamped before those Federation credits came in. Therefore, *before* the contract extension took effect. Now, if you want to tie this ship up in a court battle over who bosses who, go right ahead. But if you want to get this ship off her expensive ass to Beta Corvi to vet your lovely new power source, you'd better start moving!"

Helva should have known that Niall would neither explain or humble himself. And perhaps such an offensive was the only effective method of dealing with Railly. She could feel sorry for the Chief's aide, standing in paralyzed shock at Railly's elbow. She was glad for his sake as well as theirs that Rocco and Amiking were still there. In fact, she didn't doubt that Niall counted on their presence to force Railly to accept this bald revision of the facts.

And the Chief was going to have to accept this version. He had no choice and no recourse, not before representatives of powerful organizations that he could not antagonize.

"You'll move, Parollan," he vowed in a strangled voice, "and you'll work like you never believed a team could work."

"Naturally."

"And one day . . ." Railly grated out the words, "one day, Parollan, you're going to outsmart yourself!"

"No prophecies, Chief, just the tapes and models. Nice to see you, Rocco, Captain. Signing off."

As the screen blanked, Niall turned back to Helva, his expression oddly defenseless.

"He'd give his pension to know I already have, wouldn't he, Helva?" He spoke in a quiet, resigned voice, but his wide grin took away the sting. And the look in his eyes, possessive, proud, loving, intensely alive, made Helva's mind reel with joy.

They'd come through this crisis together after all. They could face any challenge. They knew each other better than she and Jennan ever had. They knew each other's strengths—and flaws. This was going to be bright heaven with fireworks, a constant stretching toward challenge and achievement. Helva longed to extend this ardent moment. Such pure happiness was so rare, so fragile.

The Cencom beeped to shatter it.

"Ah, Mr. Parollan? I mean, XH, ah, NH-834?" a nervous voice stammered.

"Parollan here," he said without glancing away from her column, knowing she'd open the channel.

"Sir, we can't use the lift to make delivery because . . ."

Helva cut him off as she belayed the tamper field, restored the lift power and slid the lock open.

"Fardles, what a way to take command. Look at me!" Niall swore, suddenly aware of externals again, of the filthy clothes he wore. "I'd've been cleaner if they'd dragged me back." He began to strip off the torn clothes as he strode toward the pilot's quarters. "Order me some gear from Base quartermaster, Helva. They know my size. Tell someone to pick up a small black carrier on guard post 17. And, oh yes—the perimeter sensors are shorted between 17 and 18."

He continued to give instructions while showering, dressing in the hastily delivered shipsuit, grabbing a quick meal from the galley. Neither her lift nor comcircuits were free a moment. The main cabin sprouted additional tables to accommodate the drive models and the tape files Dobrinon rushed over. Niall sent for every filmstrip from the exploratory ship. He seemed indefatigable, yet he'd been up the previous night and running half the day. Railly could never work Niall as hard as he'd work himself . . . and her.

"Hey, Helva," Niall said suddenly, squinting toward the open lock, "turn on some light. I can barely see."

"I'd no idea it had got so late." She scanned the equatorial dusk.

Just then the mellow brass voice of a trumpet from the top of Base Tower sounded the ceremonial day's end call. Day's end . . . and requiem. The rich measured notes floated over the great Service Base, out to the distant cemetery under the great trees. Once she'd heard it only as requiem. Tonight . . . each day dies, Helva thought, to let night with its darkness for sorrowing and sleep complete its course and bring . . . a new day. Taps, a simple, poignant statement of end and beginning.

> Day is done
> Gone the sun,
> From the sea, from the land, from the sky.
> All is well.
> Rest in peace,
> God is nigh!

Goodbye, Jennan. Welcome, Niall.

As the last note died away in dark space and in her heart, she saw Niall's knowing eyes on her—wary, expectant.

"Such a sentimental tradition for a modern Service," Helva murmured. ". . . Blowing taps at sundown."

"And you love it," he said, unexpectedly, in a grating voice. "You'd have tears in your eyes—if you could."

"Yes," she admitted. "I would. If I could."

"It's a good thing I'm so nasty. Balances your soft heart—partner," he said. "Helva! Don't ever change."

He might as well have been singing.

THE END

To be born as I was on April first imposes a challenge. In writing speculative fiction, I feel I have not failed the auspices of my natal day.

However, being 99 percent Irish indicates a certain perversity, so I tried out many other things before I settled down to write. I dabbled in the Theatre Arts, studied voice production for nine years before arriving at the horrifying conclusion that I was a better stage-director of opera than a singer. I capped off that facet with the production and stage-direction of the American premiere in Wilmington of Carl Orff's *Ludus de Nato Infante Mirificus,* which is not as far from speculative fiction as you might imagine.

I balance indifferent housekeeping with superb cooking; sew for anyone but myself, knit well, and (would you believe?) embroider; am currently raising three children, five cats, and a French poodle; swim, sail, ride horseback—western style by preference—collect Graustarkian romances, and resent being kept away from my typewriter by any one of the above-mentioned diversions.

My eyes are green, my hair is silver, and I freckle. The rest is subject to change without notice.

ANNE McCAFFREY, 1968

THE MARTIAN TALES OF EDGAR RICE BURROUGHS

Thrill to John Carter's exciting adventures on the
dying planet of Mars—a vast body comprising many
races, strange creatures and exotic plants.